WRECKER

Shipwrecks are part of life in the remote village of Porthmorvoren, Cornwall. When, after a fierce storm, Mary Blight rescues a man half-dead from the sea, she ignores the whispers of her neighbours and carries him home to nurse better. Gideon Stone is a Methodist minister from Newlyn, a married man. Touched by Mary's sacrifice and horrified by the superstitions and pagan beliefs the villagers cling to, he sets out to bring light and salvation to Porthmorvoren by building a chapel on the hill. But the village has many secrets, and not everyone wants to be saved. As Mary and Gideon find themselves increasingly drawn together, jealousy, rumour and suspicion are rife. Gideon has demons of his own to face, and soon Mary's enemies are plotting against her . . .

SPECIAL MESSAGE TO READERS

THE ULVERSCROFT FOUNDATION
(registered UK charity number 264873)
was established in 1972 to provide funds for
research, diagnosis and treatment of eye diseases.
Examples of major projects funded by
the Ulverscroft Foundation are:-

- The Children's Eye Unit at Moorfields Eye Hospital, London
- The Ulverscroft Children's Eye Unit at Great Ormond Street Hospital for Sick Children
- Funding research into eye diseases and treatment at the Department of Ophthalmology, University of Leicester
- The Ulverscroft Vision Research Group, Institute of Child Health
- Twin operating theatres at the Western Ophthalmic Hospital, London
- The Chair of Ophthalmology at the Royal Australian College of Ophthalmologists

You can help further the work of the Foundation
by making a donation or leaving a legacy.
Every contribution is gratefully received. If you
would like to help support the Foundation or
require further information, please contact:

THE ULVERSCROFT FOUNDATION
The Green, Bradgate Road, Anstey
Leicester LE7 7FU, England
Tel: (0116) 236 4325

website: www.foundation.ulverscroft.com

WRECKER

NOEL O'REILLY

LARGE
PRINT

First published in Great Britain 2018
by
HQ
an imprint of HarperCollins*Publishers* Ltd

First Isis Edition
published 2019
by arrangement with
HarperCollins*Publishers* Ltd

The moral right of the author has been asserted

This novel is entirely a work of fiction. The names, characters and incidents portrayed in it are the work of the author's imagination. Any resemblance to actual persons, living or dead, events or localities is entirely coincidental.

Copyright © 2018 by Noel O'Reilly
All rights reserved

HEREFORDSHIRE
LIBRARIES

A catalogue record for this book is available
from the British Library.

ISBN 978–1–78541–714–6 (hb)
ISBN 978–1–78541–720–7 (pb)

Published by
F. A. Thorpe (Publishing)
Anstey, Leicestershire

Set by Words & Graphics Ltd.
Anstey, Leicestershire
Printed and bound in Great Britain by
T. J. International Ltd., Padstow, Cornwall

This book is printed on acid-free paper

"God moves in a mysterious way
His wonders to perform;
He plants his footsteps in the sea,
And rides upon the storm."

William Cowper, Hymn (1773)

"Myreugh orth an vorvoren, hanter pysk ha hanter
den. Y vos Dew ha den, yn-lan dhe'n keth
uta-na crygyans ren."
"Look at the mermaid, half fish and half human.
That He is God and man, to that same fact let
us entirely give credence."

Louis T. Stanley, *Journey Through Cornwall* (1958)

To Sally

PENWITH, CORNWALL

TEN YEARS AFTER THE FRENCH WARS OR THEREABOUTS

I

BUDDING TIME

CHAPTER
ONE

I got to the beach too late to find anything of real worth. The gale had moved inland, leaving an icy breeze in its wake, and there was a sea stench as if the ocean bed and all its secrets had been torn out overnight and dumped on the strand. All about me the dead from shipwrecks past muttered and moaned in the tongues of their own lands. Having shaken themselves free of their unblessed graves, they shuffled about in search of some lost thing. Look upon them too long, and they'd fade into the mist that sailed across the strand.

A dead wreck it was, all hands drowned. Sounds of hacking and wrenching floated over to me on the gusts, as my neighbours took the ship apart, plank by plank. All that was left was the bare ribs of the hull, stuck between Jack and Jill, two rocks that stood like monsters' teeth at the western end of the cove. The ship's bottom was torn out and her timbers lay in piles. Alongside, casks and boxes waited, and ponies and carts laden with plunder filed from the ship up the steep track to the headland. It wasn't the first time I'd seen a ship picked clean in a single tide.

I rubbed the grit of sleep from my eyes and tied back my hair, casting my gaze all about me to make sure I was alone. On the sand a few passengers lay among the dead, but my neighbours had already stripped the corpses for the most part. Among the bodies lay cabin furniture and fittings, lengths of pipe, a binnacle and other nautical instruments of some use unknown to me. Jellyfish lay all over, like plates of glass with the grey sky trembling inside them. Queerest of all were the hundreds of oranges scattered among the corpses as if they'd rained down from the heavens. They were all the more vivid in a world grey and tired as an old garment with the colour washed out. I took my kerchief from my shoulders and scooped as many as I could carry into it.

A few yards away I saw a human hand lying palm down on the sand. Thinking it might crawl towards me and grab my ankle, I hurried off. Nearby was a severed foot still in its shoe and such other gobbets of human flesh as could hardly be named. Dogs' barks pierced the air off to the east where hounds were mauling a corpse. My best hope was to move out towards the ebbing tide, where I might find a body freshly washed ashore. As luck would have it, down where the sand was still wet and glistening I found a fine-looking man stretched out. I wove a path towards him, willing myself to touch every corpse I passed for luck. The gentleman wore a dark suit, so sombre he must have had an inkling he was on the way to his funeral when he dressed himself. A well-built fellow he was. If you stood him up he'd be head and shoulders above any man in the village, apart from the giant, Pentecost. I wondered how long he'd struggled in the cold water.

It grew lighter by the minute. Pale lichen showed on the rocks, pink crystal glinted in the seams of the cliffs and the rising sun lit the dead man's face. His dark hair lay across his cheek, covered in a slick pale rime. There was a gash down one cheek and a shadow of stubble on his chin. There was no smell off him yet, fresh out of the sea as he was. I crossed myself to show contrition before digging into his sodden trouser pockets, searching his wrists and inside his jacket, but I found only a pocket book, the pages stuck together, which I threw aside, and a watch on a silver chain which was full of sea water. Time had stopped and God had turned his back on the world.

When I was done with the man, I rose to my feet and moved through the mist, almost stepping upon a child's body that lay like a sixpenny doll on the sand. The little thing's face was turned away, which was a mercy. I went further down towards where the tide was washing out, but was stopped in my tracks by the sight of two pretty boots poking out from under the hem of a woman's skirt. Though the boots were soaked, I saw they were of the softest tan leather, laced before, with the tops reaching only just above the ankle. It was a fashion new to me. On one toe hung a little rose cut out of leather, but its twin was missing on the other boot. The woman's feet were daintier than mine, but I would gladly have put up with a bit of pinching around the toes for the chance to be seen in a pair of boots such as those.

I got down on my knees and set about working the boots off the lady's feet. The first came away easy enough but the other was the devil's own work. I tugged at the laces, but they were tightly knotted and wet, and in any case my blood was turning to ice and my fingers, usually so strong, were losing their grip. Almost crying with vexation, I pulled with all my might, but the dead woman's ankle was swollen with water and the boot wouldn't shift. If only I'd come out with a knife. By now my fingers were so numb I could barely move them, but I gave that boot one last tug and off it flew, so sudden that I hit myself in the mouth with it, and fell backwards onto my ass. For a moment I sat there, winded, my mouth stinging from the blow.

When I got my breath back I put the boots in my kerchief and knotted it. Wasting no time, I got to work searching the rest of the woman's body. Her frock had been stripped from her and her shift clung to her limbs, cambric silk by the feel of it but rent beyond repair. There was nothing else on her of any value.

A tooth was dangling from the lady's bottom lip on a pink thread of flesh, so I pulled it out, a charm I might use to cure my Mamm's windpipe of the chronic. Although it shamed me to look for long at the faces of the dead, I couldn't help but gaze at this woman. Her dainty upturned nose, black as if charred, stood out against her face that was all the paler for being encrusted with salt. Her eyes were black seams with just the whites showing between them. White sand covered her hair like a hoar frost, and there was a streak of gleaming red on a lock that fell over her ear. Looking closer, I gasped with horror to find her ear lobe had been chewed off. It was the same on the other side, the jagged edges still wet with fresh blood. For a long moment, I shut my eyes, breathing deeply to keep down the hot bile rising in my throat.

As I put the tooth in my apron pocket, I heard a noise, a low moan, more beast than human. Did the woman yet breathe? Had I jolted her back to life by drawing the tooth out of her jaw? Her eyes and mouth seemed to move, but they might have only trembled in the wind. Bubbles rose between her lips, and then — that sound again, part moan and part belch, her bosom rising and falling, and at the last only the hiss of air between her lips. Her soul was fleeing her body, and the thought gave me such a fright I screamed, which set the gulls shrieking overhead letting the whole world know what I was about. I would have fled, but right then I heard footsteps, and a crone in black widow's weeds loomed out of the fog, planting her crook in the sand at each step, her back-basket a hump on her shoulder and her shawl fluttering behind her. It was Marget Maddern, known to all in the cove as Aunt Madgie. She was the very last person I wanted to see at that moment. The old woman drew up by me and leant on her crook, panting as she looked me up and down, her creased brow crowned by a white mob cap.

"Was that you screaming just now, Mary Blight?"

I nodded. "I had a fearful shock — seeing what some devil have done to this poor lady's ears."

Aunt Madgie leant over the woman and looked her up and down, before fixing her gaze on the ragged frills of crimson where the earlobes had been chewed off. She turned and peered at me through narrowed eyes. "I hadn't thought you so faint-hearted," she said. "I see that for all your tender feelings, you were still able to fill your kerchief." She leant closer towards me, looking into my face. "What happened to your mouth?"

"My mouth?"

"It's bleeding."

I put a hand to my lips and saw blood on my fingertips. "I bumped into something in the mist and cut my mouth, that's all," I said.

She gazed at the woman's ears again. "Do you swear this is not your doing, Mary Blight?"

"I do." She gave me such a damning stare, I had to look away. I could outstare anyone but her.

"And yet I found you crouched over the body, and with blood on your lips?"

"Oh wisht! I confess that I did take the woman's boots off, and in so doing hit my face with them. I didn't tell you at first, for I was all of a tremble when I saw you. But it's the truth, as God's my witness. Some other devil got here before me and did the rest."

She gave me a still keener look. "And she was dead when you came upon her?"

"I swear to God."

"Take care with these oaths, lest they prove false. Perhaps you thought that while there was still life in the woman, you had no natural rights to take those boots. Maybe you helped her soul on its way?"

"Never! I am no murderer."

"I'd be more inclined to take your word for it, were you less renowned for stripping clothes and jewels off dead women."

"I'm not alone in that."

"Aye, 'tis true, but we must not cross the bounds of decency, or the cove will be infested with Preventive Men." A crow swooped low over our heads and croaked to harry us away from the corpse. "It doesn't belong to you to go sneaking about like this after the hard work is done, Mary Blight. I know your ways, looking for pickings from the last few bodies that drift ashore. And all for vanity. When will you learn that it's One and All in this cove and always has been? What else have you found this morning? Sovereigns? Spanish dollars? Let me see."

"Only some oranges." I swayed the heavy kerchief in front of her. "And I found this on a man a little way off. A watch that be full of water." Fumbling in my apron pocket, I brought the watch out and handed it to her.

"Maybe we can get it fixed in Penzance," she said. "Whoever owned this won't need to tell the time where they're gone."

At last, she slowly turned and hobbled away. But before she was gone more than a few yards, she stopped and spoke, her back still turned to me. "I'll have my eye on you, Mary Blight. Take heed."

With Aunt Madgie gone, I got up and threw my kerchief over my shoulder. The mist had cleared to show a mass of broken clouds flung across the heavens from the east to the west, glowing with the sun's red fire. But the pale round moon still tarried in the sky, knowing the work of the night was not yet over.

A wreck is a queer purging, when compass reckonings go awry and Nature shakes the world out of order and time out of joint. My first harvest had been in my fifth or sixth year and since then perhaps a hundred ships had broken their backs upon the western rocks. Every time I was left with an unease for days to come. That morning after Aunt Madgie had come upon me on the beach, I could find no peace. My nerves were frayed as it was, having seen the drowned woman's soul bubble up out of her throat. And then to find myself called to account by the old lady and made to suffer her dark looks! I couldn't rid my mind of the fear she might accuse me of stealing the noblewoman's earrings. To put my mind at rest, I went down to the harbour to find out how things stood.

On the slipway a fine chestnut horse with mud-spattered saddle bags was tethered to a post outside a warehouse. Its flanks foamed with sweat and its head hung low as if it had been ridden hard. The beast snorted and scraped a hoof on the stone slabs as I passed. All that was left of the wreckage was a broken old cabinet propped against a barn wall, and a couple of hogsheads with staved-in sides and spoilt cargo. No doubt, the rest was hidden away, safe from the eyes of the Preventive Man, on farms on the moor or down in tunnels, or sunk out at sea waiting to be recovered.

A huddle of men was gathered by the wall of the quayside. I was about to pass when they moved aside to

12

let two fellows through. They were carrying something heavy in a sack, one at each end, and I knew by the way the load sagged between them that it was a body. The sight of it fixed me to the spot. Not one of the men in the group gave me more than a glance, which calmed my nerves a little. The two men bearing the carcass took it to a low black shed on the slipway, where the bodies were kept before they were taken up to the graveyard.

A tall fellow stood in the midst of the men, a foreigner in a long brown cloth coat. It must have been his horse I'd seen. I knew his face from other wrecks. He was an outlier in Penzance for the wrecked ship's insurer, a loss adjuster. His trousers were streaked with mud, and his shoes covered in sand. A group of men from the village answered his questions while he looked down his nose at them and noted things in a black pocket book. The men shuffled further along the harbour wall and I moved along with them, keeping out of the way. For the briefest moment before the men hid them from view, I saw two bodies laid out on the cold, rough stone, a woman in a tattered and grubby shift and a child of perhaps four or five years old. I crossed my arms and held myself tight to stop myself from shaking.

The loss adjuster looked around at the men in his lofty way, an eyebrow raised, and spoke. "So, you'd have me believe that not a single one of you was anywhere near the wreck last night?" he said. "That a five-hundred-ton vessel like *The Constant Service* could be plundered of every last scrap of its cargo and its timbers broken up while all of you slept, unknowing, in your beds." The men shook their heads and tugged at their beards. None would meet his eye. "My client Lord S— owned the greater portion of the cargo, but this loss will be as nothing compared to this outrage," he said, looking down at where the bodies lay, and scratching out some more notes in his black book. "Mark my words, this is not the end of the matter." I wanted to slope away, but feared it would seem like I had something to hide.

"It is the very woman I'm looking for, without a doubt," the loss adjuster said. "Her face is well known in Society, that is to say the civilised world far beyond this shore. This is a foul crime, and His Lordship will not sleep easy until justice is seen to be done." His head jerked to let the men know they should remove the body. Two big fellows stooped to lift the woman up and lay her on a sheet of sacking. It was then I saw her face, and the frills of dried, blackened blood where her earlobes had been chewed off, her jewels pilfered. The child lying alongside her was surely her own. It was lucky I stood by a barn and could lean against the wall, for my legs were going from under me. But the men took no notice, just moved along the wall to look at another victim of the wreck.

My mind raced, thinking of the loss adjuster's words about a great lord wanting justice, and seeing in my mind's eye the pretty boots I'd left drying on the hearth in our cottage. I looked away as the two men passed me with their burden slung between them. All that was left of the woman was a wet patch on the stone where she'd lain.

I fled that place and turned up the lane towards home, but after a few paces I felt a feeling like a shadow passing over me, so I stopped and looked about. I found myself at the end of Back Street, the very place Aunt Madgie lived. And there she was, the old devil, as I knew in my bones she would be, standing between the two posts that stood before her ancient house, clad in her black dress as always, one gnarled hand clutching her crook and the other holding an ancient china chamber pot. When our eyes met, she shook her head slowly, before emptying the pot in the lane, making sure to throw it towards where I was standing. As she turned back to the house, she gave me an evil look before doddering inside.

CHAPTER
TWO

The following evening a feast was held to give thanks to Providence. I'd been stricken with sudden qualms all through the day and was sure Aunt Madgie was ill-wishing me, but still I meant to go to the feast. I wanted to see if there was any hint that the old dame had been about among my neighbours spreading lies concerning what she'd seen. If so, it was better to know and be able to fend off the slander.

I got ready for the feast in Mamm's old room that she hadn't used since she went wrong in her lungs, preferring to sleep in her armchair by the fire. My younger sister, Tegen, was sat in the straight-backed chair in a royal sulk, watching me. I brushed my red hair, turning this way and that to see myself in the oval looking glass that hung over the rickety linen chest. The glass was cracked and covered in blotches that no amount of rubbing could remove. The mirror was engraved and had once been fine. In my mind's eye I pictured it standing in a rich woman's chamber, but when I'd found it on the strand there was a crack running from one side to the other. Now I looked at myself in the glass, cut in two where the surface was split.

A frock and petticoat were hung on rusty nails against the damp wall to let the creases fall out. The garments looked gaudy against the faded lime wash. I dropped a white shift over my head, before putting on a petticoat and a scarlet dress. Of a sudden I remembered the scarlet chemisette I kept in the closet to stop it fading. It was of the same vividness as the dress, and only a little frayed and moth-eaten. The cloth was chill against my skin, and I shuddered, remembering how I'd come by it.

"Well now, don't you look a picture in all your finery," said Tegen, with a sour pout.

"I'll send one of the children up with meat and drink for you and Mamm later," I said, pinning a white winter lily in my hair, which I was wearing loose. The bloom gave off such a perfume it made a body near swoon. "You're better off at home, Teg. You'll only get teased."

"I don't mind a bit of teasing," she said, which I knew wasn't true. "But I'd as soon stay at home. The revels is all wrong in my eyes, celebrating when so many poor souls perished. A young child among them."

"Well now, someone's pissed upon a nettle!" I said, as I went downstairs. Tegen followed me and watched, arms folded, as I went to the hearth to fetch my new boots. They were almost dry and the leather only slightly stained with salt water. I sat down to lace them, then stood up to see how they looked on my feet.

"It'll be like dancing on that poor woman's grave," said Tegen.

I pretended to take no notice, and rushed out the door. It was almost dark. My boot heels clacked on the wooden doors of the fish cellars in our little courtyard, which stank on account of Aunty Merryn's leaky old cat. I slipped through the narrow alleyway, and headed down the steep lane to the harbour. The further I went, the more those boots pinched my toes.

The quay was lit by a row of lanterns that smoked from the fish oil that burnt inside them. Even the savoury pig on the spit had a fishy smell, having been fattened on fish offal. Every bit of the pig would get eaten, all but the squeal. Planks had been laid out across barrels to make a long table. My neighbours had become dear old friends for once, and it was one of those rare times when men and women come together as though it were the most natural thing in the world. The bettermost from the finer cottages on Fore Street sat preening themselves in a little row at the far end of the table. I saw, with a fearful start, that Aunt Madgie was among them. But none gave me a reproving look, so I took my place at the other end between Cissie Olds and the Widow Chegwidden. The first sip of rum burnt my gullet, but soon my blood slowed and a soothing feeling came over me. Cissie piled my plate with fried swine offal chopped up with onion. But I had no stomach for meat, and the sight of stargazy pie made me queasy, with the pilchards poking their noses through the pastry. It seemed that no word of my misdeeds had reached Cissie Olds or the others who sat around me. I downed one rum and then another and

18

before long lost all count. The world swam about me, and I grew reckless.

The children had grown boisterous and little lads kept sneaking over to the table for a nip of rum when their parents' backs were turned. It was time for their big sisters and brothers to take them to bed. Soon after there was banging at the far end of the table and a hush came over the company. Aunt Madgie stood up to raise the toast "One and all" and everyone but me roared in hearty accord. "Now, neighbours, if you'll excuse me, I shall take to my bed," she said, and they all cheered. The old dame knew the dancing would start soon and didn't want to witness any improper goings-on. Once she'd gone, a weight lifted from me.

Ephraim Lavin, the blind fiddler, was called on to scrape out a few jigs and hornpipes. His son, the little scarper, sat alongside him, thumping out a rhythm on a tub. The dancing began soberly enough. The men took their places in the left file and the women in the right and the shouter numbered us into couples. I had to start with Lean Jack Bodilley, but I took it in good part. When the tune was counted in, Jack took my hand and raised it and we got through the steps without tripping one another up. At each verse we changed partners, and soon my turn with Johnenry Roscorla came about. I remembered the days when Johnenry and me had walked out together and I had a sudden, fierce longing to have him back. I knew he felt the same about me because when we came face to face he was rooted to the spot, gazing into my eyes. He swayed before me and the harbour swayed along with him. He was the most handsome man on earth in the fairy light of the lanterns. I gave him a look to make his knees buckle. Then the other dancers bashed into us and we reeled in a circle with the rest, elbows locking and the men sending their partners spinning into the next man. We women held up our skirts so as not to trip on them as we stamped up and down the line, while the older folk and the lame clapped their hands to urge us on from the benches. It hardly seemed to matter what would happen tomorrow with the smears of light wheeling round my head and Johnenry's face forever looming up at me and growing more handsome as the night wore on. The men grew rough and hurled us about, some taking liberties, grabbing our waists or clutching at our behinds.

Time passed too quickly. The music petered out and the left-overs of the feast lay spoiling, fit only for flies. Men lay with their heads on the table, snoring amongst the upturned rum pots. Others were laid out on the quay. My feet were sore and my toes crushed after stomping about in those ill-fitting boots. Johnenry and I fell against a harbour post and I was glad of something to prop me up. But the post soon seemed to leave its moorings and began swaying about too. Loveday Skewes stood against another post further along with a face like a whipped dog. She had a habit of nibbling at her fingernails, and she was doing it that moment. Somewhere in my muzzy head I remembered that Johnenry was courting Loveday, and had been a long while since. I shut my eyes to think clearer, but it made my head spin even more. Down along the quay, one or two scolding wives were trying to drag their husbands home, but most people had already taken to their beds. I saw the lily from my hair lying on the stone slabs of the quay, crushed underfoot. I didn't want to go to my bed. I didn't want the night to be over and to wake up the next day with that dark and fretful feeling that haunted me, and a pounding headache to boot.

The bettermost women were gathered on the quay. Millie Hicks piped up in her pious wheedling voice. "It's time for we ladies to bestir ourselves, I seem. It don't belong to women to be abroad at such an hour." I always thought of her as a tall bird, a heron perhaps, with her long, thin neck and pointed beak poking forever into places where it had no business.

Millie linked arms with Grace Skewes, Loveday's mother and the topmost woman in the village, unless you counted Aunt Madgie. "It don't belong to women to drink strong liquor, neither," said Grace. Her little group of followers clucked in agreement, as they picked up their baskets, ready for the off. "One cup alone do fairly maze a body," said Grace, and I thought her eyes swept over me as she said it. It was all because she was sore about Johnenry preferring me to her Loveday.

Nancy Spargo, a big plain woman from the tinners' cottages on Uplong Row, wandered over from the table where she'd been larking about with some of her mates. "Well, it might belong to the bettermost to take to they beds but I be thirsty as a gull and plan on staying out a while longer," she said. She bent forward, her breasts almost spilling out of her bodice, screwed up her face and passed wind like a trumpet major. "Begging your pardon, ladies, I been fartin' like a steer all night," she said, in a mock lady-like way. "Better out nor in, eh?" She grinned, showing the gaps between her teeth.

I staggered up the steps to the quay. Seeing how linking arms was all the fashion that night, I went over to Nancy and went arm in arm with her. "We work as hard as the men, so why shouldn't we enjoy ourselves along with they?" I said, stumbling. I would have fallen if Nancy hadn't held me up.

"I be only thinking of what is seemly," said Millie Hicks, rubbing her long neck the way she did when she was about to bad-mouth a neighbour. "Others may look to their own reputations. Come along, Zenobia." She pulled her daughter away with her. The girl was her match in piety.

Loveday came over from where she'd been sulking by a harbour post. She was being mollified by her friend, Betsy Stoddern, who had stuck by Loveday and fought all her battles for her since they were little. "Some of we still care what folks think of we," Loveday muttered, glancing at me.

I wasn't going to let this pass. I let go of Nancy and walked towards her. "What's she saying of? Say it to my face if you got something to say, Loveday," I said. But someone had taken a grip of my arm and was leading me away. I tried to fight them off, but then I saw it was Johnenry, so I went along with him. He had a cup of brandy in his hand. He pulled me down from the slipway and led me out onto the beach.

"Look, you've given me the hiccups," I said, slapping him. He pulled me deeper into the night. "Wait! Let me

22

take off these boots. They're fair killing me." Johnenry took the boots out of my hand and slipped his arm around my waist. I wondered if anybody was spying on us from the dark windows in Fore Street.

"You're all hot and greasy, let go o' me," I said.

"I worked up a power of sweat jigging with you, that's why."

We moved further out to where the tide could be heard lazily washing in, some ways off. We leant against the damp hull of one of the boats, out of the breeze. The cold sand soothed my aching feet. Johnenry put the brandy to my lips, but I turned my head away. The storm that had brought the ship onto the rocks the day before had swept every cloud away, and untold numbers of stars were scattered across the night sky.

"Some pretty, ain't it, the sky?" I said. I spoke softly, but my voice was loud out there on so still a night. Johnenry took off his jacket and threw it on the ground so I could lie on it, then he lay down by me. We lay on our backs looking up at the heavens a while without speaking. A white streak bled across the sky.

"A shooting star!" he said. "I made a wish. Did you?"

I sighed. I knew full well what his wish was, but I didn't want to hear it right then. "Funny to think there were dead people lying all over the strand yesterday," I said, shivering. "When you see them lying there in their fine clothes, do you ever wonder how they must have lived before they were drowned? Don't you wish you could see inside their houses? And wardrobes? Don't you want a life like that?"

"No use hankering after what you can't have. It don't belong to us."

"Well, I'm tired of the same old life every day, even if you ain't. You be happy with too little, I seem."

"I have a dream."

"And what dream would that be?" I propped my head up on my hand to look at him.

"You know the old law that says anyone who builds a house in one night can claim the freehold?"

"You couldn't build a chicken coop in one night."

"I got some mates lined up to help. And I found the spot for it. A patch of wasteland just down from Uplong Row. There be enough ground for a one-room house and a pig sty, and a rick for furze. I been putting things by for a while, clay and poles for the walls, straw for the thatch. One night I'll build that house and the next day I'll carry my wife across the threshold."

"That's your dream, is it? A one-room hovel and a pig sty?"

He took hold of me and nuzzled his chin against my neck, chafing me. I pushed him away.

"You're strong," he said. I smelt the liquor on his breath.

"Not surprising I'm strong, slaving day in and day out," I said.

"You start housekeeping with me and you'll live like a princess, I promise."

I rolled on top of him. I had a coming-on sort of feeling, so I kissed him with open mouth. "I won't tell nobody if you don't," I said, in a whisper.

24

"I been waiting so long for this I thought I'd die," he said. He stroked my hair and kissed every inch of my face until I took a hunk of his own hair in my grip and pulled his head away so I could look right into his eyes. "It's loving I need now, Johnenry," I said.

That was all the coaxing he needed. He lifted my skirts and let his hands roam wherever they pleased. I pulled my skirts down again so no neighbour would peer out the window and see the moonlight shining on my ass. I rolled on top of him, and he ground into me like gritty sugar. I wanted to lose myself in it, forget the rest of my life had ever happened. When he was about to come to the boil, I lay quiet on him a while and put my mouth to his ear, telling him to hold off a little longer.

Afterwards he said, "I have to make an honest woman of you now, I seem," as the cold breeze blew up my skirts and tickled my tender parts. A sudden sharp pain in my temple brought me to my senses. "Let go o' me, I be about to puke," I said, getting up off him. I staggered away with the drunken stars reeling around my head, and the beach pitching and rolling under my feet.

"We be as good as man and wife," he said, catching up with me, as I staggered towards the quay.

I leant against the side of a boat, waves of seasickness building inside me. Dropping to my knees, I grasped the heavy chain that connected the boat to the quay. "You got me then," I said. "Go and have the banns read out, if you like, but leave me be. Right now all I want to do is urge."

With that I fell forward, the chain rattling in my grip. I retched, and the first of my spew splattered onto the sand.

I was in Mamm's old room, which smelt of damp and neglect after so many weeks left empty. She'd been sleeping in the kitchen since her breath had grown too short for her to get up the stairs. I climbed onto a chair and reached up to the rafters where I kept my secrets. The chair wobbled as I reached up to fetch an old stocking swollen with coins, jewellery and other trinkets. When I'd taken it down, I sat on the bed with the stocking in my lap. It was wrapped in yellowed newspaper that I had read so many times the print was worn off the pages. I blew away the dust and cobwebs, upsetting a black beetle that fell to the floor and scuttled a little way before I squashed it underfoot. I untied the string around the frayed worsted, then felt deep inside the stocking for the rag that covered my greatest prize. When the cloth was unwrapped, I gazed upon the hair pin and the butterfly that clung to it, more finely wrought than any lace. I'd taken it from a fine lady who'd breathed her last after a shipwreck a few years past and had never been able to bring myself to part with it, however scat I'd been. When I'd had my fill of staring upon the pin, I went over to stand before the oval mirror above the chest.

With trembling hands I put the pin in the back of my hair and turned my head to see it glimmer in the dusty shaft of light that lay aslant the glass. My face frowned at me, every blemish and line showing. The long winter had taken its toll. My hair was coarse under my fingers. It was both a blessing and a curse, that hair, a flaming beacon to draw the eye and set me apart from the common run of mouse-haired women. I would use my share from the wreck to buy vinegar and make it shine again. A lone white hair was threaded among the darker ones. A trick of the light, I hoped. I plucked it and found it to be silver as the hair pin.

My thoughts kept going back to the wreck, to Aunt Madgie and Loveday Skewes. At least my time of the month had passed since I'd gone with Johnenry, so that was one worry I could put behind me. To escape such dark thoughts, I let my mind drift to the man I'd seen on the beach after the wreck, the one whose watch I'd filched. If only a fellow like that were to wash ashore still alive. If not a land man, then at least a merryman. One like those who take human form on midsummer's eve and swim ashore buck-naked after dark to mate with a woman who waits on the shore in a rage of longing, only to depart from her at dawn to return to his own kind, leaving his milt stirring inside her to grow into an infant that's as much fish as human, and oh! how breathless I had become, carried along by such fancies. I'd forgotten I still had the pin in my hair, and before anyone caught me I hid it in the stocking and put it back in its hiding place.

When I felt calmer, I brought out the tinder box from under the bed, sat on the chair and took out my small ration of shag, a mix of baccie and hemp I had dried on the hearth. It was mixed with a rare kind of mushroom that has a soothing effect on the nerves and brings on curious whimsies. Such herbs can be depended on to unlock dreams and let a person glimpse the other world that is only a feather's breadth from the one we know. I took a few quick pulls on my pipe to get it smoking, releasing its incense into the air. Soon the smoke was swirling about the room and my thoughts were unfurling in its coils. The idol was at my feet, a limbless woman of stone with huge hips and breasts. I picked her up and held her in my lap. Tegen always said the idol was no more than a misshapen rock, but I knew she was an ancient goddess passed down the generations.

Weaving patterns shifted across the idol's face like light on water. Without speaking aloud, I asked the idol if I was wrong to keep my treasures hidden in an old stocking when I might buy medicine for Mamm. Was it wicked to indulge in idle fancies, to imagine myself as one of the fine ladies who wash up on the beach after wrecks? My heart raced at the thought of the liberties and luxuries such women enjoyed. How would I ever be rid of my lowly life in the cove, with ill wishers all about me?

I looked down into the idol's face. She seemed to say, "Take care, Mary Blight."

In my mind, I answered, "What's strong in the heart must out some way."

"Do not overstep thyself," the idol warned.

But the wreaths of smoke about me told another story. A man's pale naked body was slowly taking form. He groped blindly in a sea of shifting shadows while fatal currents drew him to my embrace. I put the idol on the floor, her face to the wall, and sat back in the chair in a kind of fit, letting my hands fall into my lap.

CHAPTER
THREE

The very next day I was down on the strand, raking at the tide wrack with the poorer sort of women, those forced to scavenge, just as the gulls do. A ragged line of us stretched out across the strand in the swirling haze. The work was slow, my collar stiff with sweat, my scalp itching in the close heat. With an aching back and arms, I twisted the heavy sea blooms around the end of my pole, then hoisted it and shook the seaweed onto the pile, ready for the squire's farms up on the headland. Clouds of lazy flies hovered over the seaweed, which grew more rank as it dried.

At last the mist lifted and the sun came out. I pushed my damp hair from my brow with my forearm and looked about me. Two women were approaching, black shapes against the light. As they drew nearer, I saw it was Loveday Skewes and Betsy Stoddern, both in nice, clean frocks. They had come to gloat at us poor working women.

"Here be trouble," said Tegen, at my side.

The pair of them passed the spot where we laboured. "Some people has no shame," said that big ox Betsy. "Showing her face abroad after stealing another woman's man."

Tegen gave me a look to make me keep my mouth shut.

"Never mind, I don't want him now," said Loveday. "Spoilt goods." She gathered her shawl round her with a peevish shrug.

Betsy wasn't ready to let it rest. "Her sort only ever look out for themselves."

I wasn't going to let that pass. "It be One and All in this village, don't it, ladies?" I said, digging the pole into the seaweed and twisting it fiercely. "But some get a better share than others, I seem. There's a reason why some in this village has whacks of money and others be scat."

"There's none that's poor that don't deserve to be," said Loveday.

I shook the weed off the pole so that it landed right at their feet. "If you could see yourself, Loveday," I said. "Puffed up like a bladder of lard." Tegen took my arm and tried to pull me away from them.

"That carrot-topped varmint have shown her colours again today," said Betsy.

"No father to take her in hand, that's why," said Loveday, as they wandered towards the eastern end of the beach.

"Keep your pert sayings to yourselves," I muttered to myself when they were gone.

"You shouldn't rise to it," said Tegen. "Hold your temper. Of late, you be like a river fit to burst its banks. I swear you enjoy vexing people." She stooped to gather driftwood.

"So you want to keep me in my place, as well?"

"You know I always take your side, Mary," she said. A strand of frizzy, red hair fell across her face.

"I do know it," I answered. And to show I meant well, I went over and looped the loose lock of hair behind her ear, and hugged her.

Someone signalled to touch pipe. I didn't want to sit with the other women and feel their silence so full of meaning, so I went down to the crab pools, and ate my crust and cheese alone. The sea stretched to the ends of the earth and I foresaw an empty future ahead of me, an endless round of packing pilchards, of laundry and baking days. When I'd finished eating, I slipped behind a big boulder where I couldn't be spied upon and hoisted up my skirts. I pressed my bare ass against the cold stone and let the earth's slow heartbeat throb through my flesh for a long moment. It would bring me luck. Seeing a sharp stone by my feet, I took it up and gouged a limpet from the rock and split it open. What a pang it always gave me when the sea juices spilled over my tongue.

I walked across the shingle to where the wash rolled forward in rapid shelves. The water was icy around my ankles and the foam rushed past me up the beach, sucking sand from under my toes. It was as though the land was moving towards the sea and not the other way round. I remembered the feeling from my childhood, but instead of the old giddy enchantment, I feared the outhaul would pull me into the ocean's depths.

From out in the water there was a groan, a seal perhaps. I opened my eyes and could make out a shape bobbing on the waves no more than thirty feet away.

32

But it was only a barrel, perhaps one from the ship that had struck the rocks so recently. Something made me keep an eye on the barrel, though. A new current got under it and set it turning slowly, until I saw a dark shape show against the side. Something was strapped to the tub — no, *someone*, a man, his head lying on top. Maybe he saw me, for at that moment he looked up wearily and turned his face in my direction. His face was drawn and harrowed, and the sight of this soul in torment put me in mind of the Jesu and how he might have looked if he had turned towards you on the climb up to Calvary.

The swell was pushing the barrel towards the Zarn, the great black cave where smugglers unloaded their goods. If nobody helped the man he would be broken up on the rocks, and the barrel with him. I tried to call for Tegen but my words got stuck in my throat. I ran towards where the women were sat, a hundred yards off to the east, huddled together behind a great boulder for shelter. I cried out again, more lustily, cupping my hands to my mouth, "Over here!" But there was no sign that they heard me. I called again, so loud I tore my throat and then I saw Tegen's dumpy form as she got to her feet and peered over at me.

"Quick, Teg, there be someone in the water! A man near drowned. He be heading for they rocks. In God's name help me," I shouted. She lifted her skirts and began running across the strand. I was already wading out towards the barrel, the freezing water rising under my skirts and taking my breath away. Tegen wasn't far behind. The barrel pitched in the swell, showing itself one minute and vanishing the next. The water rose above my waist and each new surge covered my shoulders and slapped my face. My skirts were soaked through and the cloth weighed me down. Being only a woman, I'd never learnt to swim, and I was fearful of being pulled out of my depth. As I got nearer to the man I saw there was an oar under each of his armpits and the oars were tied to the barrel. I had to stay clear of those oars or they would dash out my brains, so I waited for a safe moment, dived in between them, and threw my arms around the barrel on the other side to where the man was tied. The side of my head hit the barrel as I did so. Then I pushed the barrel towards the beach with all my might, but the best I could do was slow its advance towards the Zarn.

Tegen's body slammed into my back. A powerful swell climbed over us, covering our heads and lifting my feet off the sand. My sister had a powerful pair of arms and between the two of us we inched the barrel towards the beach, straining with all our might. The incoming tide was behind us but a wayward current wanted to drive us into the Zarn. We were soon almost done for, but Nancy Spargo arrived and put her broad back into it as well. In time we reached the shallows and the barrel scudded onto wet sand. Women appeared and helped us untie the foreigner from the barrel and haul him up the beach.

I lay flat out on my back trying to catch my breath. The world seemed to throb around me, the sounds now loud, now soft. When I lifted my head I saw stark shapes against the sky, and at first took them for angels in Heaven, but it was only a crowd down from the village. White clouds floated by above me while the strand rolled underneath me. The pounding in my forehead where the barrel had struck me was like a hole made of light, and the brightness hurt me the way it does if you stare too long at the sun. I turned my head and saw a world strangely aslant, a dream that might melt away at any moment, and it was then I had my first proper look at the man. He lay with his head in Nancy Spargo's lap, and what I would have given to take her place! Such a long straight nose he had, and dark eyelashes trembling on his cheeks. His wet locks were black as tar, clinging to his neck and collar. He was a big fellow, broad-shouldered and tall with it, going by how his limbs stretched out on the sand. Dazed as I was, I believed my own fancy had charmed him out of the sea.

"Should we fetch a priest to give him his rites?" said Nancy. Her voice was from another world.

"A doctor more like," said another woman.

I sat up, not able yet to get to my feet. Of a sudden, there was two of everybody and I didn't know which one to look at. Jake Spargo, Nancy's husband, was down on his knees trying to make the foreigner drink from a cup of liquor. "This be the best medicine for him," Jake said. The foreigner's head lolled this way and that, as if the smell of the drink upset him. "Take a drop of that to warm 'ee," said Jake, tipping the rum between his lips. The man choked and groaned, his features twisting in pain, as if poison were being forced down his throat instead of prime Jamaican rum. His hand flapped about feebly, trying to swat the cup away, and the liquor rolled over his chin.

"Poor fellow, who have done such a thing to he?" said Nancy, her shoulders damp from her dripping hair.

"Whoever lashed this fellow to the barrel meant to save his life and not to hurt him," said Jake. "I seen the like afore now."

"Someone should take the foreigner indoors to thaw out," said another woman.

"We'll give the man house room," I said quickly, standing up, and reeling. "He can rest up there till the doctor be fetched from Newlyn."

Tegen whispered in my ear. "Whatever do you be saying of?" She took a firm grip of my arm. "It don't belong to us two maidens to take in a man. That bang on the head have knocked all the sense out of you."

I took no notice of her. "We need a hand to get him up the hill," I called out. I was close to swooning, but tried to hide it, and in no mood to let anyone take the man from me now. Two lads came forward, keen perhaps to show their strength to the wenches round about. One caught the big fellow under his knees and the other under his armpits, and they lifted him up. It was hard work lugging him up the beach and down the quay, and then up the steep lane. The lads had to stop every so often at cottages, and take a drop of water.

It was a good while before we reached the alley into our little courtyard, which was barely wide enough to squeeze through. Mamm looked on aghast as the foreigner was carried upstairs. They laid him out on the bed. Tegen came to the doorway, not wanting to enter a room with a man lying in it.

"We durstn't leave him in these wet clothes," I said. I kept my voice steady as I could. "It will be the death of him."

"But we can't take the clothes off him! Are you mazed?" said Tegen. She was scarlet to the tips of her ears. I ignored her and went to the chest, pulling a drawer open and taking out some of Dad's old things.

"We can dry him with this," I said, throwing a shirt onto the bed. "And we can dress him in another of Dad's old shirts till his own be dry." I leant over the foreigner and began tugging the cloth up over his body. I called Tegen over. "Come here and help me lift him. Look how he's shivering, we must be quick about it." She came over to help, looking away so she wouldn't see the man's white skin as the wet clothes were peeled off him.

"Think of what folk will say," she said.

"Let their tongues wag. Have you forgot the Good Samaritan?"

"This ain't a hospital."

"You sure? You forget about Mamm, I seem."

"The man is a stranger. What is he to you? I don't follow you at all."

"Providence have brought him here. It were me that saw him first. It's meant."

We lifted him up, and with difficulty pulled the dry shirt down over his head and shoulders.

"Who, I wonder, is to do all our work if we have to nurse this man?" said Tegen.

"Don't you pity him at all?"

Tegen looked on him, but there was more of shame than pity in her face.

My head ached and all about me was a fog. I put my palm on the foreigner's brow. His skin was warm. My hands were ice cold so I rubbed the palms together before touching him again. "He has a fever," I said. I poured some water into a cup and tried to make him drink, but most spilled down his chin. Tegen left me to it and went downstairs.

I dropped into my chair and let the room turn slowly around me for a little while before it settled. I closed my eyes and was almost gone, but a sudden groan from the bed startled me.

"Is it come?" the fellow shouted. "Is this the reckoning? Dear Lord, have mercy on my soul!"

I went to the bedside. "Forgive you?" I whispered. "Why? What has you done?"

He squinted at me, and I stared into those eyes for the first time, so dark and deep and hard to fathom. His face shook and he let out a strangled cry: "Pitiless devil! Leave me in peace, for Heaven's sake. Why do you still torment me, Molly?" His strength failed and his head fell back.

"You are mistaken, Mister, I am not Molly," I said.

He moaned pitifully. "I have beaten you, Molly. God forgive me, I have hurt you, your face . . ." My fingers reached up to where his gaze was fixed, and I felt the tender and throbbing bruise on my temple where the barrel had struck me. The foreigner's eyes closed and he fell into a sleeping fit.

38

While the man was lying a-bed, I set off up the headland to buy a charm. I picked my way through the copse where Old Jinny lived. Bare winter branches creaked in the breeze, and birds pierced the cold air with their cries, warning me off. Sometimes in the night the old woman was known to take flight and soar over the village herself, not on a broomstick but with her gown open and spread out around her like crow wings. I followed the scent of wood smoke and soon I reached the passage between thickets of needle-sharp briers that led to her door.

It was dark inside, with all manner of objects dangling from the rafters and turning slowly in the draught that followed me into the cottage: dried herbs, tiny bones tied in bundles, wooden dolls, pewter pots and pans. As my eyes got used to the gloom, I saw a jumble of wicker cages piled about, and along one wall a blue dresser, the paint cracked and peeling. A fire hissed in a small hearth and a large warming pan hung over it.

Old Jinny sat in the corner on a high-backed chair with great hawks carved on the arm rests, a little wheel for spinning thread at her side. I jumped at a sudden frantic flapping of wings as a black shape ripped past me to alight in the old crone's lap. It was a jackdaw and she took it in her hands, stroking it with long twisted fingers that had dirt under every fingernail. The bird cocked its head this way and that to judge me from all sides. I had the curious notion that the bird was Jinny's own child.

"Friend or foe?" the old crone asked in a voice as light as a whistle and reedy as a child's. "What brings you across my threshold?" The sound seemed not to come from her at all but from elsewhere in the hovel. There was spittle in the corners of her whiskery mouth, and beneath her grubby lace cap her hair clung loose about her neck and shoulders. It was matted and dusty as the cobwebs that were draped in thick layers in the corners of the room. Her nose was hooked and pointed like a bird's. She wore a gown of faded blue silk, streaked with bird shit like everything else in that place. It was open at the front to show a stained quilted petticoat of faded satin, and over that an apron which looked to have been embroidered with her own needle. On it were dozens of birds — wrens, robins, snipes and choughs. Her sleeves ended in lace ruffles, stray threads hanging from them, which reached almost down to the filthy floor of beaten earth.

Seeing how dazed I was, she laughed, a piercing sound that set my teeth on edge. It was plain the woman was mad as a snake.

"Don't boggle at me, girl. Tell me, what is your business here?" She spoke grandly, like a true snot. She ruffled the pale feathers at the back of the jackdaw's head with the back of her hand, making the bird shiver.

I swallowed hard, took a deep breath. "I need a charm to cure a man in a fever, short of breath. He was at sea a long while, lashed to a barrel. He is asleep mostly, but has bad dreams and sees things before him that aren't there."

40

"Perhaps he sees things that are there, but which you cannot see? An old man or a young? Big and strong or a weakling?"

"Not young or old. But big and strong, for sure."

She opened her hands to let the jackdaw fly free, and clapped in glee. "I know the remedy you need!" She got to her feet, stiffly. She was no taller standing up than she was sitting down, and all the smaller for being so stooped. She put her hand out for payment. "Two shillings," she said.

"Two shillings!" I was dumbfounded.

She nodded, briskly.

I had just enough on me. I counted out the coins and stooped to put them in her hand. She bit each one in turn to see if it was true before putting it in her apron pocket. When she was finished she left the hovel with a queer hopping gait and went to fetch the charm from out the back. A stink of stale sweat and piss hung about after she was gone, and the jackdaw hopped and flapped all about me, shitting on everything, including my hair. Its croak was loud in that little place and had me all of a jitter. The bird could talk, too, but in strange riddles of which I could make no sense.

I waited so long that I wondered if the old woman had died out there. Through a rip in the sacking over the window I saw the hut where she kept the captive birds. Their fretful twittering could be heard all over the wood. Round about me in the shadows of the room were all manner of nasty-looking instruments among the cages. I didn't care to wonder at their use.

At last Old Jinny came back with one of the poor creatures in her hands, wrapped in a bloody cloth. It made a fearsome racket and set the jackdaw hopping and flapping about in a frenzy. My nerves were frayed.

"I be thinking I shan't go through with this matter, after all," I shouted above the din.

She burst into shrill giggles. "'Tis too late," she said, holding the little bundle out to me. "I've already plucked her."

"Plucked her? What do you mean, plucked her?"

"The bird has to be plucked, my girl, if you want the charm to work."

"That be the wickedest thing I ever heard!"

"I can't stick the feathers back into the creature, can I?" she said.

What was I to do? I had already paid her two shillings, a king's ransom. And the bird would die now, anyhow. I let her put the creature in my shaking hands, and nearly dropped it when I felt its warmth and how it wriggled inside the grubby cloth.

"A song thrush. A hen for a man, a cock for a woman," said Old Jinny, leering at me. "Tie it to the rafters in the bed-lier's room. Twenty-four hours should do it. It might take longer if there is no rash on the man. Once the fever has been spirited from the human to the fowl, the bird will turn black and bloated. And then it will expire."

I made sure nobody saw me on the way back, which was not easy because the creature was making a din fit to wake the dead. It fair pecked my hands and wrists to pieces. When I got home, Tegen wouldn't help me so I had to tie it to the beam by myself. I knew the best knot to bind its legs but it was a dreadful fiddle with only one hand spare and the little creature raging to break free of me. Once the thing was tied and hanging, it went madder still, spinning in a flurry, its feeble plucked wings flapping furiously and its screeches deafening me and echoing around the room as it tangled itself in the string. I was overcome with the horror of it then, but it was too late to turn back. The foreigner groaned in his sick bed, disturbed by the noise. When the bird had tired itself, it hung there a moment twitching, its eyes bulging and unnatural, its grey wrinkled flesh covered in bloody pinpricks.

I couldn't bear staying in the room with the wretched creature, so I fled down the stairs to the kitchen. I sat at the table and took deep breaths, waiting for my heart to slow to its usual beat. Mamm looked away from me and Tegen scowled.

"Stop looking at me like that," I said. "It's only for a day or two. A man's soul matters more to the Creator than a bird's."

Later, on the way back from the well, I passed Johnenry in the lane. He blocked my path.

"I be in a hurry," I said, nodding at the pails of water in my hands. He stood his ground.

"I suppose you're in a hurry to get back to that big fellow you fished out of the cove?" he said.

"It were only Christian to give him house room until he be better. The fellow was close to death."

"You be the last woman I ever thought would turn nurse maid."

"It fell to me, as I were the first that saw him."

"Well, don't expect me to carry him to the graveyard when he breathes his last. You be trying my patience, Mary. Think about how things stand, now. You need to make up your mind. A man can keep on fathering children until they nail him in his coffin but a woman's got to squeeze the beggars out while she still can."

"So these be the sweet wooing words you use now you've had your way with me?"

"I used up all my sweet words the other night. And you seemed to like them enough then, the way you was rolling underneath me."

"Wash your dirty mouth out."

"Let's not be enemies, Mary," he said, more mildly. "It heats my blood to think of the way some of they be slanderin' you, and I want to take care of you, that's all. To protect you."

"I got by fine without a man to protect me all these years, so why would I need one now?"

He stepped toward me as if a hornet had stung his ass. "I ain't got the patience of Job. 'Tis meant, you and me, even if you won't admit it. Why can't you lean more to the common way?"

"Maybe I don't care to. And you ain't the master of me, Johnenry. So let me pass."

He took my arm, twisting it and hurting me, a nasty look in his eyes. "What in God's name be wrong with you?" he said. "Is you sickening?"

I pulled my arm free and half a pail of water slopped over his trousers. I left him standing in the lane looking like he'd pissed himself.

44

All that night I sat in my chair and kept vigil on the foreigner in the sickly glow of the smoking tallow. On the chest was a pot of herbs that the Widow Chegwidden had given me. Earlier, I had mixed the brew with a little milk and spooned it between the foreigner's lips. The smell of the potion mingled with the odour of sickness in the room.

My head throbbed fearfully from the blow I'd taken from the barrel. Perhaps some of the sense had been knocked out of me. I thought about Johnenry and what he'd said when I met him. Why had I taken a strange man into the house and risked the mud-slinging that would follow? Perhaps I was sickening after something, as Johnenry said. But I couldn't help myself. My heart went out to the man, thinking how he'd been thrown this way and that at the mercy of the waves, lashed to that barrel. And my woman's nature stirred at the notion of this big, dark fellow, at once so strong and yet so helpless. It did trouble me, I own, the hold the foreigner had on me. I consulted with the stone idol, but her face was set in a sulk so I put her on the floor, facing away from the sick bed.

The man's breathing was quick and fretful. While he slept the bird hung quietly, twitching every so often on its string. Whenever the man roused himself with a groan and twisted in his narrow cot, the bird thrashed around as if crazed, taking on the pains of the man. The foreigner drew the life out of the bird's body and into his own, and the bird grew more and more sickly as it took on the man's contagion. I prayed for the bird to breathe its last and there were times when I almost went to fetch a pair of stones to brain the poor creature and bring its misery to an end. But I saw how the man in the bed was repairing, so I gripped the seat of my chair tight, to hold me at my post. Every so often I went over and wiped sweat from his brow with a cloth dipped in cool water. Time passed and the man's strength returned little by little while the bird's ebbed away.

In the dead of night such a hush was over the world that the wings of a moth flitting about the flame were loud as sheets snapping in the wind on laundry day. The cottages in our lane were huddled together so close that I could hear the snores of all the neighbours throbbing through the walls. At closing time the footsteps of the men staggering home from the kiddlywink — where men of the worst sort spent their time drinking and gambling — echoed out in the lane, with snatches of song, a quarrel and much profanity. The drunkards disturbed the gulls in their slumber and they made a row of their own over the rooftops.

By the time the first hint of daylight showed in the window, the man lay in a deep and settled sleep. Seeing he was lost in his dreams, I went and knelt at the bedside and took his hand in my own. He had long fine fingers, despite his bulk, soft hands that had never known hard labour. I stayed there a long while, thinking that I would never tire of looking at his face. His strong jaw was dark with stubble now, and his black locks spread out over the pillow. Without warning, his eyes opened and he stared at me.

46

"What devil are you?" he cried, hoarsely. I tried to shush him, fearful he would bring the whole village rushing to the door. "Why are you poisoning me? What harm have I done you?"

"Quiet now, don't be upsetting yourself, you're poorly," I whispered, my face close to his.

But he shouted again, as loud as before: "The boy! Scarcely more than a child, God help him. Is he saved?"

His shouts upset the bird, which began frantically flapping its little bald wings. The foreigner peered into the gloom, searching for whatever was making the sound. Then he gazed at my face as if to find out what manner of fiend had taken him capture. His breath came fast.

"If you have a single Christian bone in your body, then I beg you to get word to my wife that I am saved," he said. "Do it quickly to spare her more anxiety."

"We has sent for the doctor," I said. "He shall no doubt speak with your wife."

He was quiet again. I sat there by the bed in a slump. For a long while my thoughts were at a standstill. In the end, with a great heaviness upon me, I got up and went to my own room, where I belonged.

CHAPTER
FOUR

The next day Dr Vyvyan came to see the foreigner. He knew us Blights, because in the months since Mamm had got the chronic he'd dropped in and looked her over whenever he was on his rounds. He spent a little time with her that day, too, before I led him up the stairs. He kept glancing at the yellow swelling on my temple and my bloodshot eye.

I hadn't expected the doctor to come so soon and hadn't removed the bird from where it hung in the sick room. I made sure to go in first and stand in front of the poor thing so the doctor wouldn't see it. The room was dark and close. It smelt of sweat and musty plaster, and stewed herbs. But above all there was the sour rankness of the bird, all but dead on the end of its string. I saw then how it would look to the doctor's eyes, a pitiful, suffering thing, blackened and covered in weeping boils. The doctor's nose wrinkled as he stepped into the room. Behind my back, I heard the bird twitching.

"You are hiding something," he said right away, brushing me aside with a movement of his hand. When I was out of the way, he looked upon the bird with utmost horror, and then glared at me. He took a pocket handkerchief from his jacket and covered his nose with it.

"A barbaric custom," he said, his voice muffled by the handkerchief. "The bird is clinging to life but already in the first stage of decomposition. This abomination is to be removed. It is undoubtedly carrying mites and I am sure it is distressing my patient."

"It's taken the fever out of him, look. He's better than before," I said. We both looked at the foreigner, lying peaceful enough on the bed.

"Barbarous nonsense, a rustic superstition to the effect that the infection can be transferred from the man to the bird." He went to the bedside and got down on his knees, taking some instruments from his case. "What are we to do with these people?" he said, smiling at the foreigner. His name was Gideon Stone, and it turned out that Dr Vyvyan knew him. He spoke to him now, as if I wasn't there.

"I thank you from the bottom of my heart for making this visit, Jonathan," said the foreigner. "How is Ellie? I know I can count on you to look after her."

"She is doing as well as can be hoped."

"Let her know I'm better now, much better. Tell her I have a guardian angel who has tended me the whole while I have lain here." He looked at me and my face grew hot. The doctor frowned. I don't suppose I looked much like an angel to him.

"Whatever possessed you to get into a leaky little boat with two men and a boy in the first place?" asked Dr Vyvyan.

"Have you had news of the men who were on the boat with me?" the foreigner asked Dr Vyvyan. "Please tell me they have been saved."

"It's assumed they have perished, I'm afraid," said the doctor. "What happened to you that day?"

"I knew Hell. There was just myself, and a man and his son and an old fellow known to them. I wanted to see this place with my own eyes after the recent infamous reports, and see what good I might do here. But when we reached the cove the boat began turning in tight circles. Something was stirring the water from below, I was sure of it, the sea was so lumpy, so slippery." His breath grew thicker and faster as he spoke. "The current ran in opposite directions on either side of the boat. Unnatural! I swear that something twitched at the boat from underneath. And suddenly tearing, grinding, and a fount bubbling in the hull."

"This is enough for now. Save your energies. You can tell us the whole story when you're home again," said Dr Vyvyan. But the foreigner seemed not to hear him. In his fancy he was back on the boat again.

"The skipper asked me if the Maker would forgive him a life of mendacity if he repented at the last. I told him it was never too late. But it was the boy he wanted to save. The boy was his own son, you see? And I could do naught to save the lad. My prayers went unanswered. Before I could stop them, the pair of them had the barrel slammed into my gut. The father held me while his son coiled the rope about me and tied me fast." He fell back on to his pillow, and closed his eyes.

When his breathing steadied itself, Dr Vyvyan spoke to him again. "Well, at least you are still with us," he said. "A less robust specimen wouldn't have survived. You are the talk of Newlyn, you know. Ellie has had a visit from a correspondent of the *Sherborne Mercury*, no less. Everybody wants to know how the Methodist minister came to be washed ashore lashed to a barrel."

The doctor took out a kind of trumpet and put the bell end to his mouth to warm it with his breath. He bid the foreigner to lie on his side, and began to lift his shirt. At that, I fled the room, and waited on the stairs where I could listen to them through the half open door. It was quiet for a time while the doctor took his soundings with the trumpet. Then the bird went into a frenzy of noisy flapping.

"Will you please remove that hideous item," Dr Vyvyan shouted. With a start, I realised he was talking to me.

I went and fetched a rag from below stairs and took it up to the room. The bird was hanging limp on its string. I untied it from the rafter and wrapped it in the cloth. It seemed to weigh nothing at all in my hands. I brought the tiny bundle downstairs and out of the house, leaving it in the courtyard for Aunty Merryn's stinking cat to maul, before returning to my station on the stairs.

The foreigner was telling the doctor about his ailments. "I thought I had passed from this world into another," he said. "I was tied on some great wheel and flying demons like Furies pushed hot pokers between my ribs. Their huge wings rustled in the darkness and brushed against me."

"You have been in a violent delirium brought on by the fever, that's all," Dr Vyvyan replied. "There is congestion in the right lung, but the other appears to be clear, which is very fortunate for us. You have pneumonia, I would say. You caught a chill in the sea that made you susceptible to the infection which was carried on the unhealthy vapours of this cove." He cleared his throat. "May I speak plainly?"

"You may."

"Well then, as soon as I heard about your reckless voyage and miraculous rescue, I cancelled my appointments, at no little inconvenience, and made arrangements to travel here."

"I am eternally indebted to you."

"As a Penwith man, I know the necessity of hiring a pilot born and bred in this accursed cove to mitigate the hazards. The very reason why this village is so isolated and barbarous is the cove's unsuitability as a harbour."

"I have learned as much, to my cost."

"Your tour of benevolence has put your wife under considerable strain, and as you know I hold her in the highest esteem. If I may venture an opinion, your Bible thumping and extravagant religiosity are not the medicine these poor souls need. What is required is a dose of moral reform, attached to material help." The doctor's tone changed as he called out in a loud voice, "You can come in now, madam, from wherever you're lurking."

It vexed me that he knew I'd been eavesdropping on them, and I didn't like the way he spoke to me.

Especially given that it was me who had saved his patient and not his stupid trumpet. I took a deep breath to cool my temper and stepped back into the room.

"I am afraid we're going to have to impose on your hospitality for another couple of days," Dr Vyvyan said. "I will leave money so you can pay for any purchases you make on my patient's behalf. A warm meal wouldn't go amiss. I'll return in two days, weather permitting, and I'm hopeful I'll be able to take Mr Stone off your hands and return him to his wife in Newlyn. But before I go, I think I should take a look at that bruise of yours."

"Don't trouble yourself," I said, turning to leave the room.

"Did you hear that?" the doctor said to the foreigner. "Impertinent creature!"

I rushed back from the Widow Chegwidden's with more herbs for the foreigner, running straight up the stairs. But when I went into the room I found the bed was empty, only the old creased sheet on the bed, the clothes I'd freshly laundered gone from the chair. The house was quiet and still, abandoned. I ran back down the stairs so quick I almost tumbled, saving myself with my hand on the damp wall.

I shook Mamm to wake her up. "Where is he, the foreigner?"

"The foreigner? Oh, my pet, I told him he shouldn't be up, he's still bad." She tried to push herself out of her chair.

"Did they come and take him away?"

"Oh no, he came down stairs and took himself off."

"Where is he, Mamm? Which way did he go?"

"He wants to try his strength, he says. 'You sure you be strong enough?' I said. 'Rest up another day. Let me fit you a cup of tea.' But no, he says. Can you believe that — no to a cup of tea? Why, tisn't in a man's nature to go without tea!"

"Which way, Mamm?"

"Down the lane, I should think. He dursn't try going uphill in his state."

I ran across the courtyard, through the alley and onto Downlong Row. It was fearful close, that morning, with lazy clouds of flies hovering over the fish slurry in the gulley down the lane. I was glad to get to the quay where some little breeze blew off the sea, and that's where I caught up with the foreigner. He leant against a granite mooring post covered in slimy green moss. His face shone with sweat, and his breathing was fast and shallow. He looked up at me and I was sorry I hadn't tidied up my hair before rushing out. I put the pin in my mouth for a moment, while I pushed the tangled locks into place as best I could.

"You are better?" I asked, cross with him for running off like that in his state.

I glanced up at the quay and saw the giant Pentecost having a smoke with Jake Spargo, Ethan Carbis and Davey Combelleck. Knowing they were watching me, I kept clear of the foreigner and leant against the next post along from him, my arms folded.

"I'm glad we have met," the foreigner said. "I wanted to speak with you. I owe you a profound debt of

54

gratitude that I can't hope to ever repay. I believe it was you who hauled me out of the sea. You cannot have achieved my rescue without putting yourself at considerable risk. I will not forget that. But you needn't let me keep you from your work."

"Where was you heading when you nearly drowned yourself?" I said.

"I was coming here. I wanted to see this benighted cove with my own eyes. Porthmorvoren has achieved considerable notoriety of late."

"Porthmorvoren?"

"This is Porthmorvoren, is it not? Or have I washed ashore in another village by mistake?"

"You can call it that, if you please."

"Don't you call it that?"

I shook my head.

"Then I really am in the wrong village."

"You be in the right place. This be Porthmorvoren, right enough, though I ain't heard no soul hereabouts call it that in years."

"You must call your village something?"

"*Hereabouts*. That's all the name we need."

"I see. And every place else is *thereabouts*, I suppose. Or *uplong*?"

"Uplong, that be about right," I said. "Scarcely another village lies between here and the Land's End."

"It's the ends of the earth, then. It truly is," he said. "A place where demons lurk in the currents of the harbour, where the inhabitants continue to trust in savage pagan nostrums such as plucked birds strung up in sick rooms." He looked at me closely, so I turned

55

away. "And, above all, this is the home of the dreaded Porthmorvoren Cannibal."

"Cannibal! What say you?"

"Have newspapers still to reach this shore? All of Penwith is talking about the depraved fiend who chewed off a lady's ears to steal her earrings."

A hot, prickly flush came over me. I knew what this man would have to say if he'd known I'd filched the boots from this very same woman as she lay dead on the strand. To hide my face, I took off across the shingle. I picked up a pebble, looking it over as if to make sure it was smooth and flat. Then I leant back and sent the stone skimming across the water. It bounced half a dozen times before it sank. I wiped my hands on my apron, and went and leant against another post, further away this time.

"You're worried about those men," he said, glancing up at them. I said naught. "Good Samaritan that you are, you took it upon yourself to help me. But it concerns me that this good deed could be misunderstood by your neighbours."

"The doctor said you be one of they Methodies?"

"I am a Methodist minister, indeed." His chin fell, and his legs looked like they might go from under him. I moved to help him but remembered the men up on the quay and held back.

"'Twill take more than a Methody to stop the men round here from drinking and cock fighting and stanking on their wives," I said, low enough that Pentecost and his mates wouldn't hear. "We had a Methody here once before, but he ran off. I weren't no more nor a child. He wanted to build a chapel but left it half-finished at the top of the hill. The air in these parts don't suit all constitutions."

The foreigner pushed himself away from the post and squinted up the hill. "A chapel, you say? I should like to see that."

"You're weak still, and the lane is steep."

"Calvary hill was steep too, no doubt," he muttered to himself. He turned to me. "Can I trouble you to show me the way to the chapel? Perhaps the air in this cove will suit my constitution better than it did the previous minister's."

THE SHERBORNE MERCURY

It was with great sorrow that we reported the wreck of The Constant Service on Porthmorvoren Strand on Wednesday 2nd February 18 — . The vessel was bound for Liverpool from Charleston, via Jamaica, and struck the fatal rocks of Porthmorvoren cove with the loss of all on board. Not a month passes without a disaster of like melancholy description, but the Horror on this occasion surpassed even our worst expectations.

In the late afternoon, the Coast Guard observed the vessel fourteen miles out at sea off Sennen Cove, off course after being thrown upon a leeward shore and drifting helplessly in towards the coast. The ship of 500 tons had a crew of 28 and, furthermore, carried eight passengers, among them the wife and daughter of Lord S—. The Duke owns a number of plantations in Jamaica, and is a Member of Parliament and renowned collector of fine Art.

According to the Coast Guard, the vessel was in a most deplorable condition, part of her bulwarks gone and her sails blown to ribbons. A ferocious wind blowing across the Atlantic sent in a lumpy sea and the ship became unmanageable. Losing ground on every tack, She struck rocks on the eastern end of Porthmorvoren cove and was grounded, pinned between two crags. The sea continued striking as the tide advanced, until part of the Ship's bottom was carried away and much of the Cargo floated out. During the night the masts fell overboard, and ere long nothing remained of the vessel but her sides.

The Constant Service was laden with a cargo of dutiable goods, including eight hogsheads of Sugar, ten of Molasses, six of Tobacco, three tons of Coffee Berries, eighteen puncheons and six hogsheads of Rum, eighteen casks of Indigo, six of Oranges and Cotton Bales. Other items of property lost or plundered included sails, yards, rigging, pumps, ropes, cables, anchors and casks of candles.

The wreck presented a peculiarly ragged aspect, because the cotton became twisted and torn, and was washed onto the cliffs at Porthmorvoren strand. One country woman became entangled in cotton from head to toe and was drowned while attempting to gather the yarn.

The neighbourhood of Porthmorvoren is infested with wreckers to a degree unusual even in western Penwith, and a parcel of Cornish Barbarians rushed forth to plunder the wreck, all checks of Conscience removed. News spread quickly and the Country People came thick and fast to the fatal spot, armed with pick-axes, hatchets, crowbars and ropes to break up and carry off whatever they could.

The Human Vultures were deaf to the shrieks of the sufferers. Despite the unfeeling nature of this work, women made up the greater part of the miscreants, concealing Rum under their skirts in kettles and chamber pots. Meanwhile, men knocked in the heads of casks of Rum and dipped their hats and drank from them.

Every exertion was made by the respectable inhabitants of the cove to check this disgraceful scene of rapine, but the pressure of the multitude and the want of a military guard rendered their efforts unavailing. When the Cormorants had carried off the cargo, they took every other vestige of the ship, cutting and hewing down sails and masts, cables and anchors. To drunkenness succeeded fatigue, sleep, suffocation and violent affray. Customs officers had scant chance of saving the wreck against such a mob of obstinate and lawless villains, arm'd with rugged home-made Bludgeons.

All right-thinking Men must unite in condemning Heinous Acts of this Nature, which threaten our most Cherished Values and National Reputation. The people of Porthmorvoren are habituated to Night Work and to Defiance of Authority and Contempt of Laws, all of which are engendered by the love of Lucre. The Cornish wreckers vie with the Native Indians of North America in their Barbarism, and are unfit to be Citizens in a civilised country.

A legal precedent must be set to ensure the preservation of Property and Taxes, as well as the free flow of Commerce. Furthermore, the induction of children into wrecking is a moral outrage that must be prevented through religious education. Plundering and wrecking are a threat to English Identity, Patriotism and Commercial Prowess. Barbarity must be replaced by Civility, even in such dark corners of the land.

Yet even the depredations so far described are as nothing in comparison to the actions of the aptly named "Porthmorvoren Cannibal", a wretch who violated the corpse of Lady S— in order to steal trinkets whose value the vicious culprit could hardly have appreciated.

Those who prey like fiends on the victims of these surges

of the boiling deep, and who strip the mangled corpses almost before their Souls have departed their Bodies, must be taught a lesson in no uncertain terms.

News of the tragedy will not reach Lord S— for some weeks. In the meantime, this newspaper calls for a Public Enquiry and an Investigation to establish the identity of the infamous Porthmorvoren Cannibal as soon as possible, and to ensure a suitable Punishment ensues.

ADVERTISEMENT

MONSIEUR LEGRAND
OF CHAPEL STREET, PENZANCE, CORNWALL:

Makes and sells all sorts of Table Ornaments of spun sugar, both silver and gold, guaranteed to set off a dessert and grace a grand table. Place your order for Decorative Confectionery, including intricate Sultanes and Pavilions, as well as fully "rigged" Sailing Vessels, and Beehives populated with gum-paste Bees.

All sorts of Biscuits and Macaroons are available, as made in Paris. Mallows for Coughs, Syrup and Paste of Orgeat and Capilair of Orange Flower.

The whole in Wholesale or Retail at the most reasonable Prices.

CHAPTER
FIVE

I knew the foreigner would be back. He came roundabout Lady Day, when the green catkins dangled from the branches and the magnolia blooms opened to bask in the sunlight. A season when even a foreigner was capable of finding the winding livestock track on the moor that leads to the cove. The mating season was upon us, and the gulls mounted each other on the harbour walls. Likewise, the women of Porthmorvoren fussed about the tall dark stranger in their midst. Work began anew on the chapel after more than ten years, and the sounds of hammering and sawing filled the air. Boatloads of bricks were brought into the harbour, and women carried baskets of pebbles up from the strand for the mortar.

Since the first minister had taken sick and fled the cove ten years ago, the bettermost and a few others had kept the faith, but most had gone back to their old ways. Before he went, the old minister had got Aunt Madgie to set up a Sunday school and that was when I learnt to read. The school came to an end, but we still had a Bible in our home and I'd spent many a summer evening reading the wondrous tales in those pages.

Now we were to have a new minister. Meetings were held in Grace Skewes' house, and the bettermost were paying towards the works on the chapel. I had no part to play in any of this. It seemed that even though Gideon owed his life to me, I was cast out into darkness. But what was I to do? We Blights could hardly pay towards his chapel — we had barely enough money to feed ourselves. And what else had I to offer?

The first prayer meeting was held one night in an abandoned storeroom down by the quay. That night, when I set off down the lane, Tegen chased me and tried to hold me back. "If you go into that place tonight, it will remind all and sundry that we took that man into our house. To think of it — two unwed women! At least wait until the next meeting."

"Let them talk," I said, freeing my arm of her grip.

She lowered her voice. "Loveday's already after your blood. You know Johnenry jilted her after that night when you and he . . ."

"Loveday can go hang."

"I'm telling you to stay at home for your own sake."

"No, you ain't. You're frightened of what folk might say about us."

"Oh, how can I talk some sense into you? Your head's been turned by this fellow and it can only go to the bad."

We came to a standstill and stood in the lane a moment, face to face. "Stay at home, Teg, if that's what you want, but I'm going along tonight. Nothing like this have ever happened in the village, and I ain't missing out just to keep Loveday Skewes happy." I went on down the lane.

"If you mean to go there in spite of all, then I'm coming too," she said, catching up with me.

A minute later, we'd reached the old storeroom. We stepped into the dark and were almost deafened by the clamour of women's voices. They were packed in like pilchards in a basket and I feared we would never find a place. The only light was the bilious glow of the smoking tapers hanging on the walls all around the barn. The pews were no more than planks laid across tubs, with a rough pulpit at the front and a makeshift Communion rail. On the men's side, no more than half a dozen fellows had come. I elbowed Tegen in the ribs to get her to look at old Thomas, who was kneeling on his handkerchief in a great show of sanctity, his hands clutched under his chin in prayer.

I knew without needing to look that heads were turning towards me. The pecking order was clear enough, with Millie Hicks and Grace Skewes in the front row and Loveday Skewes sitting primly alongside her mother in a brand-new bonnet of virginal white. Soon enough, a hush came over us and down the aisle marched Gideon in his black greatcoat. I only dared glimpse as he swept past, nodding at one or two hearers who caught his eye. All that could be heard were his footsteps on the mud, the hiss of the tapers and the odd creak of a bench. He stepped up to the pulpit and fiddled with his papers, bowing his head in silent prayer before resting his forehead on a huge Bible. I saw that the Ten Commandments had been pinned to the wall behind him. Eventually he lifted his head and put his hands before him as if groping for some hidden object in the air. His shoulders shook with strong emotion. I glanced at the women down my row and saw a row of mouths hanging open.

Gideon began his prayer, his voice deep, his words filling the space up to the rafters. I took in hardly a word of it as my gaze was fixed on his flailing hands, which told me more of his passion than the dour words flying from his lips. When he was done praying, he took up a great hymn book and drew it towards him. He called out the hymn number and asked for Sister Skewes to come forward and line out the verses. Loveday Skewes stepped meek as a lamb up to the pulpit. This was the same Loveday who liked to blacken my name at every chance. There she stood, angelic, with her flaxen curls teased forward so they wriggled out from under her new bonnet. Being a dainty little thing, all that could be seen of her behind the lectern was the top of that white bonnet bobbing up and down. I noticed the minx wasn't so worldly as to wear bows of ribbons in it.

She read aloud the first two lines, tripping over every word, for the sake of them who weren't able to read. This was the greater number of the hearers, although they tried to hide it by gazing at the roll of paper over the Communion rail where the words were shown. The minister tapped a tuning fork against the pulpit and it hummed for a moment before Loveday led the singing. She soon went off key, so that those of us with a better ear were left to steer the tune back to the proper pitch.

The hymn spoke of God's mercy but any who heard it were like to abandon all hope, with its endless shambling repeats, and wailing, and the lack of aught you would take for a tune. How I longed to let my voice surge above the throng, to adorn those dismal verses with a few pretty lilts. To make matters worse, the congregation had to halt after every two lines while Sister Skewes, in her brazen little bonnet, stuttered out the next couple of lines.

When we were at last put out of our misery, the minister opened the Holy Book and began a reading on the Prodigal Son. His dark fringe fell over his face whenever he grew passionate, and he swept it back with his beautiful hand. Every woman's rapt gaze was on the handsome stranger. I was afraid of catching his eye so I cast my gaze about until it alighted on the seamstress and scandal-monger, Millie Hicks, who sat on the end of the front row. She'd turned aside to face the pulpit, and I could see the garment spread over her lap, and how she set the stitches in it, turning the fray under her thumb as she made a seam of perfect straightness. When she heard that the Prodigal Son had realised the error of his ways, she shouted "Hallelujah!" without missing a stitch.

When, at last, the sermon was done, the fattened calf slaughtered and the Prodigal Son back at his father's breast, the preacher invited others to exhort, to unburden their souls of whatever pressed heavily upon them. The first to stand was Abraham Isbell, who said that now he was under conviction he was so taken up with worship that he no longer had time to do any work. The minister got out of him that he had a family of twelve to feed, and advised him to temper his enthusiasm with due paternal duty. I'm sure I wasn't alone in stifling a laugh. Abe had always been an idle gadabout.

I was itching to get up and speak, but Tegen took hold of my arm. "Don't you dare, now," she whispered.

The next to testify was that old windbag, Henry Cutler, who all dreaded meeting in the lane for fear they would never make it home in time for dinner. He told of how he had awoken with a sudden conviction of his own sin. It happened about eleven o'clock at night on 1st April, and he would never forget that happy hour. By quarter past the hour he had gained a fearful understanding of the damning nature of sin and his many slights against God and was surprised the earth did not open up and swallow him. Alongside me, Tegen put her hand over her mouth to hide her yawn, and it must have been catching because half the women on the bench did the same.

Henry droned on. The following day, he said, he wrestled with his soul from the moment he rose and knelt to pray, at just after five in the morning until dusk at just before seven-thirty. He pondered the Redeemer's merits and saw that he must be eternally undone unless he took them to his heart, and this could only be obtained by faith in Christ. At about nine o'clock last night, Christ appeared within him and pardoned every last one of his sins, so that now he stood before us, his soul at liberty. He spoke of a great many other trifling matters besides, and each one was marked by the time of day or night that it took place as if he were more clock than man. Next the foolish dolt set about confessing each and every private shame he could recall, including at least one that did not bear repeating in mixed company. I would have died sooner than reveal the least of my own secret vices.

"Glory, glory, glory!" shouted old Thomas, whose knees must have been on fire by now after kneeling so long on his handkerchief.

Next to speak was dear old Aunty Merryn. She told the minister she had been in the world sixty-two years last Michaelmas and had never yet been saved. Having left it so long, she was now afeard the Redeemer would not hearken to her.

"It is never too late to petition for the Lord's mercy, sister, if we have faith and are fervent in prayer," said the minister, looking down on her in a kindly way. He told her to consider the Prodigal Son's example. Any fool could see the old woman was afraid of dying, and only trying to comfort herself by pretending to a faith in her Saviour she did not feel in her heart. It seemed to me that the Prodigal Son was a bad example to some, for he was sure to embolden the blackest of sinners to try to make up for a lifetime's sin by repenting at their last breath.

But I was shocked out of this reverie by the sound of hands clapping and looked up to see Abe standing on the bench with his arms raised. He had completely forgotten himself in the emotion of it all, and I had to hold onto the bench for fear of the madness taking hold of me too. Others were standing and hugging their neighbours, or shaking hands, even with their worst enemies.

The minister began his sermon, recounting in pitiful terms the great sacrifice our Redeemer had made for our salvation, coming down from his heavenly throne and letting himself be denounced, spat on, mocked with a crown of thorns, beaten senseless with a knotted rope and finally, when the human frame could surely withstand no more, nailed by his hands and feet to a cross on Calvary Hill to slowly die in agony. Every hearer was sniffling and wiping their eyes by the time he was done, grown men included. Next, the minister rounded on all of us, as if we'd been there in the crowd that called for Barabbas to be freed instead of the Jesu. He asked how we had repaid Christ's sufferings. Nobody dared to raise their head and answer him. The minister denounced the pleasures of this world, sports, revels, idle songs, card playing and dancing, in other words every little comfort that made life bearable. His creed was as hard as the bench on which I sat and the longer he went on the harder the wood ground into the bones of my backside, which no amount of squirming could relieve. I saw then why some of the bettermost had brought cushions with them. On and on the minister went, renouncing gambling, games, fairs, drunkenness, tea drinking, tobacco, wrestling, fornication and failure to observe the Sabbath. It seemed he'd learnt a lot about us in his short visit here.

Finally, he stopped for a long moment, his head bowed, his chest heaving. I watched as a drop of sweat rolled from the tip of his fine straight nose and fell onto

69

the Bible that lay before him. We all trembled, thinking he might point the finger of blame right at us, or that he had found out our inmost secret shame.

"Now I come to the heart of the matter," he said, looking out at his hearers. "The very reason why I have come here to found a chapel in this cove." He brandished a newspaper over his head, the *Sherborne Mercury*, before throwing it down on the lectern. "This journal carries an account of the infamous crimes committed in this cove after the sinking of *The Constant Service*, just a few weeks ago." I glanced around and saw the heads of my neighbours hanging in shame. "As a result of the depravity and lawlessness of that night, the name of Porthmorvoren is now reviled throughout this land. And there is one heinous act which has come to represent the darkest depths of human nature, when greed prevails over all sense of decency. Do you know that of which I speak?"

I was rigid, afraid any movement might give me away.

"Perhaps the individual responsible is among us today?" said the minister.

I knew he was talking of the stolen earrings, and all for that I was blameless of the crime, I broke into a prickly sweat. I was thankful Aunt Madgie was not in the congregation that night and able to turn on me with accusing eyes.

"Let me refresh your memory by reading from the newspaper's editorial page: *Yet even the depredations so far described are as nothing in comparison to the actions of the aptly named 'Porthmorvoren Cannibal', a wretch who violated the corpse of Lady S— in order to steal trinkets whose value the vicious culprit could hardly have appreciated.* Let me tell you, brothers and sisters, that it was this outrage that convinced me I must visit this outpost of civilisation and see what could be done to bring you under conviction. My intention is to finish the build of the chapel on the hill above the village. Together, we will light a beacon of hope where before there has been darkness. You are all God's children, even the most prodigal amongst you. You have been neglected too long. If you repent and submit to the holy fire your sins will be forgiven when you stand before the Throne of Mercy. I promise you I will work with every fibre of my being to uproot your age-old customs and plant the Holy Cross in this stony ground.

"It is late. When next we meet I will tell you about Perfect Love. About the joys that await you in the next life if you turn away from sin in this one and open your hearts to salvation. Now, who among you will offer a last prayer this night?"

Without thinking, I drew myself up from my knees onto my feet. Tegen's hand flew up and clutched my skirts to hold me back, almost sending me headlong into the row in front of us. Every face turned towards me, some with puzzlement and some with disbelief, others with purest outrage. What made me do it? Fear of hellfire or something else? I was so scared I could hardly draw breath. I had a queer urge to burst out laughing, but was able to check myself, thank the Lord. Some strange litany I had read, or overheard or perhaps only imagined, floated into my mind and I spoke out.

"Good Lord, deliver us by Thine agony and bloody sweat, by Thy cross and passion." My voice gathered its usual force. "By the crown of thorns piercing Thy brow . . ." I swallowed and looked right at the minister while he glowered at me in such a manner that my knees trembled under my skirts. It was so silent that when a hearer coughed it sounded like a thunder clap. "Dear Jesus, when I come before Thee in the final hour, if it please Thee, Heavenly Father, pray do let me know it is truly Thyself, perhaps by a sign . . ." I'd lost my way, of course, but there was no turning back. "Maybe by the nail prints in Thy hands, so that . . ." I lost my thread and stood there, seeing the open mouths of Grace Skewes and Loveday, and a whole row of other foes who had turned their heads to gawp at me. Loveday's mate Betsy Stoddern stared at me with bulging eyes as if it was all she could do to stop herself marching over and giving me a smack in the mouth right there and then.

"I offer up this prayer to thee, my . . . my . . ." I couldn't find the right word.

"My *Saviour*," Tegen hissed, at my side.

"My Saviour," I said, and dropped onto the bench with a muttered "Amen".

Murmurs of outrage passed along the front row where the bettermost sat, and then there was a coarse shout behind me. It was the voice of Nancy Spargo.

"Praise be to God!" she hollered, and suddenly the air was full of cries of "Hallelujah" and "Amen to that". I was saved.

CHAPTER
SIX

I got to the chapel, breathless after the climb from the beach, and put the basket of pebbles down. My shoulders ached and the palms of my hands were scored and red from the basket handles. The minister was on top of a ladder in his shirt sleeves, the cloth sticking to his back as he skimmed the mortar over the bricks with his trowel. Watching the play of the muscles in his broad shoulders sent me into a whoozy waking dream. But just then the huer's shout of "Hevva, hevva!" was heard up on the cliff top. I looked up and saw him standing outside his shack, waving a great bush in each hand so all would know the pilchard shoal had arrived. The little fleet of boats had been at anchor on the horizon the last four days, and now out at sea the men were shooting their nets. You could see the shoal in the distance, a dark cloud of broken water that grew till it was hundreds of yards long and, in an instant, shrunk to a small inky stain.

I left my basket and ran down to the strand. The whole village was there, from the elderly and lame to the smallest children. The copper-coloured sails were already slowly heading for shore, cork floats bobbing all along the width of the cove where the nets were slung between the boats. Already the mesh was swollen with fish, enough to feed a multitude. We waited, cheering and waving, as they inched towards the shore, the fish teeming in the nets, some leaping up and twisting in the air.

Before long, there were more than three hundred souls wading in a blaze of silver and blue on the strand, as the fish thronged and thrashed around us five deep. The fish and people seemed one and the same, the hands and forearms of the men, women and children glittering with fish scales. Boat after boat came to the shallows to empty their baskets onto the beach, not only the sacred pilchard, but ling, turbot, whiting and other barbed and whiskered monsters that you wouldn't want to see on your dinner plate. Little children wrestled with pollocks as big as themselves. I heard the minister's voice not far away and my pulse quickened.

"This is a sight to behold!" he cried. "What could be more ennobling, friends, than the exertion of hard physical labour." He came among us, throwing himself into it, rolling up his sleeves, scooping armfuls of fish and throwing them into the boxes to be carried up to the village. "Who would not marvel at this testament to the fertility of the sea and the wonder of God's creation?" he called, his dark eyes shining, his hair blowing into his face. In his zeal he was like a boy, the world all new to him, a breed apart from the men of the village, so beaten down and sly.

The very air was enchanted that day. A fine rain, no more than a soft mist, hung over us, with the sun

74

showing through the haze. Further out at sea the clouds had broken to show the blue heavens, and a shimmering rainbow made a perfect arc over all. I saw the minister gaze about him, hands on hips, proud as Moses leading his children to the Promised Land.

"Seeing how you labour together . . . I truly believe I'm seeing you all for the first time, how you throw in your lot with your neighbours for the good of all, putting aside petty resentments and rivalries, acknowledging your dependence on one another with open trust."

As time passed I drew nearer to the minister, until we worked side by side, and I might have reached out and touched him. If he caught my eye, he smiled. He didn't turn a hair when fishwives walked along the quay barefooted, their bedraggled skirts gathered at the thigh with no thought to decency. On other years I'd have done the same, but I kept myself covered that day.

Horses and carts and pack-saddled mules led the fish from the quay up through the village lanes which ran with blood, putting me in mind of Pharaoh's land during the massacre of the innocents. Every wall and door was gritty with salt and spattered with fish scales. Fish swill rolled down the gullies in the lanes down to the quay, making the ground slippery for the stout men who carried large boxes with pole handles at each corner, crammed to the brim with fish. They hauled the boxes up the steep hill to the cellars where we women stood waiting with arms folded. The banter between the women and the fishermen wasn't fit for respectable ears, but the minister seemed not to mind it. The cellar doors in the courtyards were thrown open and once the fish were tipped out, children handed them to the women down below so we could lay them out in tiers.

Herring gulls scrapped noisily for spoils and gannets swooped down to where offal lay in mounds of glistening crimson and purple, with a thick cloud of flies hovering over all. Scrums of hissing cats raked the air with their claws to shoo away the birds, and darted away to skulk in a corner and gobble their trophies. The air, always warm and sticky in the cove, felt thicker than ever that day, and even the odd gust from the ocean brought a stench of fish. Out at sea the boats were already tucking another shoal within their vast nets and I wondered if the village would be mired under fish before long.

Work carried on in a frenzy until the sun had set and the lights of the fleet twinkled far out in the darkness, not to return till daylight. We womenfolk worked away in heavy shadow lit by flickering candles, our sacking aprons smeared with blood. Walls of fish mounted around us and glinted like jewels in a vault. We squabbled and joked, and now that the children were abed, our foul-mouthed chatter went beyond even that of the men, as we packed the pilchards into the walls.

A shadow fell over me. Glancing up, I saw the tall figure of the minister standing above us looking down into the cellar. I couldn't see his face against the light of a lantern on the wall behind, but I felt his gaze upon me. What a picture I must have made, flushed from hard work, my arms, fingers and face slimed with fish juices. I brushed a stray lock from my face with the

76

back of my wrist, but all this did was smear more fish scales into my hair.

"Well now, is that you, Miss Blight?" My heart thumped hard under my filthy apron. A hush fell over the smirking women, who continued to salt and pack the fish. "If only I could do something to help," he said, "but I fear I'd only get in your way."

Nancy Spargo was sitting alongside me. "It don't belong to a man of your station in life to come down here and get mucky with us women," she said, with her gap-toothed grin. "Besides, you has done enough for us already, parson. This great catch is all down to you. It be God's blessing, I seem, on account of how you has brought so many of us under conviction."

"You has outdone King Jesus," I said, seizing my chance. "We has more fish today than at the Sermon on the Mount, and the shoal have come weeks before it were due."

"The shoals has been poor these last two years," said Nancy. "It be Divine Providence, for sure."

"You saw the rainbow, minister? That means a new Covenant, as it did for Noah," I said, growing bolder. I knew the other women were giving me looks, but I hardly cared at that moment.

"I am pleased you know your Bible so well," he said. Did he think I was laughing at him?

"I have it almost by heart." I closed my eyes and summoned up the first bit of Scripture that came into my head. "*Blessed are the poor in spirit for theirs is the Kingdom of Heaven.*"

"Blessed indeed!" cried the minister, with heat. "What a day this has been! I'm beginning to see the Almighty's design in the events of these last weeks. You were the one who hauled me out of the sea that day, were you not?" he said to me. "Surely Providence has driven me onto this shoreline. I feel God's spirit working powerfully within all of us tonight. This day I discovered the loyal and heroic natures underneath all of your rough exteriors. You are made in the Almighty's image."

He was interrupted right then by two men, the giant Pentecost and Davey Combelleck, who dropped a box of fish right at the minister's feet.

"Not on my f— toe, Davey!" shouted Pentecost. "You do that one more time and I'll stick my cock in your ear and f— some sense into you." The women cackled. I looked up to see how the minister had taken it, but he had gone.

At the crack of dawn the next day, we threw open the cellar doors in the courtyard and climbed down the ladder to get back to work. The cellar was an airless tomb, with walls of fish packed in row after row, their heads poking out and their red-rimmed eyes gazing at us. At first the stink of the fish almost made me faint, but I got used to it soon enough. We women worked alongside one another, elbow to elbow, salting and bulking, half mazed with lack of sleep, watching the wall slowly rise before us until we could no longer see over the top. We were of every age from Cissie Olds, who was barely in her sixteenth, to the Widow

Chegwidden, who must have been in her sixtieth at least. Our boots splashed about in the slurry that drained off to the pit in the middle of the cellar. A fine moist dust came off the fish which cloyed your throat and made some poor women breathless. Overhead, dark clouds raced across a sky that was tender, promising rain before the afternoon. For now, I welcomed the gusts of cool air on my face.

"I don't like standing on my feet all day like this," moaned Martha Tregaskis. "My corns be killing me." She took a good glug from the pot of Jamaican rum from the recent wreck that was being passed down the line. "All we've got at home is parsnip wine and I never could abide that swill," Martha said, belching. "This be more to my liking."

Martha was a dreadful slattern, and more than partial to a drop of hard liquor. It showed in her blotchy skin. Few would blame her for it, though, as she was married to the giant, Pentecost, that big bully. Her left eye was ringed with a fading yellow bruise.

"Corns be a sign of foul weather," said the Widow Chegwidden. There was always a soothing air about her, with her lulling voice and rosy cheeks, and her hair pure and white as lambs' wool against the black cloth of her dress. "I know a sure remedy, my dear," she said. "Gather nine bramble leaves and place them in spring water, and afterwards pass them over the soles of your feet. If that should fail, rub a piece of meat flesh on them, then bury the flesh and let it rot and by that time the corns will have gone."

Martha offered the rum to the widow, but she shook her head. I was next in line and took a good swig before handing it to Cissie Olds, who stood between me and Tegen in the line. I was fond of Cissie and knew that she looked up to me. I watched her, wiping sweat from her face with her forearm, and I thought her too young and comely for such filthy work, with her fair hair and blue eyes. Her hands were red and raw, already seasoned by hard labour. When it was Tegen's turn with the bottle she shook her head and passed the pot on to Martha Tregaskis, who took a big glug.

"This Methody talk about Perfect Love in the ever after is all very well," said Sarah Keigwin, "but a bit of a flesh-and-blood love right now wouldn't go amiss. I don't know what to do about my Matthew. I can't very well come out and say it to his face and shame him to it, and he's blind to every hint, or else he be past caring for me." Spirituous liquor freed up some women's tongues, I'd noticed.

"A woman have rights or else what be the point of conjugating with men at all?" said Martha. "If you ask me, a man is no more than a stand-by on dark nights, however much they lord it over we and stank on us. And if they can't even make a stand of a night, what use are they to the female race?" There was uproar at this, all of us stepping back to roar with laugher along with their mates. All of us except Tegen, that is. She was getting my back up that morning, with her prim and proper ways.

"Talking of men, what do you ladies say to this new preacher?" said Martha, who'd got hold of the rum pot again. She had a sly look on her face. "I reckon it be a fine thing for us women to have our own haven to go to of a night. After all, our men go to the public, like pigs to the trough. And the preacher be some handsome, don't he?" She elbowed another woman in the ribs as she said it, and there was more cackling.

"It gets a body out of the house, I suppose, although I'm not so keen on all the parson's strictures," said Sarah. "He says the men dursn't put out to fish on the Sabbath. Surely, he don't expect us to leave the whole pilcher shoal to they Newlyn skate? How would we feed our children through the long winter, I ask you?"

"He have already forbid the reading of improper psalms," said Martha. "I'd never heard of such a thing before he mentioned it. Soon as I got home, I looked up the verses in our Bible." We all chortled at this. "What do you think of him, Mary?" she said. She was slurring her words after downing all that rum. "You and Tegen must've seen a lot of him when he was laid up in your cottage that time." Tegen flushed — after we'd put the minister up in our cottage, she'd been too ashamed to show her face in the lane for days afterwards. Martha was still blithering on, the drunken fool. "I suppose you know they're a-talking about you in the village, Mary? Loveday Skewes be giving the wink of it to folk that you has set your sights on the minister."

"It's yarns. Nothing but muck and stink," I said, without letting up in my work.

"Loveday's just riled because the minister got Mary to line out the hymns instead of her," said Cissie, smiling at me.

"My Matthew told me Johnenry got into a fight the other night, to defend your name, Mary," said Sarah. That got them mumbling all down the line.

"He was defending his own name, more like," I said.

"A good man, Johnenry. And nice-looking too," said Martha.

"Mark my words, Loveday will soon get her claws in him again," said Sarah. "Speak of the devil, I heard that Loveday's to be made Sunday school teacher."

My hands stopped bulking pilchards, and I took a step back. Thinking of Loveday Skewes being the minister's favourite and simpering around him filled me with a black rage. That doltish jade was in no manner worthy of the man. In my fury, the women around me faded away and I was alone in the world. When I came round, though, I got back to work as if nothing had happened.

"Maybe you can push Loveday aside and become teacher in her place, like you did when she was leading the hymns," said Sarah, eyeing me to see how I took it.

"What say you?" said Martha, looking down along the row of women. "Can you see Mary as a teacher? The very idea!"

I looked at Martha. "And why not?" I said. That wiped the grin off her drunken face. "Why shouldn't I be teacher?"

"I were only thinking about they boys?" said Martha. "You might go and teach they the wrong things." She sniggered, but the other women saw the temper was up in me and kept quiet. "Next thing we know, Mary'll be wanting to read the sermon, like a man," said Martha, undaunted.

I heard a mild and steady voice behind me. "There were women priests once. A long time ago now, of course." I turned to find the Widow Chegwidden, sucking on her pipe. The air around her was spiked with coltsfoot, a known balm for lungs rasping from fish fumes. "We are only shadows of the women of those far-off times," said the widow. "Weak, silly creatures, easily stanked on by our masters."

"I wouldn't mind giving a sermon if I had the chance," I said, slapping a pilchard down hard on the wall. "I'd ask the men in this village how they'd like it if I had a bellyful in the public and took a piss against the wall outside. Or what they'd think if I put out in a boat, and sailed wherever I pleased, while they had to stay at home and keep house. If I ever get my hands on the tiller, I know what I'll do. I'll sail to Penzance and buy a rack of new dresses." Some of the women cheered, and others jeered. Cissie gave me a hug.

We all got back to work again. After a spell, Tegen leant behind Cissy's back and spoke to me, almost in a whisper. "You should take a little more of a care over yourself."

"For why?" I said, not caring who heard it.

"You know why. Think about Mamm and me, just this once."

"Think about you? For once? You be forgetting all the times I stood up for you over the years. It ain't my fault I've got a timid little mouse for a sister, always fretting about what the neighbours think, always running into her little mouse hole to hide from the world."

The women were quiet for a time, their hands busy salting and bulking while hungry gulls screeched overhead. After a moment the Widow Chegwidden spoke, in her kindly way.

"Might I offer you a word of counsel, Mary? Perhaps the blood of the women of old is running in your veins and, like them, you can move between the sea and the land at will. Who knows what powers you may have? But you must take care, my dear. You must learn how to balance in rough waters the way a fish does."

"A fish?" I said. "I've had enough of fish for one day!" Cissie and me laughed, while the other women looked at each other, not having a clue what the widow was talking about. Tegen shook her head at me, which only riled me, perhaps because in truth I wished I could take back my sharp words as I watched the Widow Chegwidden turn from me.

When the cellar was loaded up to the gills, Cissie and me set off, arm in arm. I saw the smart of envy on Tegen's face and was glad of it. She was a woeful figure, climbing out of the cellar and shuffling through the carpet of glittering scales that covered the path to the cottage. Cissie and me went and lay on the soft moist turf on the headland, watching the clouds roll by and laughing about Loveday Skewes, her snooty ways, and her sly way of slandering people while pretending to be kind about them. I was sorely riled that she was to be made Sunday school teacher and that was the truth of it. Only when I was walking back home to the cottage, did I feel some qualms about Tegen. I hadn't been fair to her, but knowing I was in the wrong put me in even less of a mood for making amends.

After all, hadn't I always stood up for her when we were little? Many was the time Loveday had given orders to that big bully Betsy Stoddern to pull Tegen's hair or make fun of her. They picked on her because she was a silly fretful thing, apt to start blubbing at the slightest teasing. She had no father to stank on them, and Mamm was rushed off her feet, so it was left to me as the older sister to fight her fights. I used my nettly tongue mostly, but my sharp nails too if it came to it. I got a good few bruises fighting Tegen's battles for her.

The only thing we had in common was our carroty hair. Tegen tried to keep hers hidden under her bonnet, but it was forever worming its way free and grew out of her skull as kinky as a Hottentot's. She had a thin skin, and at the first touch of sunlight, her face and arms were smattered with freckles, a thousand tiny tea stains. The slightest pinch or knock left its mark. She was blotchy and broke out in rashes, and she was prone to goosebumps and hives and heaven forfend she should ever brush against a nettle or a midge should nip her. Every little thought told in her complexion, and if a man so much as raised his hat to her, she was on fire from her face and down to her throat and all across her chest.

What a look she gave me when I came home that afternoon! She was on her knees shoving pilchards into a clay jar before they went rank. I took no notice and went up to the bedroom to wash my face and hands. I heard her pushing the broom around down below for a long while. If Tegen wanted to play the martyr, then let her. I'd had enough of her, forever worrying what people would say about me and Johnenry, or fretting about my testimony at the prayer meeting that she said made we Blights a laughing stock. When Tegen finished her sweeping, she came up to wash, pink in the face after her toiling. She groaned to see I'd left the water in the bowl yellow and greasy, and off she went, huffing and puffing, to fetch more from the well. Meanwhile, I put on a nice dress and brushed my hair.

Nathaniel Nancarrow was coming that evening for dinner. He was a great friend to the Blights and never came empty-handed. When he was due, we waited in the kitchen. A sugarloaf had been delivered that day, a reward for my part in the recent wreck. The sugar nips lay alongside it, and a few lumps were already broken off the loaf. Mamm and me warmed our hands on our cups, me at the table and Mamm in her armchair. Tegen poured herself a cup and sat across from me.

"Won't you have a bit of sugar, Teg?" said Mamm.

"I won't, she said. "It's off the wreck, where so many poor people perished."

"Oh yes, we durst pray for their souls," said Mamm. She bent down to place her tea on the floor. Perhaps her conscience had been pricked.

"A woman needs a little sweetness in her life," I said, taking another sip.

There was a knock on the door and Tegen leapt up to open it. Nathaniel's face broke into his crinkly smile as I pulled out a seat for him. He was a shy man and it showed in the way his head fell onto one side and then the other when you first met with him. Tegen let him have her chair and perched herself on the wobbly three-legged stool, which served her right for being so pious about the sugar. Nathaniel put a package on the table wrapped in old newsprint.

"What is it this time, Nat?" I said.

"Oh, only a bit of sparrow grass from my tattie patch on the hill," he said, his big hand stroking his jaw shyly.

"So you remembered me saying I was fond of sparrow grass?" I said, teasing him.

"Go and fit Mr Nancarrow a cup of tea, Teg," said Mamm. "And make it nice and strong." She sat in her frayed old armchair by the hearth, propped up by cushions. She smiled at Nathaniel. Though she was past her fortieth year, and her lungs laboured sorely, she was always keen on the company of men, her own husband now so long in his watery grave. Nathaniel was a favourite with her, as she thought him a solid, respectable man. Tegen went to put the kettle on the trivet, and Nathaniel enquired about Mamm's health.

When her long health report was done, Mamm smoothed the rug on her knees and turned to Nathaniel. "And how be they children of yours?" she asked. "The most darling little angels you could ever see, ain't they, girls?" This pleased Nathaniel, whose face broke into a hundred smile lines.

"Passing fair, Mrs Blight," he said. "And with God's help they will remain so."

Tegen stood Nathaniel's tea before him. I offered him sugar but he refused. I noticed Tegen smile at that.

"I hope you didn't go wading out to rescue people at that wreck the other month?" said Mamm.

He looked abashed, as if risking his neck to save his fellow man was something to hide. "There was naught that I, nor anyone else, could do," he said, looking into his cup. Tegen had given him a cup from Mamm's best tea set, the fine bone china harvested from a clipper a good many years ago. The dainty cup looked silly in his big hand. "A capital cup of tea, Tegen," he said.

"It goes to my heart to think of they children of yours, Nat," said Mamm. "If ever anything should, well, you know what I mean."

"My sister in Marazion would take them in if it came to that. Her own are grown now with homes of their own. And my Tamsin is in her fourteenth, after all, and a capable girl. It's hard to stand by and do naught when lives are in peril."

Tegen gave me a look, meaning I should get on and make the dinner, but I stayed put, so she went over to the hearth. She poked the faggots in the grate with the fire hook, being sure to make a lot of noise about it, then raked the embers until they smouldered, before drawing the iron trivet forward and putting the baking ire on top. She got the pilchards from the cold room and laid them out in the crock.

Nathaniel and me helped Mamm to the dinner table, each taking an arm. When Mamm had got her breath back and the high colour had drained from her face, she spoke. "We're having fresh pilchards with vinegar and watercress, Nat."

"Handsome, Mrs Blight! A real saviour," said Nathaniel.

"The Good Lord provides," said Mamm. "With help from you, of course, Nat."

"Speaking of the Good Lord, I was disappointed not to see you at the prayer meeting last week," I said to Nathaniel. "The minister were so fervent and devout, so sure in his faith, he might have set the building aflame."

"He is a man accounted powerful in prayer, that is true," said Nathaniel, quietly.

"Even *I* was moved to testify," I said.

"Aye, I did hear that," said Nat, with a little smile.

"I suppose you heard some of our neighbours blackening me afterwards?" There was a little catch in my voice, and I wondered if he'd heard it.

"I take no notice of tittle tattle," said Nat.

"So, we can expect to see you at the next meeting then?"

"Perhaps."

I didn't care for his answer. "You don't doubt the new minister at all, do you?" I asked.

"If the minister is all he professes to be, he is a righteous man, for sure."

"Speak plainly, Nathaniel. Say what you mean," I said.

"I'm only saying that life have taught me to weigh up a man's character on his conduct over time, and not judge him on first acquaintance," he said. "A plain and honest man may prove better than one who is naught but show. Howsoever, I won't reproach the minister because I know little about him."

"The minister is beyond reproach, you can count on that," I said. "There is more passion in that man's breast than in a hundred 'plain and honest men'." Nathaniel cringed, and stared down into his lap. Perhaps he was envious because I had spoken so well of the minister.

"There be more to saving souls than wild sermons," said Tegen, over at the hearth. She was almost scroached by the fire and was fanning her face with her apron. She looked more vexed than I could remember ever seeing her. "Nathaniel might not make fine speeches and lay claim to saving people's souls, but he have saved dozens of people over the years, clinging to a rope while the waves rolled over his head and the outhaul near dragged him out to sea. Think of that." Her eyes were streaming and she could hardly breathe, and I realised it was due to more than just anger at me.

"Tegen!" I shouted. "Look what you've done!" I jumped to my feet and threw the front door open, letting in a blast of cold air. I'd been so roused by Nathaniel's mealy mouthed words about the minister that I'd failed to notice the bitter smell in the room and the thick blue cloud of smoke drifting over from the hearth. Tegen had plain forgotten to keep an eye on the fire. Nathaniel was helping Mamm to her feet and taking her out of the cottage into the courtyard. I followed them, glancing back on the threshold to see Tegen cover her nose and mouth with her apron and walk through the smoke to the fireside. She lifted the lid off the crock and cried out when she saw the pilchards lying in a row, shrivelled, black and charred, no more than empty husks.

CHAPTER
SEVEN

I was in a waking dream those first weeks after the coming of the minister. He'd chosen me to line out the hymns when Loveday Skewes stood down after making such a laughing stock of herself. None could say I did not read well and, of course, I'd always been known for my singing. Sadly, I was forced to sing the dour dirges without adornment, keeping them as plain and solemn as the drab black clothes I took to wearing as a mark of my purity. At first it vexed me to go abroad in those widow's weeds, but then the mirror showed me how well my red hair looked against the black linen and I had a change of heart.

I had given myself to Christ now, and kept the stone idol hidden in a drawer. At night I lay abed, gazing at my Band ticket where my name was printed along with the minister's initials: G.S. for Gideon Stone. When I'd had my fill of looking at the ticket, I put it under the pillow and snuffed out the taper. Lying wakeful in the darkness, my mind turned over and over, wondering about Mr Gideon Stone. I was drawn to him because he was so strong and secure in his convictions. I believed his heart beat with more passion than other men's, surely more than Johnenry's, who asked for so little from the world. I knew Gideon must have climbed his own Calvary to reach the heights he now commanded. It made me think that anybody might raise themselves from their station if they put their mind to it.

I had no clear idea what I wanted from Gideon. I only wished to carry on basking in the glow of his good favour for as long as it lasted. I remembered he had a wife, of course, Ellie, and she was in good health, so I tried not to harbour any foolish thoughts on that score. But I also remembered the fervent words he uttered in his ravings when sick, about his "Molly". In the shadows of his past life there was another Gideon who could not so well control his nature. The sweetest pangs came over me when I lay in the darkness at night, thinking of this hidden weakness in the minister. Sometimes I was carried away by wild and foolish longings, seeing myself in another life than this, free from ceaseless toil and hardship, raised far above the bettermost in the village, in fine clothes like those I'd seen on rich ladies drowned in wrecks, and even, in my madness, seeing myself walking down a handsome street in Penzance, arm in arm with Gideon Stone.

While such fancies came upon me at night, in the day-time I put on a pious face and bearing whenever I passed a neighbour in the lane, and never once stopped to tease the menfolk or share a joke, as I used to. Even the likes of Grace Skewes and Millie Hicks were forced to concur that Mary Blight seemed changed since she had come under conviction, whatever the sly polecats might have said behind my back.

I was enrolled in the Society and permitted to attend the weekly Band meetings where we called ourselves "the people of God". Many is the yawn I stifled during those dreary talks on seeking perfection in spiritual matters. To begin with, I was all nerves in such grand company, but soon I saw how easy it was to frighten Millie Hicks, who was elected class leader. I was far above her when it came to citing the Scriptures, and she couldn't match my sharper wit.

In those early days, Gideon visited the cove every fortnight and attended the Band meetings. There was barely space enough to scratch yourself in that little room when the Band members were all assembled, and you had to keep your elbows at your side for fear of knocking some ornament off the mantelpiece, a china dog or tall brass candlestick, perhaps, or a strangely patterned moccasin made by savages in foreign lands or the irons for frilling Grace Skewes' caps. The corner cupboard was crammed with more trinkets, such as china, quartz crystals, a ship in a bottle and grog glasses and other heirlooms passed down the Skewes family through the generations. I had never seen such riches.

The women shuffled about muttering pleasantries, while Grace and her closest mates almost smothered the minister, keeping him all to themselves. Loveday Skewes was there with a little bunch of cronies, including that big old battle-axe Betsy Stoddern. The room was stuffy and I was worried about knocking one of Grace's illuminated New Testament texts off the wall. What a relief it was to move into the kitchen.

The time came to discuss the revival of the Sunday school. As the minister was present, the lower sort of members, such as me, and young Cissie Olds and old Thomas, were permitted to sit on the benches at the kitchen table along with the bettermost. At other times we'd been obliged to sit in the window seat like children, or on the settle at the foot of the stairs. Gideon took his place between Grace Skewes and Millie Hicks, ducking his head to avoid the herbs that hung in bunches from the rafters. Grace had put freshly cut flowers in the middle of the table that she'd picked from her own little garden. We each had a pitcher of water. The tea set was over on the dresser, but Grace hid her tea caddy inside the cupboard. She knew Gideon would surely have guessed where the tea had come from. Even Grace Skewes, for all her glitter and jaw, baulked at paying the duties on tea.

The sun flooded through the small window and dust motes floated in the stifling air. The heat of so many bodies pressed together on the benches made the women's cheeks rosy. Grace brought in a plate of saffron buns and scalded milk from her little dairy. The cream was like heaven melting on my tongue, and only pride stopped me taking the last bun off the plate. My mind wandered while Gideon talked about the funding of the new chapel.

"Money must be found to pay the masons to raise the walls, timber must be ordered for the door, the windows and the forms, as well as thatch for the roof," he was saying. "The balance of the accounts shows costs at one hundred and forty pounds, while subscriptions are only up to forty. It might take decades to clear a debt of a hundred pounds. The better-off families have been especially generous, of course."

Here, he turned with a smile to Grace Skewes and Millie Hicks, as if they weren't puffed up enough already. Their husbands were the skippers of the biggest boats, I thought, so why shouldn't they bear the brunt?

"And yet I must lean on you good people for more. You will see the worth of it once the last stone is laid, the chapel consecrated, and you are able to step inside and feel the Holy Fire."

Next he turned to his lesson from the Scriptures, which was more to my liking. It was about a woman in olden times with five husbands. When Gideon had finished, Loveday Skewes, who was sitting across the table from me, tried to explain the parable to her friend, Betsy Stoddern. Betsy turned to the minister, with a creased brow. "Will you help me get to the rights of this, minister?" she said. "How can it be that the woman in the parable was able to draw water from a well without a pail? Whoever heard of such a thing?"

"Perhaps it be one of the Lord's miracles, Betsy, like when he turned water into wine," said Loveday, giving her a stare so she'd stop making such a fool of herself.

"Aye, but that's another puzzle, isn't it, the Lord encouraging folk to drink liquor?" said Betsy. "Surely that's not good Scripture observance? I suppose it was different in those far-off times."

Gideon patiently explained the meaning of the parable. Betsy nodded, but was still out of sorts. "If you say so, minister," she said. "But 'pon my soul, I don't know why the Good Lord couldn't have looked out a more decent woman to spread the gospel among the heathens than that Samaritan. Why, the strumpet had five husbands."

"Oh my dear life, Betsy, what a base word!" said Millie Hicks, not knowing where to turn.

"Remember what we discussed before, Sister Stoddern," said Gideon. "The message of salvation is for all of us, including the poor and the outcast."

"As long as they do honest work and don't live off the parish," said Millie Hicks, with a righteous nod.

"Amen to that," said old Thomas. The women gave each other little looks, because his idea of honest work was sleeping under a hedge all afternoon.

There was a pause, so I took my chance. "Jesus scolded the Disciples for saying it didn't belong to Him to talk to a Samaritan. They said he shouldn't talk with the Samaritan woman at the well, given that the Lord himself was a Jew. But the Lord told them the gospel is for all peoples. So perhaps we hereabouts should think about being more neighbourly to one another, and even to those Newlyn skate."

Gideon rapped the table with his hand, startling the women and upsetting the water in the pitchers. At first I thought it was out of anger with what I'd said. "Precisely so, Sister Blight," he said. "We must all ask ourselves how we can remove those obstructions in our everyday life that prevent us sharing God's love with others, especially those who are different from us. We must be passionate in sharing Christ with relatives and friends, of course, but even more so with our enemies and with strangers. This is why the Lord chose the Samaritan woman to spread his Word to her people. Do you all see?"

Betsy looked as if she'd sat on a pine cone. She and Loveday looked at each other, and I could see they were in no mood to share God's love with me. The other women stared down at the table in silence, not knowing what to think. But Gideon was not a man overly sensible of the moods of women. "This rather conveniently leads me to the matter of the Sunday school class and who is to be the teacher," he said.

Grace Skewes coughed to get her daughter Loveday's attention, so that she'd put herself forward. But Loveday blushed and whispered, "Shush, Mamm!"

"Whatever is the matter with you, my pet?" asked Grace.

"Aye, Loveday, speak up now," said Betsy, giving her friend a dig with her elbow.

But Loveday only bit her lip and stared into her lap.

"Well now, do we have any volunteers?" asked Gideon.

The women fidgeted and tried not to catch his eye.

"Sister Blight, you read very well, and you have demonstrated in our meetings that you are familiar with the Scriptures. Perhaps we can persuade you to put yourself forward?"

Somebody must have kicked a table leg because a pitcher fell over.

"Mary's mother is ailing," said Grace, in her most mollifying voice. "It is asking too much of her, I seem."

I could feel all those eyes on me and didn't dare look any of them in the face. "That is true," I said, meekly.

"But we are only asking Sister Blight to give up some of her time on the Sabbath," said Gideon, sweeping spilt water away from him with his hand. "I am sure Sister Blight would not consider working on the Lord's day of rest, no more than any of you. And you have a capable sister at home, do you not, Sister Blight? These encumbrances are easily overcome."

I was cross about how little value he put on my poor Mamm's illness, but at the same time I was beside myself with excitement at this turn of events. To be put above Loveday and the whole bunch of them so easily! Grace went to fetch a cloth and began to wipe the water from the table. I saw her give Millie Hicks a meaningful look. Millie smiled at the minister, and said: "To be sure, Sister Blight is well learned in the scriptures. But she have only lately been brought under conviction and we must ask if the children will show her the proper respect owed to a gospel teacher."

That settled it for me. "I would like to give it some consideration," I said. That made their eyes pop. I sounded halfway to being a Sunday school teacher already, the way I put it.

"Splendid," said Gideon, beaming. "I am sure we can provide a small stipend for the family. We have sufficient funds, thanks to all of your generosity."

"What a turn up this is," said Betsy. "Why, it be just like the Lord choosing the Samaritan woman with her five husbands, I seem." She looked round the table for back-up.

My face was on fire but I kept my resolve. "I has no husbands at all, Sister Stoddern, so I cannot think what you mean," I said.

"Betsy, I'm sure you didn't mean that as it sounded," said Grace, with a smile as creamy as her scalded milk. "Perhaps it's time to stretch our legs in my little garden, ladies?" I suppose she wanted to get outside and start scheming against me as soon as possible.

The women rose from the table and made their way out. I followed them, but as I passed through the little dairy I heard Gideon clear his throat behind me. He asked if I could spare him a moment. We stood a little distance apart. The dairy faced the north wall of the house and the coolness that came off the stone was a blessing after that close and airless kitchen. I kept my gaze on the red-tiled floor.

"I must apologise for my presumption, Sister Blight," he said, his voice low. "I should have discussed this with you first."

"My mind is made up," I said, without a moment's hesitation. "I will do it, if you believe I am capable."

"I am convinced of it."

There was a maddening steady drip as milk plopped out of the tap in the side of the churn into a tin pail on the floor. The rich smell of the butter made me queasy.

"I will need help," I said.

"My wife teaches our Sunday school in Newlyn," he said. "She will provide some basic instruction."

"Your wife will come here?" I said, taken aback.

"No, you will have to come to Newlyn. I'm sure we can give you lodging for a few days. After all, it's only what you once did for me." He smiled. "At a brisk pace we can cross the moor in six or seven hours."

"Are we to cross the moor alone, the pair of us? What will people say?"

"Bringing a chaperone would imply I cannot be trusted, surely? Unless you request it?"

I shook my head. "I have to tell you that some hereabouts will say I am unsuited to the position of teacher," I said.

"Your knowledge of the Scriptures is exemplary."

"I know my Bible well, for sure, but there are those who will say I am not in such good standing as a teacher perhaps ought to be."

"You have shown yourself capable of Christian sacrifice and charity. How many others would have risked their lives to save me in the way you did? Who among them would have taken me into their care, regardless of the censure of their neighbours? We may need to smooth out a few rough edges, but that is a small matter compared to these virtues."

"If you say so," I said. Bright sunlight cut across the room from the little window so that I cringed before this man as he looked down on me.

"Perhaps I can give you one instance of how you might improve," he said, in a kindly, coaxing way. "I heard a woman singing the other evening, and something drew me towards the sound; curiosity, I suppose. I didn't know who it was until I reached your home and recognised that narrow alley."

"I have a fondness for certain hymns," I said quickly. "I suppose it was likely 'Praise the Lord ye Blessed

Ones' or another favourite." I shuddered at the thought of this man standing under the eaves and listening to me singing, and prayed it was not some whores' ditty he'd overheard.

"Indeed, but with so many trills and, shall we say, *sensual* flourishes, even a song such as 'Praise the Lord' cannot in all truth be sung with sincere devotion. I only remark on the matter, because, as you have implied, we must not give any envious person a stick with which to beat you."

"I suppose even the winding songs I am so fond of must be outlawed, even though they sing God's praises?"

"Such songs are the Devil's music, Sister Blight." But he smiled as he said it.

"Then I shall put these faults behind me," I declared. "From this day on I will mend my song to make it more pleasing to the Maker."

When the meeting was over, I was in a sore temper, for all my triumphing over Loveday and winning the trust of Gideon. I fled the village to break free of all the idle gabbing about me that had spread like chicken pox, to the top of Uplong Row and past the miners' cottages, where the narrow lane pressed so much upon a person's thoughts. Once I was higher up on the moor, I could see halfway round the world. It made me wish I was a man so I could sail the seven seas and be out of sight of all those prying eyes.

The higher I climbed, the more vexed I grew at Gideon's ban on me singing whatever harmless ditty took my fancy, until in the end I couldn't stop myself singing at the top of my voice, knowing I was out well of his earshot.

I was heading for Tombstone Point, where I'd always escaped to whenever my thoughts were in a fearful knot and I wanted to let them untangle. I heard the curlews' falling call, queer and unearthly, and was carried back to when I was a girl of nine or ten, my pockets full of treasures from the hillside or the beach, shells, dead field mice with the softest fur, white cuttlefish scoops, mermaid's purses with beetle claws at the corners, shards of glass whose sharp edges had been worn smooth by the tides.

I saw myself when I was older, in my thirteenth or thereabouts, when I'd often sit atop Tombstone chewing a blade of grass and watching the shifting currents down below in the cove until a calm mood washed over me. I'd wave at Johnenry down below in his jollyboat, rowing the fish ashore after fetching them from the bigger boats. I envied him, because no man would let a woman on a boat, not even a girl, for it was bad luck, like seeing a hare before putting out to sea. From time to time I saw foreigners' boats come to grief down there, too tiny to seem real, forced into a spin and slipping into the ocean's depths in a kind of dream.

In our younger days, Johnenry and I would lie on the turf on Tombstone and tell each other our heart's desire. He still had dreams back then, of joining the navy and fighting the French or sailing to the Americas and finding gold, or being the captain of his own ship with fifty men under him. I said I'd bind my breasts,

103

put on the blue jacket and be his first mate, but he laughed and said I had nothing to bind.

One summer the boys had taken to diving off Tombstone Point on days when the sea wasn't too rough. They'd hurl themselves over the cliff edge, sometimes turning somersaults, or diving with their arms straight ahead of them or else rolling themselves into a ball before they hit the water so the surf blasted around them like cannon shot. Johnenry would open his arms and legs wide and swoop down like a bird.

A dark mass of clouds had gathered a mile off the coast and rain as black as soot was falling into the ocean. The storm was heading towards me. Why had I come out on such a day? I had seen the warning signs and ignored them — Aunty Merryn's stinky old cat lying on a step giving its ass a lick, a sure sign of rain; the rooks diving towards the trees and the geese honking; and a spider darting into a hole in the wall. A hard rain began to sting my face and soon there was a deluge like in Noah's time. I could barely see through the downpour and feared losing my way and never finding the path back. I couldn't go to Tombstone Point on a day like this or I'd risk stepping over the edge into the vacant air.

At the end of the lonely rock coomb I saw the ghostly shape of the little church tower and ran towards it. It had stood there since the times of the saints, and was haunted by them still. Mass was rarely held there any more, unless there was a funeral or wedding. On such occasions the rector would come over from Paul, for a price. I crossed a stubble field where the first green shoots of the year were peeking out of the sodden earth. Reaching the churchyard, I leapt over the wall and jumped between overturned gravestones. Two cows stretched their necks down over the crumbling wall and chewed on wiry plants, the rain dripping from their eyelashes and rolling down their long, black faces.

At the top of the tower was the little old hag, carved out of stone, squatting under a turret, her legs wide apart and her hands holding the gaping hole between her thighs open to the four winds. Rain was shooting out of her as if she was pissing down on the big stone cross that stood directly beneath her. Over time the hag had loosened the moorings of the cross and now it was listing. How I loved that old hag!

I rushed over to shelter in the porch, but more water was dripping through the old porch roof than out in the open. The church door was swollen with damp and needed a push to get it open. Inside, an ancient chill came off the musty stone, making my nose run. Little puffs of mist poured from my mouth, and a thin film of steam rose from my shawl. Up above, rain rattled on the slate roof, a pleasing sound when you were indoors and not outside getting drenched. When my eyes were able to see better in the gloom I walked further into the nave, my footsteps echoing. People were buried underneath the granite flags, their names and dates of birth and death almost worn away as if time had forgotten them. I heard something move high above and started, but it was only a pigeon roosting in the roof beams.

Down the aisle I went, humming to keep myself company. A spirit echoed me, so I stopped. I passed the row of spindly stone arches and reached the back of the church where I could look up into the shadows of the tower. Plaster was hanging off the walls. Folk said there was once an older temple on that same spot, where animals and even people were sacrificed to the ancient Gods. Thick straw bell ropes hung down around me, the ends frayed as if they'd been chewed. Up above me in the tower, the cracked old bells were hanging somewhere in the darkness where the hoot-owl hid. The bells had never been taken and melted down because nobody had ever thought it safe to climb such a tower. You sometimes heard them toll late at night when the ghosts of dead fishermen returned from the sea. I wished I could climb up those ropes to Heaven and see the face of King Jesus. But when I closed my eyes and tried to summon the Jesu, it wasn't him I saw. It was the face of Gideon Stone, with a crown of thorns around his head and his life blood rolling down his face. I had to sit down on a rickety pew to quiet myself.

The Maker had shone a light into the darkest shadows of my soul and brought my hidden desires into the light of day. I wanted Gideon to save me, but not so that I could kneel at the throne of King Jesus and kiss the holes in his feet. I wanted him to help me flee the village so I could parade among the snots in all my finery in a grand town. I longed to be able to look down with scorn on the bettermost of Porthmorvoren cove. Other desires lurked in my heart as well, dark longings that I dared not let out into the light.

106

Looking round me, I saw an old stone tomb on one side of the nave. A knight of old in a suit of armour lay on top in deep shadow. A heavy mood fell over me as I remembered the time the boys had wheedled me into playing a trick on Pascoe Hurrel. They'd been teasing Pascoe because he was a soft and sickly boy and afraid to jump off Tombstone Point. The truth is Pascoe was afraid of everything. The boys put me up to saying I'd meet him in the church and let him kiss me. We were to meet by the tomb of the old knight. When he came looking for me, the others jumped out from where they'd been hiding and chased him out of the church and down the hill, jeering all the way. A week later Pascoe leapt off Tombstone Point. I don't suppose he meant to drown himself, only to show he was as bold as the others. As I sat alone in the pew thinking back to that time, rain water dripping off my skirts onto the stone flags, my eyes filled with hot tears for I knew I shared the blame.

There was a sudden loud crash behind me and I near jumped out of my skin. The church door had wrenched open and a flurry of leaves and twigs burst inside. I fled that place with a righteous haste and ran home through the pelting rain.

The next day I was summoned to Aunt Madgie's house on Back Street to attend a meeting of the Methodist Society that had been called without notice. I was in a dark mood as I turned off Downlong Row into that dreaded lane, knowing a gathering behind the minister's back didn't bode well for me. The old woman's house stood in the middle of the street, held up only by two stout columns to the fore that supported the upper floor. The place had once been grand, but had long since fallen into rack and ruin. People said it was the only building left standing after the Spaniards put the village to the torch in olden times, so it went back even further than Aunt Madgie herself. On dark winter nights when neighbours gathered around the fire, an old tale of dark imagining was told, about a room in the back of the house that had long been kept locked. At nights, the spirit of a dead noblewoman was heard inside that chamber, pacing up and down in all her finery, her heavy skirts rustling and her jewellery rattling.

I hadn't set foot in that house since I was a child and had no wish to do so now. It was where I'd first learnt my letters, under Aunt Madgie's instruction when she was Sunday school mistress. She had kept a stick hanging over the door but seldom reached for it, not even for the boys. A look was enough to quell us. I was the best learner among the children but the crone would always save her praise for Loveday Skewes, who was her kin. That was more than ten years ago, before the first minister fled the cove and left his chapel behind, with only the foundations built. He wasn't tall and handsome like Gideon Stone, but old and ruddy-faced with a dusty smell off him. It was said Aunt Madgie scared the old fellow off after he tried to put a stop to free trading and wrecking. The old dame was devout, but not when it took food out of the villagers' mouths — or tobacco out of their pipes. With the old parson gone, we children dropped out of the school one by one and went back to our old ways. But I carried on reading in the years after, the Bible and anything else I could lay hands on.

I stepped between the two stone columns and took a deep breath before reaching for the rusty knocker, dreading the moment when the door would creak open and Aunt Madgie's face would loom before me. It was a relief when Dolly Stoddern opened the door instead, but her false smile told me all was not well. I followed her through the dark hallway with its queer echoes, my heart fluttering the same as it had done in the days I came there as a child. The kitchen door was ajar so I could hear the women's voices. The talk was always the same in those weeks, about that wretch the Porthmorvoren Cannibal. The women broke in on one another to have their say.

"If you ask me, 'twere one of they tinners from up the lane. They'll stop at naught . . ."

"What makes you so sure 'twere a man though?"

"'Pon my soul, no woman would do such a thing, surely."

"Whatsoever, 'twill only end when the culprit's flushed out. Someone round here knows who did it, you can be sure of that."

"Aye, but nobody will snitch on a neighbour. 'T'ain't done. 'Tis one and all in this village . . ."

"And yet all our good names are blackened. I'm ashamed to show my face at the market in Mousehole."

The loose talk stopped when they saw me come into Aunt Madgie's kitchen. I shuddered in that chill room,

109

the feel of the old days flooding back to me. And who did I first set eyes on but Aunt Madgie herself, sitting grim as death in her yellowed mob cap at the head of the table. Up and down the sides of the table were all the ladies in Grace Skewes' clique, the bettermost of the village.

A seat had been left for me at the other end of the table which meant I must look straight down at Aunt Madgie's unflinching gaze. I might as well have been brought before the Magistrate. To one side of Aunt Madgie sat her daughter Grace Skewes and next to her Grace's daughter Loveday, with Betsy Stoddern alongside Loveday as always. Dolly was next in line, then Millie Hicks, her sewing in her lap and her thimble on her thumb, her daughter Zenobia beside her. Aunt Madgie aside, they were all smiles, which only went to prove they'd been catting about me.

"How is your Mamm keeping, Mary? She must be a worry for you and your sister?" said Grace.

"As well as can be hoped," I muttered, taking my seat.

"'Tis always hard when there's a bed-lier at home," said Millie Hicks, looking up from her stitching. "You and Tegen must be forced to take on all work to earn your meat." She rubbed her long thin neck, slyly.

I was tongue-tied, for once, twirling a strand of hair in my fingers, a childish habit that came upon me when jittery.

"You look ever so pretty, even so," said Grace, with her creamy smile. "Don't she, ladies?" A few of them nodded. "That dress you've taken to wearing suits you

110

fine — the black linen against that pale and delicate skin of yours, not to mention all that red hair!" She looked about her at the other women, and some smiled.

"Enough to turn any man's head," said Loveday under her breath, to her mate, Betsy.

"And it's not long since she went to the feast with a huge flower in her back hair," Betsy muttered back. Grace gave them a sharp look.

"Why have you called me here, Grace?" I asked. "I've heaps of work to do, as you say."

"Oh 'tis only that we mean to talk Society business and, with you being a Band member now, we could hardly leave you out. I just wanted to say how pleasing it is to see the change that's come over you of late, Mary. We're quite taken aback."

"I'm under conviction," I said.

"Of course you are, my dear heart," said Grace, looking down her nose at me, her eyes narrowed. "And of course there's a place for you here in the Society. We trust your conversion is sincere, but we mustn't throw all reason to the wind now, must we?"

"What are you saying of?" I asked.

"I'm talking about what came about yesterday, of course. What a rum turn of events! How are we to put things right?"

So that was it! I saw the rotten black-flies had sent for me because they meant to stop me being Sunday school mistress.

"We're only thinking of you, Mary," said Millie. "What a fright you must have got when the minister asked you to become school mistress. You, of all people! He must have taken leave of his senses."

A few women sniggered, and my face was on fire. They made me feel a fool to think I could ever truly become school mistress.

"I'm sure Mr Stone means well," said Grace. "It's just that he don't know the neighbourhood. He can't see how hard it would be on you if this madness came to pass."

"I made a promise to the minister," I said, fighting to keep my voice steady. "He put his trust . . ."

Grace cut me off. "The minister means well and has done right by us women," she said. "He has brought us together, given us a haven in that old barn, but he don't know people hereabouts."

Millie backed her up. "A shrewd woman like you, Mary," she said, "lettered as you are, and always so fine and fond of reading, surely you must see that right-minded people won't want you teaching their children."

"I know the Bible better than any here!" I said. "I know I'm no angel . . ."

"Far from it," said Betsy.

"Hold your tongue, Betsy," snapped her mother.

"Remember the Prodigal Son," I said. "He had a change of heart and his father forgave him . . ."

"I never heard tell of any Prodigal *Daughter* in the scriptures," said Loveday.

"Hearken to me now, Mary," said Grace, folding her arms. "It is already decided. All here agree that

Loveday should be school mistress. It don't belong to you to do it."

"Because I'm poor?"

"Because you put people's backs up, stealing their men and . . ." snapped Loveday.

"Quiet now, Loveday!" said Grace, before turning to me. "Now, Mary, listen well to what I have to say. You don't have the standing in this cove to be Sunday school mistress, and well you know it. You must ask your conscience if you have the cleanness of heart for such a task. Then you must tell the minister you mean to stand down. It must come from you."

I was sick of the whole parcel of them. "Cleanness of heart?" I said, fixing my gaze on Loveday. "I could name a good few in this parish who are no cleaner of heart than me. Half the women hereabouts are with child when they go to the altar, and none here can gainsay it."

"You never once thought to become a Methodist until the minister arrived!" cried Millie. "Some of us have kept the faith these ten years."

"As long as the minister thinks me fit to be school mistress, I will stand firm," I said.

"Very well. Be it on your own head," said Grace, her smile gone. "I must inform you that the Sunday school classes are to take place here, in my mother's house."

"Here? Why not in the old barn?" I cried.

"The barn ain't safe for children, and it's too cold," said Grace. "This kitchen is the only room in the village big enough to hold the class until the new chapel is built. And it means Mamm can keep an eye on things.

So, you'll promise to tell the minister you're standing down then?"

I shook my head. There were gasps around the table.

"Is that a yay or a nay?" said Grace.

"I will be teacher. The minister chose me."

A sudden loud grating sound at the other end of the table set my hair on end. It was Aunt Madgie pushing her chair back, the legs scraping over the stone floor. She got to her feet and stood, laying her palms down on the table to support her, the crooked fingers and swollen knuckles spread out, the black veins bulging on the back of her hands.

"Blood of the lamb, fire of hell which goes not out!" she snarled. "I have heard enough. This varmint will never yield, unless made to." She gazed hard at me and pointed a shaking finger at me. "As for you, I rue the day I taught you your alphabet. If I'd known your wanton ways back along, I'd never have given you the Holy Bible so you could use it to charm a weak and doltish preacher into thinking you virtuous. You'd better think upon what has passed between us lately, Mary Blight, and think hard!"

"Naught has passed between us!" I cried.

"What is this, Mamm?" said Grace. "If you have some sway over her, then you must use it."

"All in good time," said Aunt Madgie, putting out her hand for her crutch, which Grace gave her. I waited for the old woman to dodder out of the room, before I got up and hurried out of the house.

I was lost to all around me as I dashed up and down the lanes afterwards. When my anger abated, I began to

114

fret over Aunt Madgie's dark threat. Would she tell the Preventive Men that she'd seen me steal the earrings? It was a black lie, but the hateful look in her eyes made me more than uneasy. Hadn't she seen me leaning over the noblewoman's body, a picture of guilt? It was my word against hers, and she was of a good family, while my word wasn't worth the squeak of a pressed pilchard. If she lied and snitched on me, I'd be hauled before the Justice, sure as time and tax. I was in a beggar of a hole and there was no getting out of it.

But then again, I thought, if there was no other proof, her word might not be enough to send me to gaol. And in any case, nobody in the cove had ever informed on a neighbour. It was One and All, and Aunt Madgie, of all people, never missed a chance to tell us so. We might stank on our own, but we didn't hand them over to uplongers. And if her false word did send me to gaol, she'd surely go to hell twice over. So, in the end I told myself she'd made the threat idly, to frighten me into standing aside for Loveday.

The truth of the matter was that nothing, not even a hurricane, could have kept me from going to Newlyn with Gideon Stone when the time came.

II

WHITSUNTIDE

CHAPTER
EIGHT

As soon as we got up the slope onto the moor Gideon started his sermonising. He barely gave me time to get my breath back, or to let my ears pop after the climb, and he wasn't gallant enough to walk at an easy pace, but set off briskly, so I had to work up a sweat to keep up with him. The hot sun glared in a sky that was clear apart from a few scattered clouds, and my scalp itched under my bonnet. I wore the boots that I'd taken from the woman who'd been washed ashore lifeless in the winter wreck. They were too small for me and pinched my toes. I carried my basket with two dresses inside, as sober and as seemly as I could find.

We tramped in single file between the stone hedges, following the miners' mule track that wound up and down the moor. Sometimes we rounded a bend and startled some sheep so that they scrambled off in panic. Gideon wove a long and twisting lesson as I followed him along that narrow path.

"There are many ways that a man can judge whether he is a true child of God or only deceives himself," he said. "Some men lead themselves to believe they are witness to the true and genuine testimony of the Spirit, but they mistake their own pride for God's grace."

"Then how can we know for sure that we do God's work?" I asked.

"That is not easily answered. Even Wesley could not find words to describe 'the deep things of God'. The Spirit is like the wind, which you can feel without knowing from whence it came or wither it will go." As he spoke, leaves rustled in a hawthorn bough beyond the hedge.

"So we cannot tell if we truly act in God's grace?"

"To know His grace is akin to a change from darkness to light, a passing from death into life," he said. A dark cloud must have passed and hid the sun because a shadow fell over the moor and I felt a sudden chill. "The Scriptures laid down clear and obvious marks for the children of God," he said. I kept my thoughts to myself as we listed these marks for God's children.

"We are to keep His commandments, and love our neighbour as ourselves."

I smiled to myself at that.

"We are to honour the Sabbath day," he said.

"What, and starve?" I thought.

"We are to do unto others as we would have them do unto us."

So if a neighbour blackened your name and tried to keep you low, was it fair to do the same to them?

"One must possess one's body in sanctification and honour."

Too late for that, I thought, recalling my spree with Johnenry.

"Be temperate in eating and drinking."

Chance would be a fine thing!

"And do all to the glory of God."

Well, Amen to that, at least.

We reached a place where the old pannier lane took off in a different direction, and we walked out across open moorland. All the while Gideon spoke, I heard a skylark overhead urging its endless stream of song from its throat, toiling high in the air as it chased after flies, as tireless as the minister in his preachifying. My mind wandered and I found myself lost and drowning in a sweet reverie where I groped my way through a huge draper's store, like the ones with big plate glass windows in Penzance. Almost swooning, my feet scarcely touching the ground, I swam among armies of dresses stretching away in rows forever and swaying softly and slowly, beckoning me into their midst. At either side of me were great billowing puffed gigot sleeves, and embroidered collars, and high-waisted full skirts with twisted satin hoops around them so that they seemed to twirl, and the hems high enough to show the dainty ankles and feet of the ghostly forms that moved underneath the cloth. My hands reached out to stroke the folds of muslin, satin gauze and silk, the heavy cotton and calico, all tingling under my fingertips. All about me were garments drifting upwards towards a queer, misty light high above, wide-brimmed bonnets, gloves, parasols, sashes, ribbons and bows, while below me on the sandy ocean bed lay great oak chests, the tops flung open and dazzling jewellery of every kind you could desire spilling over the sides.

I heard a man's voice and realised he was speaking to me. "Sister Blight? Are you sick? You are pale and seem to stagger." Jolted out of my stupor, I grew mindful of the bleating of sheep, the smell of sheep dung, the wind buffeting my ears and the skylark's song still pouring forth overhead. I felt the hot pain of my poor toes cruelly crushed together, as if the dead woman's spirit was punishing me for taking her boots. On the brow of the hill I saw the minister, a brooding shadow against the light so that I couldn't know for sure what look he had upon his face.

I hobbled up the hill to join him and caught a glimpse of soft blue sea, which lifted my spirits a little. Another time I would have filled a basket with the thrift that grew in the boulders, the blue dog-violets clinging to the stone hedges, and all the other glories of high summer that blushed in a bed of rose and purple heather: devil's buttons, lady's smock and the pink ling that was only just opening.

"'Tis pretty, the view from here," I said, more to myself than to him.

"When I enjoy a vista such as this I am filled with wonder at God's creation, and how we can see His glory in all things," he said, without troubling to look at anything at all. He stood there stubborn and rooted as an ancient oak, and as empty of feeling. I wished that the fat bumble bee that was buzzing around the minister would see fit to sting his ass.

"Why must you turn everything in creation into a cold sermon?" I asked. My sore feet were making me bad-tempered and I risked getting above myself, but I'd had my fill of the minister for one day.

"I beg your pardon?" he said, looking at me askance.

"Can't I look at a pretty view and enjoy it without thinking Bible thoughts? You can pick a leaf off any tree and wonder at its colour and shape, at the veins that run through it, so like those on the backs of our hands. The Maker lets the skylark soar and sing her heart out in any way she pleases, so why must we cage our feelings and not let them out. This land lives in me, is in my soul."

He stared at me for a moment. I was afraid I might have troubled him so much he'd change his mind about making me teacher.

"Sister Blight, you have good qualities and I have put my trust in you," he said, at last. "If you are to assume the responsibilities I have in mind, you must attempt to rein in this propensity for . . . for what I might call unbridled sensual arousal. You must learn to channel your feelings into worship of the Almighty."

"Didn't God make us the way we are? I know you have feelings too. I see it when you stand in the pulpit. How strong you are up there — strong *here* in the heart." I gave my breast a thump.

"But that is not the same. When I preach the gospel, the Almighty works through me. What I was referring to is self-seeking lust for the pleasures of this world. It leads us to the worst excesses of Fallen Man's corrupted nature, to intemperance, abandonment, darkness . . ." He broke off for a moment, frowning at the distant patch of sea. When he spoke again, it was more softly. "What is the love of Nature but a form of pagan idolatry? Without an awareness of God, we are lost. We must learn to know Him in all things. I have chosen you, Sister Blight. I have come to see you as a beacon of hope in that poor benighted village of yours. Pray, do not disappoint me."

"Well, I will try my best — as long as I can be permitted a few little comforts."

He nodded, smiling. "Perhaps, weariness has made us both ill-tempered. I only wish I could show you the higher joy awaiting us in the next life. Let's rest awhile on these boulders." He pointed at some rocks that giants had thrown down in far-off days.

Grateful to set my rump down on the stone, I could at last let the cool air soothe my feet. I peeled the first crippling boot off, and recalled with a shudder the instant that same boot had come off the noblewoman's foot on the strand. It came upon me so strong I smelt the seaweed and heard the wash of the tide, and was lost to the world around me a long moment. When I came out of it, I looked down at my poor swollen ankles, and the great white blisters blooming on my heels and soles. The blisters were tender to the touch, even more so now I'd stopped walking. I looked about me for dock that would ease the smarting. The minister sat with his back to me, looking out over the moor, having seen nothing of my unease.

When I'd soothed my feet with a cool leaf, I took my crust of bread and cheese out of my basket. The minister ate naught, perhaps God's grace alone was enough to sustain him. He passed me his water flask and I drank deeply from it. As I chewed the dry crust, I thought about all the minister had said as we'd walked along. The Scriptures commanded the children of God to show a soft, yielding spirit, to be all mildness and sweetness and long-suffering. All around me were stunted trees that bent to the prevailing wind, just as I must bend to a higher will. I remembered the minister saying that a true child of God was saved from the pain of proud wrath, but I was in no mood for mildness at that moment. Would the Maker save me from the pain of blistered feet? Or a guilty conscience?

Gideon stood up and gazed this way and that, then stood overlooking the vale beneath us, as if he bestrode the world. "This is the way, I believe," he said, pointing down across the moor.

"That is the wrong way," I said.

"I think you are mistaken. That coppice over yonder is familiar to me."

"My feet are badly blistered and I don't want to walk any further than I must."

"I've made this journey several times in recent months and I've taken note of the landmarks," he said. "I will admit that I allowed myself to be distracted momentarily today, but I'm sure we haven't strayed too far from my preferred route." He did not turn to look at me as he spoke but kept his gaze fixed on the land below him.

"I have no need of landmarks," I said. "I have walked between the village and Newlyn many times since I was a child, and I know the way by feel alone."

He made a sound, a kind of laugh. It was the only time I'd heard anything like a laugh come out from him. "I am sorry, but relying on 'feel alone' is not sufficient," he said. "If we lose our way on this moor and cannot find the route by nightfall we will find ourselves in dire circumstances. I imagine the temperature drops considerably."

I suppose he was thinking about the scandal it would cause, the pair of us huddled together for warmth while we lay in the darkness and the midges bit us raw.

"Since you won't take heed, I will not waste my breath," I said.

"Well, we shall see. Let us go down and cross this brook."

I knew ill fortune would follow a man who took a woman across water but I kept my own counsel, and followed him, step by painful step. The further we walked, the more barren and rocky the land became. My ankles turned and I tripped over hidden stones. Now and then my feet would sink into a foul-smelling mire. After a long while our route was blocked by a high ridge. It was steep and when I reached the top I had to rest a long while until my light-headedness eased off and the blood stopped thumping in my ears. From the top of the ridge we looked down on a world so grey, bleak and Godforsaken, that it might have been the moon. Only the hardiest flower could show its face in such a wilderness. Great marshes choked with reeds stretched as far as the eye could see. Put a foot wrong down there and a quagmire would swallow you up to your chest and devour you bit by bit while you clung to the weeds for dear life. Only a fool would try to cross such land. Further along, the ridge was smothered in low cloud that threatened to wrap itself around us and take away all hope of ever finding the way home. I could still hear the skylark overhead, but now its song was fretful and forlorn. A fear gnawed at my gut, the worry that I had not enough strength to make it either to Newlyn or back to the cove. I didn't say to the minister that we were lost and that we should turn back. It would only make him more fixed on following his own hopeless route.

"Were I alone, I would continue down this hill and find a path through the marshland over there," he said. "However, given the difficulty you are having in those boots, I think it better that we retrace our steps."

We finished the last drop of water. I was loath to get back on my feet and put my weight on those blisters, but had no choice. Down we went, the way we had come, and it was even harder on my poor aching calves inching down that breakneck hill than it had been climbing up. After a while I saw a livestock trail that passed by an old ruined barn and a dry tree, an old hollowed-out elm. I recognised the place and knew it led to the highway. I called to the minister who was walking on ahead of me. The long silence that had passed between us was broken. This time he didn't gainsay me, but agreed to follow my route with a nod and a far-away look in his eyes, like one whose mind was on higher matters. I was almost beside myself with weariness and agony, a martyr to those pretty boots. The sight of Gideon marching ahead, too high and mighty to walk alongside me and show companionship, inflamed my wrath. He stood waiting for me at a place where two tracks crossed, unsure which path to take.

"We might be the only people on this earth, like Adam and Eve," I said.

He ignored me, which spurred me on.

"I've always thought men were awful hard on poor old Eve. Didn't Adam bite the apple too? And suppose Eve hadn't bitten the apple, then where would we be? Walking about naked as the day we were born and not even knowing it, or caring."

He gave no answer, but I fancied his shoulders hunched a little.

"Look there," I said, wishing to goad him further. "Perhaps that's where the Serpent is waiting, in that ash tree."

"I think you'd be better conserving your strength," he said. "You're beginning to rave, Sister Blight."

I told him which way to go and he walked on. We were silent a while. "Aha!" he cried, of a sudden. He'd spotted the road up ahead of us, the highway that led to Newlyn. I struggled on till I reached the roadside then threw myself down on the verge.

"We'll wait here until a vehicle passes that can take us the rest of the way," he said. "You needn't walk further."

I took off the boots and sat in a slump, letting the cool grass calm the stinging sores on my feet and ankles. For a long while I waited, willing a Penzance-bound coach to appear on the horizon, or a jig that might at least take us part of the way. My parched throat longed to swallow cup after cup of cool water. In the distance I saw black puddles glimmering on the road, but it was only a phantom of the low sun and the dust. Likewise, ghostly vehicles took form in the distance before melting into the shimmering air. The long grasses whispered as the breeze rippled through them. Near where I had laid down my head, a red ant slowly climbed a tall blade of grass. The creature took an eternity to reach the top, and dangled there as the grass swayed in the breeze, the bristles on its head trembling. It seemed the minister and me had stepped outside of time and that we were truly as alone in the world as Adam and Eve had once been.

When I'd forsaken all hope and the sun was looking to set behind the far-away hills, I heard the tinkling of a distant bell, thinking at first that I'd dreamt it. I prayed it was a horse's neck bell. A little later the clattering of wheels was heard and a farm wagon appeared, laden with hay bales, slowly lumbering towards us. It was heading the right way, towards Newlyn. Eventually, it pulled up and I heard the voices of Gideon and the farmer conversing. The minister came over and told me the man was heading for Paul but he would make a detour to Newlyn for a small fee. I tried to raise myself, but the searing pain was too great, and I burst into tears, whether in thanksgiving or suffering or confusion I couldn't have said.

Gideon came over to me, holding out his hand to help me to my feet, but when I tried to stand my legs went from under me and I dropped back on the grass, sobbing with vexation.

"I regret that we have been at odds with each other," he said. "On reflection, I believe you were correct about the route. I fear I allowed myself to become distracted and forgot to take note of the landmarks I've followed so faithfully at other times. I hope you'll forgive me. Now, Mary, will you allow me to help you over to the wagon?" I wiped the tears from my face, got up and grasped the minister's hand, which was wonderfully warm and dry. We took a step or two towards the wagon, but my legs shook under me and I almost fell. The minister caught me in time, and put an arm round my waist to hold me up. In this way we made it over to the wagon. He stooped and lifted me up, holding me under my knees, so that my feet dangled like a child's for a moment, and then he set me down, almost tenderly, our faces close together. We looked at one another — his eyes were black as sloes. I turned from him and lay my head on the prickly hay, closed my eyes and waited for my heart to slow to its usual beat.

I woke up, curled up on the hay and shivering. It was night and we were in Newlyn. This time Gideon gave me no help in getting off the wagon, but leapt off himself to pay the wagoner. It was dark but for the murky light of the window of a house where we had pulled up. The minister knocked on the door and soon a plump woman appeared.

"Poor Mrs Stone is sick with worry, sir, you being so late," she said. Gideon sighed and went inside, leaving me to climb down and follow him. Every step pained me in those boots. Once in the narrow hallway, I saw the woman take the minister's coat from his shoulders. She looked me up and down, leaning backwards as if afeard to go anywhere near me, before leading the minister through a door into another room. I didn't dare follow them, but stood there, wishing I was back in my own home.

A woman's high and peevish voice cried: "I've been frantic with worry, we expected you hours ago." She sounded like a true snot. I supposed it must have been Gideon's wife. "Rebecca is here. I sent Susan for her, not knowing what else to do," she said.

"Heaven knows, poor Mrs Stone have been some brave," said another voice — the woman who had opened the door to us.

"And where is our Sunday school teacher? Are you hiding her?" said the woman with the peevish voice.

"Sister Blight, please be so kind as to enter the room," called the minister.

I had no choice but to limp in. The candle light dazzled me at first after being in the dark so long. After a while, I picked out a standing clock, too big for the cluttered little room, and three women huddled together on a settle. I couldn't help but gawp at the woman in the middle, knowing it was Mrs Stone. She looked dressed for a ball in her blue silk dress, wide across the shoulder with padded sleeves, the skirts frilled and plumped out all about her. I had never seen the like, not even in Penzance. On one side of her was the plump woman who had let us in and on the other a big girl with buck teeth. I supposed they were Mrs Stone's maids. Mrs Stone stared at me, wide-eyed, holding a handkerchief to her bosom as if she might faint away at the sight of me.

I looked to Gideon for help, but my gaze fell upon a distressful vision in a round gilt-framed mirror on the wall behind him, hanging over the fireplace. I saw a bedraggled, drooping woman, who looked as if she'd been dragged by her hair through a hundred gorse bushes. She might easily have been taken for a wild woman in a sideshow at the fair. It would be hard to find anyone who looked less fit for the role of teacher.

The women around me sighed and mewed with pity at the state they found me in, and Mrs Stone shook her head to let the minister know it was shameful of him to have put this sorry creature through such an ordeal.

"Why, the poor thing! Is she lame?" asked the plump woman.

"We've had quite a journey of it. Miss Blight's feet are somewhat blistered," said the minister.

"Oh, Susan, go and fetch a bowl of warm water, quickly now, and salt," said Mrs Stone to the buck-toothed girl, who rushed out of the room. "Miss Blight, do please sit down, I hope my husband has not been too severe. He forgets we women aren't as robust as he is. This is Mrs Gurney," she said, meaning the plump woman at her side. "She'll look after you during your stay. Now, Mrs Gurney, help me get these boots off this poor woman."

They brought a chair out to the middle of the room for me to sit upon, and I let them peel the bloody boots off me while I wailed.

132

"Oh, wisht! Look at the state of her poor feet. They be cut to bits and seams," cried Mrs Gurney.

On a straight-backed chair across the room, another woman watched me. She had long sharp features, and sat very upright in the chair. She smiled, but her eyes looked sorrowfully over at me, and seeing how she pitied me made me sorry for myself and brought a tear rolling down my cheek. Seeing that, she put both her hands over her mouth, then stood up and crossed the room to stand before me.

"My dear woman, I do hope to make your acquaintance soon, but fear I am only in the way here tonight," she said to me. "I'm sure you will make an excellent Sunday school teacher under Ellie's instruction, and I greatly look forward to finding out all about you." She smiled and put out a hand for me to take. "Rebecca Vyvyan." I gave Rebecca Vyvyan's hand a quick shake, before looking back at my bleeding feet, shy at being spoken to in such a familiar way by a proper snot and unsure what I was supposed to do.

"I was on the point of taking my leave when Mr Stone arrived," said Rebecca Vyvyan, hugging Mrs Stone. Then she gave Gideon a little nod and went out. Was she the kin of Dr Vyvyan who often came to our cove, I wondered.

With her gone, Gideon at last went over to his wife where she sat on the settle. She turned away from him as he kissed her on the cheek. I smelt her perfume from across the room. She said nothing to her husband, but stood up and walked over to me. Mrs Gurney positioned an upholstered footstool so she could sit by me.

"I expect my husband has told you all about me," said Mrs Stone, sitting down. I shook my head, as Gideon had told me nothing at all about her. "Really, Gideon, what is the matter with you?" she said. She wrinkled her nose and I wondered if it was because she could smell my sweat and the foul bog water that stained the hem of my skirts. As for her, every part of her seemed to twinkle in the candlelight.

Susan pushed through the door with a bowl of warm water in her hands, slopping half of it over the rug as she squeezed through the doorway. All three women stared at me as I put my feet into the water, closed my eyes, threw back my head and moaned. When I opened my eyes again, the water in the bowl had already turned brown.

"Perhaps Susan should take you upstairs where you can scrub yourself clean at my wash-stand?" said Mrs Stone.

"That can wait until tomorrow," said Gideon, quickly. "At this moment, what Miss Blight needs is a good night's sleep."

"The nursery is prepared," said Mrs Stone.

"Oh, don't you think of climbing they stairs now, my dear," said Mrs Gurney to Mrs Stone. "I'll help the lady up to the room."

"Might I trouble you for a glass of water, pleasing you, ma'am?" I said. How rough and country I sounded, after Mrs Stone.

"I am going to wash in the kitchen," said Gideon. "I'll see to everything, so you needn't trouble yourself, Susan. It's late and I expect you ladies will want to be getting on your way." And without another word he left, closing the door behind him.

With him gone, the smile fell from Mrs Stone's face.

"Nothing at all to say about the new dress I was wearing, from my father's shop," she said to Mrs Gurney. "Cornflower blue is the colour of the season, although I wouldn't expect my husband to know that, or to recognise genuine Macclesfield silk when he sees it."

"You look charming, my dear," said Mrs Gurney. "Even Miss Rebecca said so, and heaven knows, she cares little for fashion — you need only look at her to see that."

Mrs Stone glanced at me, all her twinkle gone, before turning to the buck-toothed girl. "Susan," she said. "Would you be so kind as to take my husband's teacher up to her room?"

CHAPTER
NINE

The next morning Mrs Stone let me go into her bedroom to use her wash-stand. I knew this was because she couldn't abide the smell of poor people, but I'd have put up with any slight to get my hands on her scented soap. Standing in her little tub in clean, warm water from the kettle, I lifted my shift and rubbed myself all over with a glassy lavender soap-ball. I didn't spend as long at it as I'd have liked because there was no lock on the door. When I was done, I used a linen towel that hung on the wash-stand to dry myself. It was damp from Mrs Stone's own bathing. She even had a little brush for cleaning her teeth, and a dish of soot she used for it.

Her bedroom was like Heaven itself, all dressed in white, the walls, the window curtains and the bed curtains. Even the dresser and the wash-stand were white, with a white basin and pitcher on top. On the dresser she had bottles of scented hair oil which is where her nice smell came from. I drew back the curtain to peek at the bed, and saw it was just wide enough to fit Gideon and his wife snugly.

As I stepped away, I saw something on the floor behind the hem of the counterpane, the corner of a book that had been pushed under the bed. Treading ever so softly I went to the door, opening it a crack. The house was quiet, the door to the parlour shut. I got down on my knees and pulled the book out. It was called *Virtue Rebuked* by Mrs Catherine Fitzherbert. Afraid someone would come before I got a good look at it, I didn't get dressed right away, but knelt at the bedside and leafed through the pages, almost sick with the thrill of it and the fear of being caught.

It was a book of letters from Lady Rosemount, a woman who was in the first bloom of youth, but who had experienced a disappointment in love and had gone to Italy, a dark country of great mountains, castles and forests full of howling wolves. She was writing to her friend in England, and the pair of them wrote such grand words I couldn't make sense of the half of it. Lady Rosemount was *in a frenzy of passion which the strong chains of prudence could not hold*, and was having an intrigue with a Count from that land, which meant they were lovers, I supposed. Such fine words Lady Rosemount used, even if she was a strumpet, and afterwards I remembered some, such as *I was ever feelingly alive to the beauties of nature*, and, *What is a woman when she neither loves nor is loved?* But I had no time to dwell on her story, so I went straight to the last pages to discover what became of her. Before I could find out, I heard a door open down below, and pushed the book back under the bed.

When I'd dressed, I went downstairs and was about to knock on the parlour door when I heard muffled voices. It was Mrs Stone and Mrs Gurney.

"No, ma'am, not what I expected at all," said Mrs Gurney. "She's quite a beauty, though, wouldn't you say, in a common sort of way?"

There was a peal of laughter from Mrs Stone. "Perhaps you mistake her species of gypsy glamour for true beauty, my dear, but she has none of the self-restraint and dignity of a lady."

"Oh no, of course not . . ."

"She displays all the rude simplicity of a country girl, with a freedom in her movements that isn't at all becoming."

"I was just about to say the very same myself, Mrs Stone."

"She has no waist to speak of, did you notice? And wears no stays."

"I imagine that's to allow her to move about free when she's at work."

"In any case, she's so straight and narrow that stays would do little to improve her figure. From the rear, you might easily mistake her for a boy, apart from all her red hair, enough to set a hay rig on fire. And Blight? What a name! One hopes it is not symbolic. Now, where is the woman, for heaven's sake?"

I knocked on the door, and was called in. Mrs Stone glanced at my bare blistered feet, and looked away quickly with a little shudder. Mrs Gurney left the room, giving me a curt nod as she passed. Mrs Stone pointed to where I was to sit at the little dining table and we took our places. She had laid out the Bible with some books of sermons and catechisms.

"You won't mind me remarking that I was a little surprised when my husband sent word, without any prior discussion with me, that he was bringing a woman to stay with us and I was to instruct her," she said. "I have to say, I had imagined a person somewhat older and considerably more sober in demeanour."

I sat still, wishing I could scratch my hands for I'd come out in a nervous rash.

"I will begin by explaining the simple doctrines you are to impart to the children," she said. "You will recite them back to me, word for word. This is to ensure you don't depart from the Good Lord's intentions when you are teaching the children. Is that understood?"

I nodded. She was staring at my hands, so I looked at hers, so small and white with not a mark upon them, then back at my own, which showed the marks of work and were larger than a fine lady's, the fingernails cracked and yellowed, and bitten to the quick. Ashamed, I put them under the table.

"Very well then, let us begin."

Mrs Stone near ruined the Bible for me. As a child, I'd turned the pages with no other wish than to find out what would happen next, to see if Noah got his Ark built before the flood, or Abraham cut his son's throat, or Lot lay with his daughter. But this woman made every story into a dismal lesson about right and wrong. She talked in the main of Jesus and his Disciples, forgetting the Old Testament stories which were far better for quickening the pulse. But the Bible was a stale old yarn after Lady Rosemount's letters and I swore to myself that I'd read the rest of her book if ever I got the chance.

I listened, straining to follow her, my hands twisting in my lap. As the morning wore on, I stumbled over the words she made me repeat, not knowing their meaning. The only sound was the tick-tock of the standing clock, which grew more vexing by the minute. Every time it chimed at the quarter hour I near leapt out of my skin. My mind was forever straying to the minister, and wondering when I would next set eyes on him.

She could tell when my mind had wandered, and tried to catch me out. "Now, what do you think the Lord means here in John when he says: *And other sheep I have, which are not of this fold: them also I must bring, and they shall hear my voice; and there shall be one fold, and one shepherd?*"

"The sheep are us, his children, I suppose?"

"Of course the sheep are his children! But what is he saying in regard to them?"

"Not to forget about poor folk — who live far away and might get looked over?"

"Wrong, again. He means that all people must become part of his church. All people, everywhere."

When she was done with the gospels, she told me her notions of schooling. "It may interest you to know that I once paid a visit to the Sunday school in Redruth, which I believe was the first in all of Cornwall," she said. "I encountered various children on my travels, and there was a marked distinction between those who attended the school and those who did not. The latter were quite evidently disinclined to submit to the

140

restraint and discipline that a good school imposes. So we can have no doubt that instruction in Sunday school is the surest way to inspire a more respectful behaviour in children."

I nodded, but my fists were clenched under the table.

"Now, will you tell me something of your own church-going history?"

"Well, I have been to Mass quite often, at Easter or Christmas or for a wedding or a Christening betimes."

"And that is all? Heaven help us! What about the Sabbath?"

"The old church in Porthmorvoren has fallen into rack and ruin, and we have had no rector for a good many years. Sometimes we have to walk to the church in Paul."

"But that must be ten miles, at least. You take the Sacrament, I hope?"

I looked into my lap, ashamed because I did not get her meaning.

"You take Communion?"

I shook my head.

"Oh dear, oh dear!" She began gathering together the books on the table. "Well, I think that will be enough for today. In fairness to you, your knowledge of the Scriptures is a little better than I feared it might be."

"Thank you, Mrs Stone," I muttered.

"However, your notions of the moral lessons to be drawn are rather fanciful and misled. Especially your understanding of the parables, which is often far from what the Good Lord intended."

Before lunch, Dr Vyvyan came to look at my feet. It was strange to see him there, when before I'd only ever seen him on his visits to the cove. Remembering the last time I'd seen him, I blushed. Now that he was here, Mrs Stone was all smiles, and seemed much more bothered about my feet than she'd been before.

"I am somewhat surprised to find you here," he said to me. "I hope your doubts about the efficacy of modern medicine have lessened since our last encounter. Or perhaps I should hang a poor plucked bird from the ceiling?"

At this mention of the bird, Mrs Stone put a hand to her mouth, as if in horror. I noticed she'd turned quite skittish since the doctor had arrived, not at all like how she'd been with me.

"I'll tell you the story some time, Ellie," Dr Vyvyan said to her.

He asked me about Mamm, and I said she was doing as well as could be hoped. The thought of Mamm, wheezing in her chair so far away, brought the tears to my eyes, and when the doctor saw this he put a comforting hand on my shoulder.

"I'll make sure to drop by the next time I'm in Porthmorvoren," he said. "Now let's have a look at those feet of yours." He took one ankle at a time and turned my foot in his hand to look at it from all sides, prodding the blisters with his forefinger and making me wince.

"There's nothing here that won't heal in a few days," he said. "You're quite right to leave the skin exposed to the air, and let Nature do her work." He put a little

142

round pot on the table. "Here is some balm. You're to apply it to the blisters morning and night."

For the rest of Dr Vyvyan's stay, Mrs Stone and he talked among themselves, as if I wasn't there. When he was leaving, I heard her out in the hall, seeing him off.

"You've been an absolute saint as always," she said, her voice light and girlish. "Let me fetch my purse."

"I won't hear of it, Ellie."

When he was gone, she came back into the parlour, prim and stiff as ever she'd been.

"You will eat dinner with me at six," she said.

"Will Mr Stone be having dinner too?"

"I'm afraid Mr Stone will not. He has been obliged to absent himself during your stay. He'll be abroad on his visits to the stewards of the Penwith societies for the coming week. It's most provoking for him, of course, but he has rather neglected his circuit work due to his labours in that cove of yours. What is the matter with you, Sister Blight? You're a peculiar colour all of a sudden. I sincerely hope you're not about to fall ill?"

I was so miserable at dinner, Mrs Stone sent me to bed early. Most of that night I lay awake, and all my vain hopes unravelled in the darkness. Without owning it to myself, I'd dreamt that while I was in this house Providence would somehow throw me into Gideon Stone's path. My hopes were raised when he picked me up bodily and put me in the cart, looking into my eyes a moment longer than was proper. And later, when I saw how his wife's play acting and falseness irked him, I let myself believe it was all proof of some secret feelings he had for me, like those I had for him. But now Gideon had run off and left me here for a whole week with a woman I loathed, and who looked down on me, and I saw that all along he wanted no more than to make me Sunday school teacher in the cove. Almost without admitting as much to myself, I'd hoped Gideon would help me flee the cove and raise me above the bettermost of Porthmorvoren who ill wished me and wanted me brought low.

The next morning, I had some peace from Mrs Stone because she went on a trip to Truro with Miss Rebecca Vyvyan, the tall woman I'd seen the night I came. As Miss Vyvyan was the sister of Dr Vyvyan, the two were able to go in his carriage. Mrs Stone got back again mid-afternoon with flowers that she put in a big urn in the hearth. I was dazzled, so lovely they were, violet asters and white roses, with bleeding hearts trailing over the sides. When the blooms were all arranged to her liking, Mrs Stone wearily sat on her settle, while Mrs Gurney pushed a cushion behind her mistress's back. I watched them from the window seat, a book of sermons in my hands.

"Such artistry!" said Mrs Gurney to Mrs Stone, beaming at the flowers.

"I do what little I can to bring art and delicacy into this modest home," said Mrs Stone.

"And such a perfume! Why, the parlour smells like Lemon Quay on market day," said Mrs Gurney. "A pity you have no grand acquaintances to visit and see what you are capable of."

"More than a pity, my dear. Miss Vyvyan and I took a stroll down Princes Street today. Balls are held there most weeks. The Boscawens and the Lemons were in attendance at one only last night. Happier people than I, able to enjoy the Theatre and the Assembly Rooms. Miss Vyvyan would admonish me if she knew I hankered after such amusements, but surely I can be forgiven for imagining the sensation I might make among new people?"

"You certainly may be forgiven, Mrs Stone. A fine lady like you shouldn't be hidden away from the world."

"Well, tomorrow, at least, I will have some company. There is a reason for my unaccustomed extravagance with the flowers. I am having a little tea party, and have invited Miss Vyvyan and Mr Dabb, who is the new Justice of the Peace."

"I'd better come over early and start baking, then," said Mrs Gurney. "We'll want scalded milk too. And the house will need a good clean, of course."

"No effort will be spared in achieving an impression of careless negligence," said Mrs Stone, with her silvery laugh.

There was a knock on the door, and Susan went out to answer it. People were always calling, I'd noticed, selling their wares. A moment later, Susan came into the parlour and handed a note to Mrs Stone.

"Who gave you this?" she asked.

"It were Miss Vyvyan's maid."

Mrs Stone looked at the envelope. "Yes, I do recognise Rebecca's hand." She opened it and took out a note. When she had read it, she turned pale, and the hand that held the note fell to her side. "Shall I fetch the salts?" cried Mrs Gurney.

Mrs Stone shook her head.

"Will I plump up your cushions for you, my dear? Or bring you a slice of heavy cake? You haven't overdone it, have you?"

"Please don't fuss!" said Mrs Stone, waving her away. "Find something useful to do. I wish to have a moment to myself. I'll call you if I need you."

Mrs Gurney looked most put out, but did as she was told. I rose to follow her out, but Mrs Stone's voice stopped me dead, just as I got to the door.

"You stay here, Miss Blight," she said. "I have a matter to discuss with you. Sit down over there."

I sat in a straight-backed chair, as ordered, and waited. Mrs Stone looked me over, her head on one side. It set my nerves jangling, being inspected like that, so I took hold of the cloth of my skirt and twisted it into a little pucker, a habit I had.

"I am sure it will surprise you to learn that my dear friend Rebecca has requested that you join us tomorrow," she said.

"Join you?

"At the tea party. You might well look alarmed. I'm afraid that Rebecca is nothing if not capricious. Of course, you'll find yourself out of your depth in such company, but you'll have to put a brave face on it. Naturally, Mrs Gurney will be most disconcerted that you're invited and she is not. I shall have to think about how to break it to her."

"But what would Miss Vyvyan want with me?"

"Oh, she's quite taken with you. She spoke of little else in the carriage this morning. I imagine she wants a new mascot for her benevolent society. But rest assured, she'll tire of this latest whim soon enough. Just make sure you do nothing whatsoever to embarrass me in front of my acquaintances."

Just before the tea party was due to begin, I went into the parlour and found Mrs Stone putting a book on her French coffee table, *Thoughts on Slavery* by Mr Wesley. I'd never once seen her peruse the book, yet she put the stem of a pressed flower in one of the pages as if she had. There was a loud knocking on the door and suddenly the room was full of noise. Her visitors had come at one and the same time. Miss Vyvyan came into the parlour and gazed open-mouthed at my bare feet.

"Do forgive Miss Blight's feet," said Mrs Stone, hurrying in after her. "They got dreadfully blistered crossing the moor. As soon as they are better I intend taking her to Penzance to have her fitted for a new pair of boots."

"Bare feet? Oh, but that's sublime!" said Miss Vyvyan, laughing. "I hope you succeed in starting a new fashion. Nothing would delight me more than wandering about bare-footed. Or perhaps even dancing to a gypsy guitar?" Mr Josiah Dabb, the Justice of the Peace, grinned at this, as they all moved towards the dining table. "Such unadorned simplicity and elegance," said Miss Vyvyan, taking her seat.

"You're too kind," said Mrs Stone.

"As if a Grecian nymph had wandered out of a grove in a painting," Miss Vyvyan cried, beaming at me and showing her crooked teeth. Mrs Stone looked most put out, realising it was me being praised. Abashed at all this talk of my feet, I pushed them out of sight. Miss Vyvyan sat at the head of the little table facing Mrs Stone, while Mr Dabb was on the other side to me.

"Miss Blight will hardly gain the respect of Sunday school children looking like an indigent. So new boots she will have," said Mrs Stone, laughing and twinkling with all her might. I caught Mr Dabb giving her a little wink as he put his napkin in his lap. He was a short, thickset man with a red face and white mutton-chop whiskers.

"Miss Blight, would you mind if I called you by your Christian name?" asked Miss Vyvyan, leaning towards me and smiling.

"It is Mary," I said.

"And you are from Porthmorvoren, Mary? Is life harsh for you there?"

I looked at Mrs Stone, not wanting to say the wrong thing, but her gaze was on Miss Vyvyan.

"Mary, do tell me about your family," said Miss Vyvyan.

I cleared my throat, remembering to put my hand in front of my mouth at the last moment. "There's only me and Mamm, and my sister Tegen."

"No father or brother?" I shook my head. "But that must be dreadfully hard on you."

"It is hard, ma'am. But we do the best we can."

"Such quiet stoicism." She looked at Mrs Stone and Mr Dabb, and they both nodded assent.

"Your neighbours help you, I suppose?"

"Some do. And some don't."

"Oh dear! And what is your work?"

"Whatever we can find, depending on the time of year, packing pilchards, mending or tarring nets — filthy work, that is. Or tracing rushes to make them into maunds for field work just like you trace a little maid's hair."

"Maunds?" said Miss Vyvyan.

"Baskets, I mean. And smashing the lode-stuff at the mine, and stitching sack, and making the wicks for candles and fish-oil lamps." Miss Vyvyan was nodding away at everything I said, so I went on. "And when food's short, ma'am, me and Tegen go shrimping at slack water, or looking for crabs. Then there's always baking to be done, and fetching water from the well, and laundering and darning and weaving."

"Well, that has given us all a very good idea how Miss Blight spends her time," said Mrs Stone, to put a stop to it.

"And how do you endure all this?" asked Miss Vyvyan, still set on quizzing me.

"Well, now and then we might have a rummer of brandy grog. As for me, a little scrap of a song helps cheer me."

"Songs, how lovely! Which are your favourites, Mary?" asked Miss Vyvyan.

"Oh, any lively catch that takes my fancy."

"Well, we should hear you sing another time."

I looked into my lap, wishing she'd leave me be.

"How delicate you are, Mary. I suppose that sometimes you must go hungry, despite all your labours?"

I nodded.

"What would you say to me paying a visit to your village? I should love to see it with my own eyes."

"You might find my neighbours a bit rough and ill mannered, ma'am."

"Come now, Mary, no more of this 'ma'am'. I insist on you calling me Rebecca. Now tell me — is Ellie a splendid gospel tutor?" I nodded, but not as quickly as Mrs Stone would have liked, going by the look on her face. "Ellie tells me you have a quite remarkable knowledge of the Bible?"

"I'm fond of the stories, ma'am."

Miss Vyvyan turned to the Justice. "Well, Mr Dabb, don't you agree that this young woman is an excellent example of an individual from the poorer classes making efforts to improve herself?" she said. Mr Dabb smiled. The man had a loud, gruff voice and a way of speaking that was foreign to me. He began telling Mrs Stone that he was a benefactor to Miss Vyvyan's Benevolent Society for the Relief of Indigence, and that he hailed from somewhere called Hanley which he said was in the north, and full of converts to Methodism. He was in Cornwall to advise the mine owners about steam pumps, and had only lately been made Justice.

Miss Vyvyan turned to Mrs Stone. "Ellie, you must let me borrow Mary so I can present her at our next public meeting."

Mrs Stone tried to force a smile but I saw her tea party wasn't going quite as she'd hoped. To my relief, at that moment Susan came in with the tea tray wobbling in her hands. The scones were still warm and the smell made my tummy rumble. And there was sugar for the tea in a pretty crystal bowl.

"Ellie, I hope you'll join me on our visit to Porthmorvoren?" said Miss Vyvyan, buttering her scone. Mrs Stone nodded, spreading jam on hers.

"I wish you luck with it," said Mr Dabb, slurping his tea. "The mental darkness of these isolated villages is the shame of all Cornwall. We Methodists must work to subdue all degenerates who yield to the influence of wickedness. It's our duty to show that a man may raise himself up through learning and sober application."

Mrs Stone nodded her head heartily at this.

"Let me tell you the problem with the country people, this young lady notwithstanding," said Mr Dabb. "It's not want of employ, or short wages or dear provisions. The problem is the extravagance of the vulgar in the unnecessaries of life. Their children go about in rags, yet they think nothing of having three score snuff boxes in their homes. Alehouses contrive to let labourers live above their condition, crediting them till their account is so large that the bailiffs come after them, and the wretch must pay a fine as well as settle his scores."

"Surely we should look to the temper of the times in forming rules for conduct," Miss Vyvyan said.

But Mr Dabb would have none of this. "Take care that doling out funds to beggars doesn't make them

151

worse," he said. "Let them first show they are capable of fulfilling their moral duties and of showing a more correct feeling towards their superiors. When you make your trip to Miss Blight's village, ladies, make sure that before giving alms to the country people you enquire into their character and habits."

Just then, Mrs Gurney came in with a jug. "What am I to do with that girl! She plain forgot to bring the scalded cream," she said, putting the jug on the table. She stood behind Mrs Stone's chair wiping her hands on her freshly laundered white pinny.

"Surely Mr Dabb is right," said Mrs Stone. "The poor should save for their luxuries and pay their duties, just as respectable people do. And as for that ghoul in Porthmorvoren who chewed off a fine lady's ears to steal her earrings . . ."

Miss Vyvyan was looking at me, which made me tremble, seeing in my mind's eye the dead noblewoman lying on the sand. "Let's not upset Mary, who I'm sure is as horrified as anybody about the crime," she said.

"You know my feelings on the matter, Rebecca," said Mrs Stone. "When you catch the Porthmorvoren Cannibal, I hope you will make an example of him, Mr Dabb."

"P'raps it's not my place to butt in," said Mrs Gurney. "But if it were up to me, that cannibal would get a salutary whipping, followed by transportation and twelve years hard labour. And that's letting the varmint off lightly."

I took a sip of my tea, but it had gone cold and bitter.

★ ★ ★

After three days had passed, my feet were healed enough to walk the mile to Penzance, so Mrs Stone and I set off to buy new boots. I was forced to wear the ill-fitting boots one last time, but it lifted my spirits a little to be out in the air after being pent up so long with the minister's wife. The sky was bright with screeching gulls, and I could hear the cries of the merchants and fishermen down on the beach. A forest of masts could be seen where the boats were moored, the rigging clanking against the masts in the breeze. As we walked along the coast road, all of the bay opened out around me, and across the water I saw the castle set on a hill in the sea, and thought of Lady Rosemount in her castle in Italy.

Mrs Stone wanted me to know what a great sacrifice she was making, paying to have me reshod with brand-new boots. She hoped I didn't think by it that she was well off. A minister's salary was very modest indeed, she said. I let her talk wash over me while I enjoyed the light feeling that had settled on me that morning. A gang of Newlyn fishwives in scarlet cloaks came bounding past us. They carried their fish in their back baskets, which were tied to a broad band on their beaver hats, something I'd never seen in my own village. I feared they would be able to tell I was an enemy from Porthmorvoren just by the look of me, but they went past me without a glance.

Before long, we were climbing up Market Jew Street in Penzance through bustling crowds. I felt I could lose myself among so many souls. The different sounds thrilled my senses, the rattling of coach wheels and the clomping of hooves, the stallholders hollering, "Cotton, sixpence a yard!" and "Shirt linen, only a shilling to you, madam!" In the stores I saw gingerbread and hardbake, and candies of every colour under the sun, while other stores sold chapbooks and Bible prints, and I wished I could have bought the one that showed the animals lined up, two by two, before the Ark. We passed Moses and Son, conveyor of used clothes, a shop Tegen and I had been to in the past. Looking at the dresses hanging on the railings in the street, I had a giddy feeling that I could put on one of those garments and become somebody else altogether. Nobody would look strangely at me, or know or care who I was or where I'd come from.

On the broad, raised pavements, rich and poor rubbed shoulders, the better off in their fine coats and the poorer women in their worn and patched-up red cloaks. Behind the glass front of the draper's shop there was a haughty wooden manikin, put there to show the latest fashions and what the establishment was capable of making. The manikin wore rich velvet mantles, and a dress that fitted tightly to the body. Underneath the bodice, the skirt fell in gathers, with crimped hems at the base.

But a moment later I was brought to a standstill by a notice nailed to a post. It was tattered and torn, but the words shouted out their message, and as I took in the meaning, the world reeled about me. I'd have fallen to the pavement had not a gentleman taken hold of my elbow. I stood there a moment, blood pumping in my ears and drowning out the noises of the street.

"Miss Blight? Miss Blight? Whatever is the matter with you?" said Mrs Stone, who had rushed to my side. "You look as if you've seen a ghost."

"If I might just sit a moment," I said, sitting down on the stone steps by the town hall. The words of the poster cast a shadow over me. A rich Lord was offering a reward, a huge sum, to any informer who would snitch on the evil-disposed person who'd robbed his wife's boots and dress and jewellery, not to mention other foul deeds done on her person. The foulest deed of all was chewing off her earlobes to steal her earrings. In my mind's eye I saw the bloody jagged edges of the lady's ears, and saw Aunt Madgie stalking through the mist. I heard the old dame's voice, *Is this your doing, Mary Blight?*

"You do realise this is most inconvenient?" said Mrs Stone, jolting me back to the here and now.

"I'm sorry, ma'am. Really I am."

A kindly woman handed me a cup of water, and I took it and sipped. Slowly I recovered, and became aware once more of all the folk going about their business. The light-heartedness I'd felt before had gone, and in its place a heaviness weighed on me. I watched the snots parade by in their finery, holding their breath so they wouldn't have to smell the stale sweat of the poor people, or see the ragged hems of their skirts or trousers as they shuffled past. And I no longer believed I could escape into the crowd. The collar of my own dress was stiff with sweat from all the times I'd worn it before, and it rubbed against my neck. Under my skirts, the coarse worsted of well-darned stockings made my limbs itch. But even as the wretchedness of my life chafed with me, I told myself that all that mattered was to hide from danger, to stay safe and accept my lot.

I got to my feet and looked around for Mrs Stone, but I couldn't see her in the street or on the steps. Then I looked back towards the post with the reward bill pinned to it, and there I found her standing before it, her nose inches from the printed words, the corners of her mouth turned down in disgust.

Shortly after, as I sat in the shop with bare feet waiting for the cobbler to find some second-hand boots that fit me, Mrs Stone picked up my ill-fitting boots from the floor, and looked them over closely. She frowned and mouthed some words, her voice so soft I had to read her lips: "Half-boots laced before . . ."

"I'll hold onto these boots," she said. "I'm sure Miss Vyvyan and I can find a deserving woman to donate them to on our next tour of the parish."

"I was hoping to pawn them, myself," I said.

"Given that I'm purchasing a pair of boots for you out of my meagre housekeeping money, the least you can do is allow me to pass these on to someone whose feet they actually fit."

With that, she asked the shopkeeper to parcel up the boots for her so she could take them home.

50 GUINEAS
REWARD

ROBBERY AND FOUL DEEDS
to the inhabitants of
PORTHMORVOREN
And its Vicinity

WHEREAS on 2nd February

A certain evil disposed Person, or Persons, did steal Articles of Clothing, amongst them a silk dress, wherein were fifteen guineas and jewellery and other effects; and also earrings and a necklace, and half-boots laced before; and furthermore did

maliciously molest and most heinously desecrate

the drowned body of Lady S— of S— Hall, who perished in the wreck of The Constant Service on Porthmorvoren Strand.

NOTICE

Is hereby given that whoever will give such information as may lead to the discovery and apprehension of such offender, shall receive the **REWARD**

OF 50 GUINEAS On the Conviction of one or more of the said Offenders. On Application to *Lord S— Duke of S—. Member of Parliament, at S— Hall, Lower R—, Hampshire*.

CHAPTER
TEN

The next day Mrs Stone was barely an hour into her lesson when Susan came into the parlour with an envelope for her. She got to her feet, took a penknife from a drawer in her corner cupboard, prised open the envelope and took out a card. Whatever was written upon it made her turn pale and start tapping the card against her palm. She read it a second time, but must have found it no more to her liking because, without a word, she put it down and swept out of the room. I heard her footsteps on the stairs and a door slam shut upstairs. After waiting a short while, I crept over to the cupboard and picked up the card. On one side, these words were written in a fancy swirling hand:

> To Mr and Mrs Gideon Stone,
> and Miss Mary Blight

and on the other it said:

> Mr Jonathan and Miss Rebecca Vyvyan
> Request the pleasure of your company for dinner
> Seven p.m. on Friday, June 10th
> Orchard Lodge

Belle Vue
Newlyn

What a flap those words put me into! I was jittery enough as it was after seeing the reward poster in Penzance, and now I would have to suffer a lot of snots gawping at me for a whole evening. Mrs Stone was sorely put out that I'd been made invited, it was plain, and she'd be colder than ever with me after this. But at least it meant Gideon would be coming back to Newlyn and I might find out why he had taken himself abroad.

How slowly the hours passed that day and the following. Mrs Stone was more scornful of me than ever as she worked to drill the true sense of the gospels into my head. On the evening of the dinner party, she put on the blue silk dress she'd been wearing the night I arrived. I wore the same dress I'd been wearing all that day, a simple black one, faded with sweat patches under the armpits. Gideon left it until the last minute to come home, which put Mrs Stone in a foul temper. He was too late for his ablutions or to change out of his clothes, which were crumpled and dusty from the road. When she scolded him, he said the clothes he wore to do God's work were good enough for the hosts of any grand dinner party.

The pair of them spoke not a word to each other as they climbed up the hill, me tagging behind them. I would have liked the walk better if my nerves had not been so frayed. The air was much sweeter up in the orchards than it was down in the cramped cluster of lanes where the Stones lived. Orchard Lodge had fine green gables, and was the biggest of the old manor houses that can be seen from the harbour.

Miss Vyvyan herself came to greet us at the door, and seemed not to notice the coldness between Gideon and his wife. I was surprised to see her in a black dress as plain as my own. She led us into the dining room which was big with a high ceiling. The other guests were in their places on the long table set for dinner. Dr Vyvyan sat at the head of the table and Miss Vyvyan led me to the other end so we could sit next to each other. How my heart soared when I learnt I was to sit between her and Gideon.

"May I introduce Miss Blight," she said, as we took our seats. I looked quickly round the table at the smiling faces of these well-to-do snots. Miss Vyvyan told me their names, but I took none of it in. I tried to smile at each in turn, but I couldn't look them in the eye. There were three ladies from her benevolent society on one side of the table, very grand women, and opposite them three physicians, which I learnt is a sort of doctor, who sat alongside their wives. With dread, I saw that Mr Josiah Dabb, the new Justice of the Peace who'd had been at Mrs Stone's tea party, was next to Mrs Stone, right across the table from where I was to sit.

I hardly dared open my mouth in such company as it would show how common and stupid I was, so I stared down at the plate before me. There was a row of knives and forks on either side of the plate. I had no clue which I should pick up. Another smaller plate was set to one side with a bread roll on it and a knob of butter that was going runny. Three glasses on long stems were standing before each person. A young woman came and leant over my shoulder to pour some wine into one of the glasses. The wine was clear as water with bubbles rising in it. I took a gulp, grateful for the mellow, warming, tingling feeling that spread through me.

Miss Vyvyan spoke to me as if I was her equal. She told me about the work of the benevolent society, but I kept losing the thread with all that was going on about me and, most of all, because Gideon was next to me. Miss Vyvyan was not what people would call a handsome woman, but tall and thin, with big crooked teeth and a nose that was curved and sharp as a hawk's. Even so, she seemed comely to me. When she turned to chat to Mrs Stone and Mr Dabb, I wondered if the minister would say something to me, but he did not. I didn't suppose it was my place to speak to him, so I looked all about me at the room.

On one side there was a window that opened onto some grounds. It looked out into the bay far down below, where a broken path of moonlight danced on the water. Heavy, great, mustard-coloured drapes hung at the window, with velvet tie-backs. Over the fireplace was a large painting of a fine chestnut stallion. His haunches were painted so artfully I thought I could see the muscles rippling, and the horse's long face looked so clever it wouldn't have surprised me if he had opened his mouth and spoken in the King's English. On either side of the fireplace were big, gloomy portraits, an old man and woman staring out of the sooty darkness in their black clothes and white collars.

162

They had the likeness of Mr and Miss Vyvyan, so I thought they might be their dead parents.

Every wall was filled with shelves of old leather-bound books. It tired me to look at them. A handsome Turkish rug covered most of the floor, frayed in places, and there were fine old chairs, all of them scuffed with wear. It puzzled me that while this house was far grander than the Stones' little place, it was quite shabby, whereas in theirs everything was buffed up to a shine.

The food came, a thick, oily, orange-coloured soup with chunks of ox tail floating in it. I watched to see what spoon the others picked up, and followed after them, moving the spoon from the front of the bowl to the back and sipping from the side of the spoon. I was already better bred than Mr Dabb, for he sipped from the point of his spoon, bending low over the bowl and even slurping a little. I took bites from the bread roll but didn't dare dip the bread in the soup as I would have done at home. With the slightest touch of my spoon, the flesh of the ox tail fell away from the bones and it was more tender than any meat I'd known. It was rich fare, though, and I wondered how I would ever find room for pudding.

Down the table from me, the doctors were talking about whatever dull things such gentlemen discuss, and their wives, thank the Lord, were too far away to bother with me. Miss Vyvyan was talking to the minister about the business of the Newlyn Methodist Society, and asking him about his hopes for the new chapel in

Porthmorvoren. He said little, and I noticed his hand go to his mouth now and then to hide a yawn.

Miss Vyvyan turned to Mrs Stone. "We are neighbours in Newlyn, aren't we, my dear?" she said. She caught the eye of her philanthropical ladies. "Ellie lives in a charming house in the lanes by the harbour, which she maintains in perfect order, while I am a dreadful sloven," she told them.

"Oh, it is only a modest property," Mrs Stone said. "I must confess that when we first went to look it over, I was disappointed to find it so small and plain. But as the wife of a minister one must learn to want no more than will suffice and make that little do, and put what is committed to your care to the best advantage."

Gideon sighed when he heard this.

"You are a veritable saint, Ellie," said Miss Vyvyan, giving Mrs Stone's hand a squeeze.

Across the table, Mrs Stone turned to chatter with Mr Dabb. Her twinkling that night was the brightest I'd yet seen. I looked to see how the minister felt about his wife's flightiness, but he just stared, heavy-lidded, at his soup, which he'd hardly touched.

Mr Dabb's voice was too loud to ignore. "Not long ago I sent a man from Lansallos to the assizes for stealing a watch, and when the jury found him guilty the judge sentenced the poor wretch to death," he told Mrs Stone. "Nor was this the first occasion that I've encountered such harsh treatment in my time on the bench."

"I wonder if I would know any of the offenders by name?" asked Mrs Stone.

The serving girls arrived to take away our soup bowls. Then, to my amazement, they brought in two large joints of beef and put them down at either end of the table. Dr Vyvyan got up and began carving one joint and putting bits onto people's plates, while at our end one of the doctors did the same. The girls then brought pickles and jellies, and trays of potatoes, carrots and sparrow grass, enough to feed a family in the village for a month of Sundays. For a while, all were quiet as they cut and chewed their beef. I could manage only a slice or two. The meat got stuck in my teeth, but I thought it would show bad manners to get the gristle out with my fingernail. I noticed Mr Dabb had no such qualms.

With a jolt, I realised Gideon was speaking to me, his head bent towards me and his voice low so that only I would hear. "I trust this is not too much of an imposition," he said.

"It's no trouble. I have never eaten so well."

"Well, don't grow too accustomed to it, Sister Blight. I wouldn't want you spoilt by luxury, like these people." He looked at his wife as he spoke.

Just then, one of the philanthropical ladies called to me: "Miss Blight, won't you tell us about your famous cove?"

"Infamous cove, more like," said Mr Dabb.

All of them had turned to face me, waiting to hear what I would say, but every thought flew out of my head. Staring into my lap like a half-wit, I felt a bead of cold sweat roll down my neck and under my collar.

"If it wasn't for Mary, Gideon wouldn't be here today," said Miss Vyvyan. "She rescued him from the sea, at great risk to herself."

"Bravo!" said the philanthropical ladies, and everyone clapped — all except for the minister.

"Mr Stone enjoyed his dip in the Atlantic so much he has decided to go back and make the folk there into decent law-abiding evangelicals," said Dr Vyvyan.

"Wasn't it the very same cove where that incident of so-called cannibalism took place?" asked one of the doctors' wives. "Some devil chewed a woman's earlobes off to steal her earrings. One supposes his hands were too cold for the task. Naturally, public opinion is in uproar for miles around."

"You will no doubt be aware that the victim of the outrage was the wife of Lord S—?" said Mr Dabb.

"This sort of thing does nothing for the reputation of the Cornish," said the doctor's wife. There were murmurs of agreement.

"It was because of this scandalous behaviour that my husband decided to go to that dreadful cove and begin building his chapel," said Mrs Stone.

"I'm not building a chapel in response to sensationalist reports in the *Sherborne Mercury*," said the minister, scowling. Judging by the way the dinner guests glanced at one another, he had spoken out of turn.

"Did you know his lordship has a private agent making investigations?" said Mr Dabb.

"With all this nonsense about the so-called Porthmorvoren Cannibal, don't you think the public

166

would be reassured if they encountered our Mary?" said Miss Vyvyan, smiling at me.

"I don't suppose you would ever dream of chewing off a fine lady's ears to steal her earrings, would you, Mary?" said Mr Dabb. He spoke to me as you would to a naughty child or a simpleton, and he gave me the kind of look that must have made the accused tremble when he sat on the magistrate's bench.

"Now, now, Mr Dabb!" said Miss Vyvyan. "You're frightening Mary, who has already shown herself to be a devout Christian."

"I don't suppose any of your neighbours have let slip who the cannibal might be?" Mr Dabb asked me, a nasty look in his eyes. I shook my head.

"Such a terrible loss for Lord S—," said Mrs Stone. "I understand he is a great patron of the arts, with a fine collection of paintings and rare *objets d'art*. I hope they're some solace to him in this sad time. What I find most affecting is that Lord S—'s unfortunate wife was held to be a woman of uncommon beauty. And I must say her reputation was well deserved if the engraved print of her is true to her likeness. She was a religious woman too, of superior blood, and presented at court. I believe his Lordship sent her home to England because he was concerned she might catch a terrible tropical disease."

Mrs Stone's mention of the uncommon beauty jolted me back to that morning on the beach, when I'd crouched by the lifeless body of that very same woman, struck by her rare beauty even in death, and dreaming of the fine life she must have led. Yet I'd searched her body with little more feeling than if she'd been a manikin in a store in Penzance. I thought how these people around that table would look if they'd seen me pull the boots off the noblewoman's feet, and my heart near came to a stop. It was silent in the room, and I stared down the table, all of a tremble, thinking they might all be looking at me. After a while, I glanced at the minister. He was slumped in his chair, glowering at his wife as she sipped from her wine glass and patted her hair into place.

Miss Vyvyan broke the silence. "My dear Ellie, your only vice is that you are too tender-hearted to see mendacity in others," she said. "I'm afraid for once I find myself at variance with you. I don't believe Lord S— is the blameless victim you portray him to be."

I could breathe a little more easily now, knowing that none of them thought me responsible for what had happened that morning, not even Mr Dabb, but the hands that had pulled off the lady's boots were shaking in my lap.

"We must pay due respect to the gentleman, especially at this time of loss," said Mr Dabb. "He is a Member of Parliament, remember, and the nation owes much of its esteem to the sugar trade, whatever reservations we might have concerning it. We can't have common people giving up all respect for rank and degree, can we?"

"I can't vouch for the character of Lord S—, but he has spoken in the House against the emancipation of slaves," said Miss Vyvyan. "As well he might, given his fortune is founded on their sufferings. As a member of the Abolition Movement, I find myself somewhat at odds with his views. Perhaps you are unaware that six Methodist chapels have been attacked and destroyed in Jamaica where Lord S— has his plantations? The preachers were imprisoned for educating the island's slaves."

"These are weighty matters for a dinner party," said Mr Dabb, smiling and looking around the table.

"Perhaps you believe women are not competent to debate the duties of legislators, Mr Dabb?" said Miss Vyvyan. "Would you prefer to continue the discussion later when the gentlemen retire for cigars?"

"I do not say that, madam," he answered.

"Mr Stone might want to convert the people of Porthmorvoren, but I take more of a scientific interest," said Dr Vyvyan, heading off the quarrel. "I'm thinking of contributing a paper on the unique epidemiology of the inhabitants of that cove to a new journal in London. Have you gentlemen come across *The Lancet*?"

Dr Vyvyan's doctor friends said they most certainly had. They began talking about dropsy, malaria, yellow fever and the like. I reached for a wine glass. The serving girls had been topping up the glasses whenever my head was turned, so I had no idea how much I'd drunk. I took a big glug, but it did little to steady my nerves, which had been on edge since Mr Dabb had turned on me.

"Consider the environment," said Dr Vyvyan. "A moist and enervating climate, overcrowded cottages packed closely together and insanitary conditions. What

169

better way to allow the easy communication of contagious diseases?" He sounded quite pleased about the diseases. "What's more, there's a higher than usual incidence of intermarriage among the inhabitants. I've no doubt my records could form the basis of a study into hereditary patterns of disease. In fact, I sometimes aspire to publish a larger and more ambitious volume, perhaps taking in the entire west Cornish littoral. The idea would be to classify the country people's racial characteristics, and discuss how these correspond with their intellectual and moral faculties."

"I hear the cove is also infested with mermaids," said Mrs Stone. One of the philanthropical ladies rolled her eyes at this.

"Oh yes, and half the families in the village will tell you they are of mermaid descent," said Dr Vyvyan. "Every cove in Cornwall has its own mermaid legend, derived from smugglers' stories designed to keep rivals away from the shores where they ply their trade."

"Don't be such a spoilsport, Dr Vyvyan," Mrs Stone said. "I much prefer to believe the cove is haunted by sirens." She laughed too loudly, and I saw she was quite drunk.

The servant girls were putting out bowls of nuts, sweetmeats and fruit. Next they placed a ship with three masts made out of spun sugar in the middle of the table. I'd seen the like once in a shop window in Penzance. Would the food ever stop coming? My dress was already stretched tight across my belly and my insides were churning. If I'd been forced to stay in

Newlyn for another week, I'd have needed to take out my dresses.

"Oh, but it seems a shame to eat it!" said one of the doctors' wives, gazing at the sugar ship. But Dr Vyvyan was already tapping it with a spoon to break it into small pieces. The tray was passed around so we could put some onto our dessert plates.

Mr Dabb coughed, and looked at Gideon. "Will you not take a drink, parson?" he asked.

"No alcohol is permitted to pass my husband's lips," said Mrs Stone.

"Most commendable," said Mr Dabb, swirling the brandy in his glass before downing it in one. "Mr Stone, I wish you good fortune in reforming the manners of the cannibals in that cove of yours," he said. "It's a worthy project to instil frugality and prudence among people of that ilk. Our ends are one and the same, yours and mine, although we work through different channels."

"I'm not sure I understand you," said Gideon.

"What I mean to say, sir, is that in my travels up and down this land, I've seen how a dose of evangelicalism can transform the indigent class of people into productive, sober and self-reliant individuals. The nation is on a path of progress, even here in Cornwall. For evidence, you've only to look at the steam pumps in the mines hereabouts. All over England we have new roads and canals. You must visit the north when you have leisure and witness the factories that have sprung up there. The efficiencies of these institutions in comparison with home looms and cottage industry is the wonder of the age. Dare I propose that this nation can lead the world into a new era, and improve the conditions of the poor as we make progress?"

"My concern is with the life beyond this one, not with filling the pockets of factory owners and speculators," Gideon said, leaning across the table towards Mr Dabb. "I've seen these mills you talk of, with women and children at work all hours of the day and night, risking life and limb. I have no appetite for turning human beings made in God's image into cripples or slaves of industrial production. What's more, I ask if it's fair to subject the poor to standards of behaviour which are not countenanced by their betters."

The wine was warm in my veins and I was faint and muzzy with weariness after getting such a shock when the talk had turned to the Porthmorvoren Cannibal, and from being so long among these people far above me in rank. I saw Gideon was no more at home in this company than me. To them he must have seemed ill-bred and churlish, but I saw a man who was not afraid to speak his mind, a man who would not be swayed from the path of Godliness by fine living and false prizes.

"Perhaps we should allow that Mr Stone has a point," said Miss Vyvyan. "Progress will be gained at too heavy a cost if greed for material wealth takes precedence over all else. And if I might be permitted one last remark in relation to our friend, Lord S—. With my own eyes, I have witnessed worse-than-negro treatment of the poorest class of people right here in

Penwith, and it's my conviction that even the most depraved acts reported in the newspapers are not necessarily proof of a vicious character. Isn't it possible such deeds are engendered by desperate poverty and ignorance?"

"I shan't argue with that," said Mr Dabb, wiping his shiny forehead with his napkin. "People can be reformed and civilised, if we first convert and educate them."

After that, the talk turned to safer, more trifling matters, and I was left to my own thoughts. It had grown darker, the candles burnt low and some had sputtered out. It came to me that I had seen Gideon as he truly was that night. I'd heard him speak out for poor people like me, and against our hard task masters. And I saw that he and Mrs Stone didn't see eye to eye, and that she thwarted him in his desires. They were not happy, but what was that to me? The minister sat so close to me that we were almost touching, yet I felt as far away from him as ever. I looked over at Mrs Stone. She had a fierce look on her face, and held a shard of the sugar ship in her hand. She must have felt my gaze on her, for her head turned and she looked right at me, and as she did so the brittle piece of sugar she was holding shattered, and the broken pieces fell upon the table.

CHAPTER
ELEVEN

Mrs Stone and I sat at breakfast. All that could be heard was the chink of spoons in teacups, knives scraping butter onto toast and the ticking of the standing clock.

"I haven't seen that hair pin before," she said, looking at me askance. "I wonder if it's the best choice for today."

I should have known better than to wear the pin, but it was Sunday and I was to observe her teach the children. I didn't want them to know I was a low-born woman.

"We must consider what the children will think of any improper fondness for show. Apart from any other consideration, the benefactors of the Sunday school might see you, and it might reflect badly upon me."

Not wanting to cross her, I kept my own counsel.

"If I'm not mistaken that pin is genuine silver, and of a quality I would have thought beyond your means."

Was she calling me a thief?

"What is the matter with you this morning, Sister Blight? Have you lost your tongue?"

"Shall I take the pin out?" I took my napkin from my lap, wiped the butter from my fingers, and threw the napkin on my plate.

"Such peevishness! I hope the blandishments you received from Miss Vyvyan at the dinner party haven't emboldened you to this unsuitable self-display?"

I saw she was taunting me out of envy, and made no reply. The air in the little parlour thickened.

"If we're to instil duty and restraint in the children, we must avoid anything that betokens pride or luxury, which can only equate to idleness and improvidence when worn by the poor."

"It's only because I don't want to go before the children looking shabby."

"This only proves my point. It is your pride that's at fault. We must learn to submit to Providence. Might I ask you how you acquired this pin?"

"I bought it with my own money."

"You would need a great deal of money to afford such an ornament."

"It was bought second-hand."

"Be that as it may, I must insist on you removing the pin and replacing it with something plainer," she said.

I stood, pushed back my chair and stormed out of the parlour and upstairs. In the nursery, I threw myself down on the cot in a rage. When my anger was spent, I took the pin out of my hair, and opened the door to go downstairs. Down below, there was a knock on the front door.

As Mrs Gurney had not yet come, Mrs Stone went to open the door herself. I heard a woman speak, a plain country woman by the sound of her. I waited on the landing to eavesdrop.

"Begging your pardon, ma'am, is the minister about? I must speak with him."

"Would you mind telling me what business you have with the minister?" asked Mrs Stone.

"I don't like to say, ma'am."

"I'm afraid he isn't at home at present. Would you like to leave a message for him?"

I went down a few steps until I could see the door and Mrs Stone, and beyond her another woman whom I didn't know. Her clothes were of the meanest sort, her face drawn and her hair loose and dishevelled. She wiped the sweat from her brow with her sleeve, and spoke.

"You be his wife, I suppose?" She looked Mrs Stone up and down quickly.

"Indeed, I am his wife. May I ask from whence you came today?"

"St Buryan. I set off at dawn, leaving my little one with my mother."

"But that must be fifteen miles or more! And on so warm a morning. You must tell me what has brought you all this way."

"When will the minister be back? I shall wait for him."

"The minister is not expected home for a day or two."

"That's no use to me," the woman said.

"I am not in a position to offer charity, if that's your purpose in coming here," said Mrs Stone.

The woman shot a look at her. "Can I trouble you for a drop of water, at least?" she asked.

Mrs Stone turned and walked towards the scullery. When she came back with a tumbler in her hand, I went down the stairs.

"Wait for me in the parlour," she told me, as I passed her. I went in, leaving the door a little ajar so I could stand behind it and eavesdrop.

"Would you like to leave your name?" Mrs Stone asked the woman. "So I can inform my husband of your visit."

The woman faltered, before saying, "Anne Treveil." And then I heard the door close.

On Monday morning, the day before I was to return to Porthmorvoren, Mrs Stone told me she was going out to attend a meeting with Miss Vyvyan and would not be back until late afternoon. I was to consider my instruction over and done with. It meant I would be left alone in the house until Mrs Gurney came two hours later.

When she left, I was so skittish I hardly knew what to do with myself. I sat on her settle, which was like her throne, and found out how it felt to be queen of her little house. The place seemed strange now I was alone in it, full of little sounds, soft thumps within the walls, the sighing of a draught in the chimney breast, and all the while the ticking of the clock that stood guard in the room. I fell to wondering what I should do with myself for two whole hours. My thoughts quickly fell upon the one thing I had wanted to do ever since my first morning in the house — to find out what happened to Lady Rosemount at the end of *Virtue*

Rebuked by Mrs Catherine Fitzherbert. The more I tried to will away the notion, the stronger my desire grew. Unable to stop myself, I crept up the stairs, almost every one of which creaked. At the door of Mr and Mrs Stone's bedroom I stopped, my hand on the handle, and almost lost my nerve.

Once inside the bedroom, I left the door slightly ajar so I'd be able to hear Mrs Gurney if she showed up earlier than expected. Next, I went to the window and looked down at the street to make sure nobody was coming towards the house. The street was empty, so I opened the doors of the wardrobe and gazed upon Mrs Stone's frocks hung all in a row. When I'd had my fill of that, I moved over to the chest. On the top she had laid out her boxes of jewellery, a silver hand mirror and little bottles of coloured glass with scented oils in them. I took off the tops and sniffed one or two, but didn't dare to dab any on my wrists or neck.

I realised I was only putting off the moment when I must find the book, so I got down on my knees and reached for it under the bed, but there was nothing to be found. Sorely vexed, I lay down on the floor, lifted the counterpane and looked underneath the bed but again found nothing. I knew the book must be somewhere in that room, so I got to my feet to search for it. Hardly daring to draw breath, I opened one of the little drawers at the top of the chest. It was stiff and scraped noisily. Inside were gloves, scarves, muffs and the like, but there was no book. I tried a bigger drawer underneath and found only the minister's small clothes and stockings. Finally, I tried the very bottom drawer where Mrs Stone kept her neatly folded linen and woollen blankets. I had a hunch and felt underneath the layers of pressed cloth until my fingers butted against the corner of a hard-edged object. Listening for a moment to make sure nobody had come into the house, I pulled out the book, leaving the drawer open so I could put it back quickly, if disturbed.

After opening the bed curtains a little I sat on the edge of the bed and opened the book with shaking hands. I turned to the last few pages, the final letters that Lady Rosemount wrote to her friend. It seemed that her ladyship had tired of her intrigues and had found her conscience at last. She had tried to escape the castle to live in a convent, but that fiend, the Count, had hired some brigands to ambush her coach on a mountain pass, so he could pretend to rescue her, when really all he wanted was to have his way with her. My blood pumped hard in my ears as I read, so that I didn't hear footsteps on the stairs until it was too late. I thought that busybody Mrs Gurney must have come early, to keep an eye on me no doubt, and was just about to come barging through the door. I jumped to my feet, but before I had a chance to put the book back in the drawer, the door swung open and there before me she stood — not Mrs Gurney, but Mrs Stone herself. She saw the open bed curtain and peered through the gap as if she expected to find someone on the bed.

"May I ask what you are doing in this room?" she said.

"I was reading." She looked at the book in my hands and then down at the open drawer. "I was only looking for a blanket, ma'am. I was cold in bed last night and I thought I might find one in the chest. I should have waited and asked you, or got Mrs Gurney to fetch one, but as there was nobody about I went to look for it, thinking you wouldn't mind. I found this in the drawer and wondered what it might be."

"What on earth made you think you could sneak into my room and look through my private belongings?" she said, flushing.

"Your belongings?" I said. "This book is *yours*? I supposed it had been taken off Susan, for her own good. Or else from Mrs Gurney."

"Don't you dare trifle with me," she said, her mouth quivering.

"Please, ma'am, you mistake me, I was only . . ."

"Be quiet!" she snapped.

"Oh, please don't tell Mr Stone, I beg you!" I cried, thinking this would surely end my hopes of becoming Sunday school mistress. "He thinks well of me and I was only a little curious as I've never before seen such a book."

"How dare you suggest the novel is corrupting you!" she shouted. She lunged towards me and slapped my face so smartly that I screamed. I had never before been hit by a woman and let her get away with it.

"I told you to be quiet," she said. "Do you want me to call for a constable and have you arrested as a common thief?" She stepped back from me towards the door. "Pay attention to what I say. I won't let you drag me down to your level. I will not stand for it."

"I've done nothing wrong, really I haven't," I sobbed, wiping my running nose with my fingers.

"If you are such an innocent, then how do you explain the silver pin in your hair yesterday? Not to mention the fine pair of boots you were wearing when you arrived, boots that didn't fit you. Well?"

"I bought the hair pin in the market in Penzance with some money I had put by. The boots were second-hand, and cheap as they'd been damaged."

"Damaged in a wreck, you mean. You took them from a dead woman's feet."

"Oh no, ma'am, I didn't, I swear."

"Do you think me a fool? Admit what you've done."

"I would never do such a thing, honest to God, I wouldn't." Again, I broke into tears, as if all the feelings I'd held inside me since coming to Newlyn were pouring out at once.

"Calm yourself and dry your eyes," she said, handing me a pocket handkerchief. "Mrs Gurney will be here soon. You needn't let her see you like this."

I dabbed my eyes. "Shall I say I fell on my face?" I asked, touching my hot and stinging cheek.

"Say whatever you like." She reached out and took the novel from me. "This novel is mine, as you well know. It was in my possession when we moved into the house and I had forgotten all about it until now. I never intended to keep it a secret from my husband. We do not have secrets. In fact, I will put the book here on the chest for him to see. It is no more than a silly romance, after all.

"You have quite a gift, don't you, Miss Blight?" she continued. "My husband has seen fit to pass you off as a Sunday school teacher, but I think myself a better judge of your sort. Once you are back where you belong, do not ever think to return here. When the works are finished on the chapel, Mr Hawkey will take responsibility for leading prayer meetings in that village of yours and there will be no need for my husband to ever set foot on that shore again."

CHAPTER
TWELVE

My week in Newlyn came to an end. On the walk home across the moor I had to listen to Tobias Hawkey, the tinner preacher, tell me at length about his thirst for mental improvement. He'd started out as a buddle boy in the mines and later turned to smuggling before his conversion and submission to the Lord's will. The man wittered on and on about all manner of learned men, but Wesley was the only one I'd ever heard of. An hour or two of silence let him know he was wasting his breath and we passed the rest of the journey without a word. Afterwards, I felt sorry, though, as I'm sure he meant well and few men would even think of educating a poor low-born woman.

What tears of joy were wept when I walked through the door of my home and into the arms of my Mamm and Tegen! We had never in all our lives been so long apart.

Meanwhile, two guineas had been raised from the Society to buy catechisms for the new Sunday school. Now that the time had come, I realised I'd never wanted to be the Sunday school mistress at all. I'd gone along with it due to my pride and wanting to spite Loveday Skewes, and most of all so I could be tied in some way to the minister. What hope was there of that now, after he had steered clear of me all the while I was in Newlyn?

The day of the first class arrived and I had not slept all night. I got to Aunt Madgie's house, went through the two sturdy stone columns that held up the top floor, and knocked on the door. It creaked open and the old woman appeared in the shadows. She offered only a withering look for a greeting, barely glancing at me. I followed her to the kitchen door, where she stood and let me pass into the room, before disappearing into the back of the house, her crook sounding on the stone floor and echoing down the hallway.

I took my seat at the head of the table, feeling the squitters coming on and wanting the chamber pot, but not daring to ask for it. In a short while the children began to arrive in twos and threes. There were thirteen in all, crammed around the kitchen table with the latecomers on the settle by the hearth. It was the coldest kitchen I had ever known because the old dame was too mean to light a bit of kindling and furze in the hearth. The children sat on the hard wooden forms, the boys on one side of the table and the girls on the other. I saw how they cowered in that dark place lit only by the feeble light from a tiny window high on the wall, the corners of the room in such deep shadow that a ghoul might leap out at any moment. A great crucifix hung on the wall as a warning of what might happen if any child incurred God's wrath. I made sure to take a seat where that cross was out of sight and I would not be judged by it. Along the opposite wall was a huge dresser of dark stained wood, which loomed over the room and seemed to draw what little light there was into its depths. I saw how poor little Sarah Pengilly trembled and when nobody was looking I gave her a smile, and she returned it. Aunt Madgie entered, trailing a cold draught behind her. Without a word, she placed a stick on the dresser, a horrid thing. I was sure I could never bring myself to strike a child. When she was gone she left the kitchen door ajar so that she could overhear us.

I passed around the catechisms. Only a few minutes of the class were done and there was almost three hours to go. How was I to keep control of the children for all that time when by rights they should be running wild outside? The cloth in the armpits of my dress was damp with sweat, in spite of the cold. "Now which of you can read a little?" I asked. All stared down at the table in silence.

When the class was over I was more tired than I had ever been in my life. Throughout, as I'd given the children their instruction, I'd felt Aunt Madgie's dark presence behind the kitchen door, finding fault with whatever I did. At the end Gideon came to pay a visit. The children stood to attention, the girls curtseying before him in the sweetest way you could imagine and the boys tugging their forelocks like the dearest little men. I felt proud of them at that moment, as if they were my own children.

"Do you know that you are very special children because you are the first in over ten years who have had the opportunity to go to school?" he told them. "I am sure you will all attend well to Sister Blight's lessons. Under her instruction you will learn your ABC. More importantly, you will become habituated to a regular and devout attendance upon the public worship of Almighty God, and the ministry of His word. You must pay attention to whatever Sister Blight tells you, because it will enkindle a thirst for mental and moral improvement, and train you for Heaven. I hope that this school will become a nursery for the chapel and a bulwark of the Protestant faith in the village, and that its influence will be reinforced in all your homes."

When he had finished the children stared at each other, not having understood a word of it. "And perhaps next week we will bring some wood for the fire," he said, with a smile, and they all cheered. The children went, leaving me in the shadows of that dark room with the minister. No doubt Aunt Madgie was outside listening.

"I hope this morning wasn't too much of an ordeal," he said. He must have seen how I shook, having hidden my nerves so long from the children. "I don't want you to feel abandoned. I regret that I was unable to spend more time in Newlyn during your stay." He cleared his throat, and I knew he meant to broach some weighty matter. "You have heard something about my home arrangements, perhaps?" I shook my head. "Well, you will do soon enough. Hearsay travels quickly in these parts. My wife has moved out of our home and gone to stay with her parents. She is indisposed, and may be gone a little time. However, I trust in Providence that she will recover before too long."

This news pleased me, but not wanting him to see, I set about gathering the catechisms and putting them in my basket.

"Of course, the work must continue on the chapel," he said.

I nodded, but said nothing.

"Sister Blight," he said, in a way that called for my full attention. "I must be sure that you are undertaking this work in good faith."

I put the catechisms in my basket, and turned to him. "What do you mean to say?" I said. "Mrs Stone hasn't said anything about me?"

"One or two things, but they don't overly concern me. However, if you are to continue as Sunday school mistress, I must be assured you are not bound by the chains of superstition, as so many of your neighbours are. I will never forget that poor plucked bird you hung from the rafters. Some of these pagan notions are merely quaint, such as children baptising their dolls on Good Friday or sacred rocks with curative properties. Others are more concerning, women offering pardons and protections, for example, or animal sacrifices. I must be persuaded that you have surrendered to faith in the Redeemer's love."

"I've always held with King Jesus, and the angels. But I own that I have at times used herbs and charms. I thought it would do no harm and perhaps some good would come of it. But I will stop now, if you ask it."

"The Creator is not to be compared to piskies, spells or spirits. But this is not all." He was quiet for a moment. When he spoke, he didn't look me in the eye.

187

"We must also disavow our pride, the secret and selfish desires of our heart. We must forget the vanities of this world, and look to the next. There is a great liberty in this, I promise you." His voice became softer. "Mary, I have put my faith in you. I know you will not fail me. I have brought something for you." He glanced over at the door, which was ajar, to make sure we were not spied upon. Then he took a scroll of paper from inside his coat, and handed it to me. "It is one of Mr Wesley's hymns. You will be familiar with it from our prayer meetings. I have made a copy of it. Often times, when I've been low in spirit, I have found these verses comforting."

I took the scroll from his hand, but didn't unravel it until he'd left.

I am no longer my own, but thine.
Put me to what thou wilt, rank me with whom
thou wilt.
Put me to doing, put me to suffering.
Let me be employed for thee or laid aside for thee,
exalted for thee or brought low for thee.
Let me be full, let me be empty.

Let me have all things, let me have nothing.
I freely and heartily yield all things to thy
pleasure and disposal.
And now, O glorious and blessed God,
Father, Son and Holy Spirit,
thou art mine, and I am thine.
So be it. And the covenant which I have made

on earth, let it be ratified in Heaven.
Amen.

In the days after, I read the hymn over and over until I had it by heart. One day I was singing the verses as I went about my chores, trying to think of the Maker and not Gideon Stone. Then I remembered the visit of the woman from St Buryan to his house while he was abroad. She'd come begging for money, which made me think she must have been something to him in the past. And of a sudden I saw what had been right before my face all the while, and had to sit down on a chair. Gideon had stayed away from Newlyn while I was there because he felt something towards me, and he wanted to put himself beyond temptation. As I recited the verses of Mr Wesley's hymn in my mind, I began to feel Gideon had given me the verses to hint at another kind of love than church love, even if he hid it from himself.

I got the knack of taking classes over the weeks that followed. I tried to sound like a teacher and have the bearing of one. Luckily, I had always been a good mimic and often made my neighbours laugh by taking off my betters. When in doubt I thought of myself as Lady Rosemount in *Virtue Rebuked*, only a little less grand. To begin with, only the children of the bettermost on Fore Street came, but soon a few others joined, even some from Uplong Row, most likely because their parents wanted to get the little devils off their hands for three hours. They turned up with their toes showing through their boots or else no boots at all, and with nothing at all inside their bellies. Some were forever scratching their heads because lice were tormenting them. The next week I brought biscuits along that I'd baked myself the night before. I turned a blind eye when the children from the poorer families dropped off to sleep during the lesson, knowing that they had likely been looking after their younger brothers and sisters since dawn. I wouldn't chastise them, even though I knew that black-hearted old woman was listening behind the door, scheming to be rid of me so she could put Loveday Skewes in my place.

If I'd had the little mites to myself I'd have spiced up the lessons with a few old yarns like those Mamm used to tell us on stormy nights when we were small. I'd have taken them out into the little yard for a while so they could play a few rounds of Thread the Needle or Twos and Threes, or I'd have brought an old rope so they could have a tug of war, the boys against the girls. One time, while the children took turns to piddle indoors, I let a few of the boys play a game of marbles in the gutter. When the class was over, Aunt Madgie took me to one side.

"I see you have allowed the boys to play at marbles," she said, fixing me with her cold grey eyes.

"An innocent pastime, I would say."

"Far from an innocent pastime, it is a game that leads to ungodliness, to cheating and tricks and all manner of deception. In time it will lead to the heinous sin of gambling. *Lying lips are abomination to the Lord, but they that deal truly are his delight.* Proverbs 12:22. I shall have to mention this matter to their parents. There will be no marbles in this house. Am I understood?"

Another week, Sarah Pengilly stayed behind once the class was finished and the others had run home.

"What is it, Sarah?" I asked.

"Only that . . ." she said. She bit her bottom lip and wouldn't say more.

"Speak up now, you can say what you like to me."

"Never mind, it's no matter. I better go."

"Wait, Sarah. Is there something you want to tell me? Is anybody telling tales about me? I won't say anything if you tell me."

"Oh no, Miss. Not that I know of."

"Is there something else then?"

"Just . . . Can I help you next time, Miss? To give out the books." I couldn't stop a tear welling in my eye. "Oh Miss, don't be sad," she said.

"I'm not sad, Sarah. I'm happy. You have made me so. And of course you can help me hand out the catechisms."

My heart swelled with pride. The children took me for a proper teacher. But Aunt Madgie was watching my every move, waiting for me to falter. And the more able I proved myself, the more she would want to bring me low. And I could never forget she had a secret she might one day use against me.

At the start of the next class I told the children that Sarah was to become class monitor. And from now on there would be an extra biscuit for all who attended for four weeks together. At the end of that class Aunt Madgie came and leant against the frame of the doorway. I carried on tidying away the books, then put on my shawl.

"Don't be too soft on them," she said. "*He that spareth his rod hateth his son, but he that loveth him chasteneth him betimes*. Proverbs 13:24."

"Must we only frighten them into learning? All we ever have them do is learn verses by heart, words they cannot hope to make sense of."

"You think you can win them over but they will turn on you at the first sign of weakness, mark my words. You won't get the children's respect by appointing monitors and doling out biscuits to bribe them."

I was in such a passion I couldn't trust myself to speak, so I pushed past her and almost ran into the lane. Before I had turned the corner into Downlong Row, she called after me, "Mind that every word you teach them is sound Bible doctrine, young lady!"

CHAPTER
THIRTEEN

Five bleeding wounds He bears,
Received on Calvary;
They pour effectual prayers;
They strongly speak for me.
Forgive him, O forgive, they cry,
Nor let that ransomed sinner die!

The sound of women's voices singing "Arise, My Soul, Arise!" echoed around the cove for all to hear, as a bunch of us womenfolk climbed the hill out of the village. Gideon walked before, blending his deeper voice with ours, as we followed him to the kiddlywink. There was me and Tegen, and Cissie Olds, the Widow Chegwidden and Martha Tregaskis. Halfway up the hill, Nancy Spargo joined us, her big arms swinging at her sides, along with a couple of her mates from the tinners' cottages, both as stout as she.

The journey came about because Gideon had asked for hearers to come forward to make a deputation to visit the kiddlywink. "My work here will not be accomplished until I have brought the vilest class of sinners under conviction," he told us. We were to go and persuade the ruffians who loafed about in that filthy shack to choose temperance and go home to their wives and children. I put my hand up quicker than any to enlist, for this was a chance to be near the minister. He had kept well out of my way since he'd given me Mr Wesley's hymn. But I had little faith that our visit to the kiddlywink would make the men who drank there into God-fearing Christians.

We were still singing, although more raggedly, when we reached a blighted orchard of dry and twisted trees, where only a few hardy sea cabbages and silver ragwort had taken root, together with tangled shoots more suited to the ocean bed that had wound themselves around the tree trunks. Beyond this was the lane where the miners lived, two rows of cottages facing each other across a narrow lane that the sun's rays never reached. A couple of children scampered ahead of us and disappeared from sight. We found them in a narrow alley between two cottages, shadowy figures lurking in the gloom. The minister stood at the entrance to the alley, seeming much troubled by what he saw.

"They are brother and sister," I said, as I pushed my way through the women to stand at his side.

"A most distressing sight. How did the boy lose his hands?"

"It was when he was an infant. His mother nipped out to fetch something and forgot and left the door open. The family pig got in and his Mamm couldn't pull the animal off in time."

"Oh, but it's a blessing in disguise, really," said Martha, squeezing herself between me and the minister. She stank of liquor. "The little scarper will never have to

194

work, and his father have made a fair wack showing him at fairs and markets."

Gideon stared, frowning, at the boy's sister, whose face was badly pock-marked.

"Smallpox, minister," said Martha. She lowered her voice to a whisper. "It's been visited on the child because someone in the family have angered God."

Gideon shook his head, and sighed heavily. "She is an innocent child, Martha. How will I ever break the chains of superstition and barbarous custom that bind you people?"

We moved on and before long, we were within reach of the kiddlywink. The tap boy came running out. "You can't come in here. Women ain't allowed. Now get on home, or else!"

"Out of the way, scrimp!" said Nancy, bowling him over onto his ass. With the minister in the lead, we filed into the shack. In the airless hovel, it was too dark to see at first. The fusty smell of the men's clothing and the reek of sweat, tobacco and strong liquor were hard to stomach. One of the women had a coughing fit. When my eyes grew used to the light, I saw perhaps a dozen men through a dense haze of tobacco smoke. Several of them had got to their feet and stood there, gawping at us women in disbelief. Others perched on piles of brick or on empty ale firkins, staring at us, looking none too pleased. One fellow lay passed out on the floor behind the barrels, only his legs showing. A group sitting around a tub were frozen in the midst of a card game, one fellow's hand hanging in the air at the point of throwing his card down on the table. Piles of coins lay on the barrel. One huge fellow sat with his back to us, and there was no mistaking that bald, misshapen head and those broad shoulders — it was the giant, Pentecost, the husband of Martha Tregaskis, who was cowering behind the other women.

Gideon took a step forward, stooping to miss a low beam with hops hanging from it. He took up a place by a row of barrels, and cleared his throat. "Gentlemen, may I have your attention!" he called.

"F— off out of here!" shouted Pentecost.

"You has a nerve coming here, parson," said another fellow. It was Ethan Carbis, who sat in the middle of the hovel, his pipe held to his mouth. He wore a filthy sacking apron smeared with dried blood. "Can't an honest working man enjoy a quiet drink with his associates without being pestered by Bible thumpers?"

"As I have yet to see any of you gentlemen in attendance at our prayer meetings, I thought I would come along and invite you to worship with your neighbours," said the minister. Some of the men shook their heads with disbelief.

"I has a mind to swing by one of these nights. I hear it's full of women," said Ethan, which made them all laugh.

"Your missus would have something to say about that," said Nancy.

"She can go hang," said Ethan. "You know how it is, parson. Us men forget the wedding vows when the first storm of fervour have died down. You got a missus yourself, I heard, so you get my meaning." He winked at the minister. "A man needs a few pots of ale of an afternoon to get through the marriage scrimmage with no tiles off the roof."

"It's the custom hereabouts for a stranger to stand a drink for one and all," said Ephraim Lavin, the blind fiddler. He had his fiddle on his lap and no doubt he came to this filthy place to play airs, hoping the drinkers would throw him a few coins. He sat with his back against one of the barrels that were stacked at one end of the room, and his cloudy yellow eyeballs looked out at nothing in particular.

"I'm afraid I must disappoint you, then," said Gideon. "My purpose in coming here is to persuade you to take a pledge of temperance."

"Go to hell, then!" said Ephraim, raising his pot for the tap boy to take away and fill. "Here's a health to the barley mow!"

"Since you has showed yourself to be a sportin' man, parson," said Jake Spargo, "why not make a wager tonight? I has the pluckiest devil of a rooster, and you can watch him flay the life out of Henry Trenhouse's cock. As guest of honour I'll save you a place in the front row. You'll be liberally sprayed with blood, I promise you."

"Take no notice of him, parson," said Nancy, glaring at Jake, her husband. "He'll get a piece of my mind when he gets home tonight, never you fear."

"I might come home more often if she was less of a scold," muttered Jake.

Gideon spoke. "I came here this evening, as you gentlemen well know, to speak out against cock fighting, and against wrestling, and against every species of barbarity that plagues this village. Against wrecking and smuggling, breach of the Sabbath, intemperance, gambling and above all against disrespect toward women folk. My work here will not be finished until I have brought the better men among you under conviction."

"Any more sermonising from you, rector, and I'll give you syphilis of the mouth," said Pentecost, looking over his shoulder as he slammed a playing card down on the barrel in front of him. The women were in uproar at him using such lewdness with ladies present, but his mates only laughed.

Ethan puffed on his pipe. "It do seem to I, parson, that your doctrine is hard on poor men like we, whose only pleasure in life is to partake of a pot or two of porter with our mates every once in a while. From what I hear, King George himself is fat as a hog from gorging on cake and sherry. And he keeps a harlot round the corner for his own convenience." He blew a long stream of smoke up into Gideon's face. "There be one rule for the bettermost and another for the poor, I reckon. And a word of advice to you, parson: we men here take great offence at you calling us 'wreckers'. We ain't wreckers; we're *salvors*."

"If the goods you plunder are salvage, then why do I see them on sale in Penzance?" asked Gideon.

"That be the King's fault, I seem. It were he that put duties on every basic necessity, just so he could service his debts from the French wars. The King's Coast Guard would rather sink a ton of tea than let we poor folk enjoy a drop of it. And we has scarcely salt enough to cure our pilchards. You can forget your Methody notions, parson. They don't take hereabouts. You ain't in Newlyn now."

"They Newlyn women is all whores," said Davey Combelleck, who was one of the card players. "Exceptin' your good wife, of course, parson."

"Newlyn is the Home of Sin," said Ethan. "A fact which admits of no gainsaying. They Newlyn wenches is only half human. They has poison in their spit so when you kiss them you lose your senses and are helpless to stop 'em dragging you down off the quay to drown you." He stooped towards the spittoon, and his phlegm rang on the metal like a pellet. "It's a matter of common knowledge that they Newlyn women can make babes all by themselves, without need of a man at all."

"Your conversions hereabouts has been mostly among the women folk, if I ben't mistook," said Jake, looking slyly at the minister.

"Show some respect, you dirty stop-out!" said Nancy, wagging a finger at him.

"It don't belong to women to go out nights to prayer meetings when they should be at home taking care of the childer, and that's the gospel truth," said Jake in a wheedling, self-pitying voice.

"Did Christ die on the cross to save the likes of you men? Shame on you!" said Gideon. As he spoke, I saw Pentecost get to his feet and turn to look at him. The big oaf loomed out of the smoky haze, his eyes no more than tiny hollows, his face hewn out of granite, his nose broken in at least two places and his great slab of a chin jutting before him, deeply dimpled. At the sight of him,

Martha, who had the bad luck to be his wife, tried to hide herself behind the other women.

"Come out here," he shouted at her. She made a bolt for the door, but he stopped her with another yell. "I'm speaking to you. Come over here this minute, or I'll show master and lay on you so hard you'll wish yourself dead — and I don't care who sees it." Martha turned and pushed her way through the women to stand in front of her husband, clutching herself and not daring to look up at him. "What are you doing here, you slack old lump of misery? You want to shame me in front of my pals, do you?"

"I am come with the minister." Her voice was so soft it could barely be heard.

"That's right, you're here with me, Martha," said Gideon, putting his hand around her shoulder.

"To tell us to stop drinking? Is that why?" Pentecost said to Martha.

First she shook her head, but then she looked up at Gideon and nodded.

"You come here stinking of liquor and has the nerve to tell me to stop drinking?" said Pentecost. "Go home, before I break your neck."

She shook her head, and muttered, "I can't, Pent. We've come to ask you men to come home to your wives."

"What is this? A mutiny?" He took hold of her arm.

"Don't you be hurting me! Not in front of my friends," she cried. "Please, Penty!"

"I'll show you hurting!" The back of his hand struck her hard across the face, and every woman in the alehouse screamed. Martha would have fallen if Pentecost hadn't held her up, gripping her by the arm. Cissie Olds and the Widow Chegwidden tried to pull Martha away from him. She was panting, her head thrown back and blood pouring thick from her nose. There were red specks over Cissie's apron.

Gideon stepped right in front of Pentecost, looking up into the giant's eyes. "I warn you not to lay another finger on this woman!" he said.

"What's this world coming to if a man can't beat his own wife without a ranting preacher getting in the way?" said Pentecost, with a sneer. He let go of Martha and turned to walk away, but then quick as lightning threw a punch that caught Martha in the ribs. Nancy leapt on the brute's back and tried to pull him away, shouting, "Leave her be, you dirty bullswizzle!" But he shrugged her off, and she fell heavily to the floor, groaning. Everything was happening at once. Martha was bent double, making sounds like a wounded animal. Gideon was grappling with Pentecost, and barrels were overturned. The women scattered to get out of the way, the men rose to their feet, and somewhere in all this Martha fell to the floor.

Pentecost held Gideon in a bear hug, and pushed him up against a wall, making the whole hut shudder. "Come outside, milksop, and show me what you're made of," he taunted. "Let me get you in a hitch and make a man of you. I'll learn you a few throws, the foreheep, or the flying mare, maybe." With a sudden lunge he got Gideon's arm twisted behind his back and his head locked in the crook of his arm. He began banging Gideon's head against the wall, making dents in the cob. I ran over, and tried to pull him off, hearing my own voice as though it were somebody else's. "Leave off, you devil, let him be!" I near tore the shirt off Pentecost's back but to no avail, so I reached around him to grab hold of his face, and tried to dig my nails into his eyes. He shook his head and let go of Gideon, who fell in a heap on the floor. Then he turned around and stood there, opening and shutting his eyes one by one to see if he could still see through them. There were scratches on his brow and cheek.

"Which one of you bitches did this?" Pentecost looked around at us, one eye shut and the other squinting, and every woman looked down at her feet. I was the nearest to him, and he peered at me through the little slit of his good eye for a while, sweat dripping off the end of his nose. "You'll pay for this, whichever one of you it was. I'll find out." Then he stomped out of the shack, leaving his wife lying on the floor, her hair caked in her own blood. The women crouched down by her.

I rushed to Gideon and got down on my knees by him. "Let me have a look at you," I cried, taking his head in my hands. I could feel a big bump under his scalp, but saw no blood. I helped him to his feet, and he looked around, dazed, touching the top of his head and wincing. His gaze alighted upon Martha lying on the floor, with Sarah Keigwin and Tegen squatting down beside her. He went and stooped over Martha, looking at her nose, which was purple and swollen.

202

"Will one of you take in Martha tonight?" he said, standing upright. "She shouldn't go home after this, not until I've had words with that bully."

"I will take her in," said the Widow Chegwidden. "I have remedies that will comfort the poor creature."

"And I will look in on her children," said Cissie.

Gideon looked around the room, swaying, so I took his arm, worried he might swoon. He squinted at the men, as if puzzled to find himself among them.

A voice was heard, one I knew very well: "So this is the lay of the land." It was Johnenry's voice. He stepped out of the gloom and staggered towards where I stood alongside Gideon. Johnenry was greatly changed since last I saw him, his face gaunt and smeared with dirt, one of his eyes black and bloodshot. I realised it had been him I'd seen before, lain out cold behind the barrels.

"Such a big brave fellow," he said, sneering at Gideon. "I suppose Mary thinks you a proper snot with your fine words and foreign ways."

"Do I know you?" Gideon asked.

"No, but I know you well enough," said Johnenry. "Look at the pair of you, arm in arm."

"Come, we should get out of here," I said, tugging Gideon's arm, but he stood his ground.

"Who is this fellow?" Gideon asked me.

"It's of no matter," I said.

"No matter, say you?" said Johnenry, glaring at me. "I be naught to you, then." He turned to Gideon. "What are you doing by her, preacher man? You want to watch your step with this one, I tell you. You think you know Mary, but you don't. Not like I do. Look at you! You be mazed by her, same as I were."

"Take no notice of him," I said, pulling Gideon towards the door, before Johnenry could say more.

"We should speak another time," the minister called to him, over his shoulder.

"Save your breath, parson," said Johnenry. "I don't want to hear your measly sermons. King Jesus and all the Angels can go to hell for all I care, but if you hurt Mary I'll make you sure you pay for it."

I got Gideon outside. The Widow Chegwidden and Cissie were a good way down the hill, helping Martha home, with a straggle of other women in tow. The fresh air seemed to go to Gideon's head, for he was staggering sidelong in one direction and then the other, as if the world was tipping up and down beneath him.

"I'll never get in a boat again," he cried.

"Nobody's putting you in a boat," I said, gripping his arm to stop him falling on his face.

"I won't go near water, mark you! I'd walk through hellfire first." He groaned loudly and clutched his head. "Such a pressing on my skull. And these lights. Is it glow worms out early to torment me?"

"You're muzzy, is all. You've taken a few blows to the head. Or don't you remember what's just befallen you."

He stopped in his tracks, shaking his head. "I hit my head on the barrel out there on the swell," he said.

"That was months back. We've just been in the kiddlywink, not five minutes ago. That brute Pentecost took hold of you and banged your poor head against the wall."

"That's a damned lie! I've not set foot in an alehouse in ten years. No since . . ."

"Have it your own way, then," I said, startled to hear an oath like that from him.

He reeled again, unsteady on his feet. I saw a boulder up ahead and pushed him towards it. "Look, sit yourself down here," I said, when we got there. "Sit quiet a while now. You're dizzy. We'll wait here till it wears off."

Gideon's chin dropped to his chest and he closed his eyes. He sat that way a long while, me beside him. Meanwhile, the sun sank lower in the western sky, the grasses of the headland took on an amber glow and long shadows were thrown behind every tree and boulder. Gideon's face was bathed in soft light and I was free to stare to my heart's delight at his long, dark eyelashes quivering on his cheeks, the care lines on his brow, his long, straight nose. At last, he roused himself and looked blearily about him, rolling his shoulder and rubbing his neck. "That big oaf has done me grievous harm," he said.

"So you remember now?"

"I remember the brute bashing my head on the wall, but not how I got here."

"What you did today was terrible brave," I said softly. "All on your own among those ruffians — and standing up to that big devil, Pentecost. To turn the other cheek was braver still — no man hereabouts would have done such a thing."

"Over the years, I've had brickbats thrown at me, and pisspots emptied on my head from windows as I preached. I've had to leave towns in the dead of night for fear of my life." He turned to me, squinting into the sun's glare. "I see Christ in you, Mary, as you sit there before me, with the sun for a halo. His light is shining from within you. It was Providence that drew me to this shore so you could haul me out of the sea."

"You must be feeling better if you're back in the preaching way," I said.

"There was a young fellow just now in the alehouse, the one who accosted us as we were leaving. Who is he?" he asked.

"That ain't worth talking of."

"He has a claim on you, it would seem." He winced, touching his head gingerly. Gideon was in a queer mood after what had happened, and it struck me that he might be envious of Johnenry, or of what had once gone between Johnenry and me. I felt the scroll that hung on a string around my neck, the copy of Mr Wesley's hymn that Gideon had given me after the first Sunday school class. It seemed to throb against my breast.

"We've known each other since we were children, Johnenry and me," I said. "And we walked out together a while ago, but not anymore."

"Yes, of course. You'll have had dalliances. It occurs to me I know nothing of your past life. I should like to know more."

"Oh, there's little enough to tell. Not like you. Who was that Molly, who you cried out to in your fever? Forgive me, it is not my place to ask such things."

He was quiet a moment, looking down at his feet, before looking up at me and answering. "I thought Molly an Irish Magdalen, but her heart was as black as her hair. Perhaps I was looking for somebody to save, even then. She told me she was putting aside the money I gave her so that we could emigrate together. One day it was Canada, the next Australia. On her account, I left a man with his skull cracked open and his life blood spilling over the straw of an alehouse floor. And all to defend the honour of a woman who had no honour to begin with."

"Can this be so?" I cried.

"My fall from grace came when I was twenty years of age. My father, for whom I was an eternal disappointment, had me apprenticed to an engineering draughtsman in Plymouth. My dear doting mother would have contested it, had she not been confined to her room by a seizure of melancholy. That draughtsman's office was as good as a prison to me. My shackles were the lines and angles I was forced to put upon the paper with pen, rule and compass. I wasn't fit for such work. And it was all for no higher purpose than to serve mammon, to fill the pockets of the merchants and speculators whose goods I saw loaded and unloaded on the quay. They built fine houses in the country for themselves, while men, women and even children ground away their short, wretched lives in their mills and factories. Before long, I took to spending my days in the alehouses around the fetid alleys haunted by Molly and her ilk.

207

"So it was, that one cold, black night I came to be walking in steady drizzle through the meanest alleys of the port, lanes frequented by press gangs, cutthroats and harlots, and I'm ashamed to say these by ways were well known to me. I was intent on one thing only — to bring my wretched life to an end in the place where I'd first met Molly. But as I approached, I heard the voice of a preacher, and thought bitterly that I was to be thwarted even in death. A throng of people of the lowest sort filled the little courtyard: indigents, pickpockets, convicts, smugglers, men who made their living from the immoral earnings of women, all peering through the murky light at a stout little man in their midst, the kind of ranting preacher my father despised.

" 'Friend!' the preacher cried. 'Some great trouble weighs on your heart, I see it in your eyes. Don't be afeard, now, feel the Lord's grace. Your saviour is here for you. You have found a true father in God. Take him to your heart, and save yourself. Make Christ the sole object of your wishes!'

"The preacher seemed to look into my soul. You have found a true father in God. Those words, and others he spoke to me that night, set my heart beating like the pendulum of a clock. The power of Our Lord Jesus Christ seized every limb and laid me flat out on the floor. The crowd, coarse as they were, gathered all about me, offering consolation and friendship. In that moment Heaven and earth appeared to me in a new light."

He was quiet a moment, rocking back and forward where he sat, and breathing hard. There was a sheen of sweat on his face. I thought I knew his meaning. At times, I too had seen another world, glimpsed through a veil as fine as spiders' webs.

He turned and looked at me closely. "You're a rare individual, Mary Blight. A poor country woman who knows the Scriptures better than many a country cleric. This will set you in good stead. But your friend back there says I don't know you. What was it he said — I'm *mazed* by you?"

"I haven't always been as good as I should be. You're not alone in your sinfulness," I said, unable to look him in the face.

"All can be saved! Open your heart to Christ Our Saviour, Mary."

"I have often wished I could raise myself to a better life, but I hankered for base things, to be rich as the bettermost, to put myself above my neighbours out of pride, and even . . ."

My hands trembled in my lap, for as I spoke I saw myself on Porthmorvoren strand on that grey winter's morning months ago, pulling the tooth out of the noblewoman's mouth, and seeing the bubbles rise in her mouth, and wondering if she had still been breathing as I pulled the boots from her feet. The memory gave me such a fright, I forgot where I was for a moment.

"I've filched things from the dead who washed up in shipwrecks," I said. "Can the Maker forgive even that?"

Instead of blaming me, he gave me a weary smile. "Your conscience is even now awakening. The essence of perfection is perfect love for God and neighbour, not sinlessness. This is not a religion of hard doctrine, but a religion of the heart. Perfection begins with the new birth. You can be born again."

He spoke on, most of it too hard for me to grasp. Yet I felt a new day dawning, a new birth, as he'd called it. I had always thought myself far beneath others, no more than a worm delving in the dirt, eking out a poor living, my heart full of spite and envy for my neighbours among the bettermost — not that they didn't deserve it, mind. Yet, now a great surging hope sprung in my heart.

"We must bear witness, even as the stones rain down on our heads," Gideon said. "All around is evidence of the Fall. Industrialists who plunder and rend this earth, poor wretches in rags slaving long hours in black mills. You too, Mary, you must bear witness of the spirit working within you when you teach the children in the Sunday school."

His passion was spent, and he slumped where he sat. My rump was sore from sitting so long on the hard rock, so I got him up to his feet, and led him down the hillside. The sun was now all but sunk under the far horizon and the sky was streaked with clouds of rose and deep blue that spread far and wide over the heavens. Above, a great many birds, gulls and geese and crows and starlings, flew in flocks across the sky, their screeches and croaks piercing the air, all heading the same way as if called into the swirling golden haze in the west. Gideon and I tramped down the hillside, two weary pilgrims side by side. And though I had no wings to fly, my soul soared as darkness began to spread over the waters.

The man who walked beside me had been a sinner too, in his time, and he had been reborn. In his weakened state, he had opened his heart to me and I cared not if on the morrow he was back to his old puffed up ways. He'd wrought a change in me, and I swore I'd submit to Christ's saving grace and never more go wrecking for the rest of my days.

At the next prayer meeting in the makeshift chapel down in the harbour, two men turned up just as Gideon was mounting his pulpit. I recognised them from among those who had been in the alehouse the night Martha took a beating. The men took off their caps and fumbled with them. "Begging your pardon, parson, if it's all the same to you, we should like to attend your meeting," said one of them.

"You are very welcome to join us," he cried, showing them the men's benches. The man who had spoken went and stood under the pulpit, glancing about him furtively before looking up at Gideon. "We wanted to say . . ." He seemed to lose courage, but found it again. "What I mean is . . . Your words struck at our hearts that night. We be tinners, Jack and me, and must go and work the second night core in the bal tonight. We has often wondered, stuck down there in that black hole, if this were all life holds for men like we. And it seemed awful hard. Your words has given we hope."

Almost as one, the hearers rose to their feet, shouting hosannahs and alleluias and clapping the men.

When the shouting had died down, Gideon said: "Gentlemen, I cannot tell you how much your appearance here tonight has lifted my spirits. You are very welcome here."

A few more women came through the door at that moment, but the women's benches were full so they went to sit on some corn sacks that had been put along the walls for latecomers.

"Sisters, there is room on the men's benches," Gideon called to them. "It will not breach decorum or anger the Maker, I promise you." But the women looked horrified at the notion and took their place on the sacks, where the grease from the tapers up on the wall was like to drop on their shoulders.

With a little shake of his head, Gideon began the meeting. "Now, I have some wise words for all the young maidens here," he said. "Let me remind you to put a sprig of myrtle under your pillow tonight. That way you'll know the man you are to marry." The hearers looked at each other, not able to believe their own ears. Some of the girls looked at their friends and couldn't help giggling, until they were told off by their parents. "And if there is any old widow among you suffering with heartburn, the remedy is to grind up a black spider into powder and put it in your tea." I saw he was laughing at our old ways, but some looked at each other, not knowing how to take it. "As you will have surmised, my friends, I am not in earnest," he said. "Such foolish superstitions may be harmless in themselves, but I know of other pagan customs that are of more concern to me. This very day I learned of a family whose members, wishing to cure a grandmother of a malady, had cut a live pigeon in two and placed the bleeding parts against the soles of the old woman's feet. Such barbarism has no place in a civilised Christian country. I commend you to turn your backs on primitive beliefs and customs and trust instead in the divine truth of the gospels."

After that, the rest of the meeting went as usual, with Gideon ending with the dismissal prayer and a reminder of the tender mercy of God's love.

"Before you go, I have an announcement to make," he said. "Next month, we will be holding a Lovefeast, the first ever in this village. All will be welcome. I bid you to invite those of your neighbours who, for whatever reason, have not so far joined us at our meetings. There will be cakes and tea for all at the Lovefeast!"

There was a great hubbub about this as people filed out of the benches towards the door. But then, word got about that the bells in the old church up on the headland were ringing. I strained my ears and heard that it was true. It sounded like lunatics had got in and got hold of the bell ropes. I thought of that lonely hilltop at this late hour and of phantoms in the old church where I'd spent so many hours, and it chilled me to the bone. Instead of stopping awhile to chatter, all the hearers were pushing and shoving to get out of the door.

"What is the matter?" said Gideon, as he came to the scrum of panicking people jostling to get out.

"Do you not hear the bells ringing in the old church?" said Millie Hicks, her sewing bag under her arm.

"Dead sailors leave their graves at nine bells and go to ring the bells," said Dolly Stoddern, pushing past.

"And you believe these old yarns? Even after all I've said about superstition? I hoped for better from you, Millie."

"I ben't no ways particular about the tale," said Millie. "But just the same I'd sooner be tucked up inside my home if there's any chance of spirits haunting the lanes."

"Lord, have mercy!" he shouted. "There is a rational explanation for this bell ringing. It is no doubt a few drunkards playing a prank on you all."

"We have so many lost souls on our consciences," said another woman. "So many who has been buried in unblessed ground over the years, or lost at sea."

"Listen, friends," Gideon cried. "I can put this nonsense to rest if a few stout men and women will go up to the church with me this night and discover the true cause of the disturbance."

The men were no more keen to go up to the church than the women. Outside, the two tinners from the kiddlywink loitered after the other hearers had fled.

"Are you coming?" Tegen asked me.

"Not just yet."

"You're not thinking of going up to the church?"

"Maybe."

"Mary, what's got into you, of late? Well, I'm off, and what happens to you is your own lookout."

Gideon emerged, locking the barn doors behind him.

"If you want to go and take a look at the church, we'll go with you," one of the tinners said to him, the one that did the talking. "We must walk across the moor anyhow to get to the mine."

"And you, Sister Blight? We have two witnesses already, so there's no need for a woman to go roaming around on the headland in the dark."

"If you want people to believe the church isn't haunted, you must bring a woman along. Everyone knows women have the sight more than men do, and can better see if there are spirits abroad in the world."

"And you really believe this — about 'the sight'?"

"Not I, no. But there are others that do."

"Oh dear. Then perhaps I'd better let you join our party."

And so it was decided that we should set off for the church right away. It was a clear and quiet summer night, well lit by the moon, so we were able to climb to the headland without fear of a mishap. Scarcely a breeze rattled the branches of the stooped little trees that clung to the slopes. The moon was low in the sky and cast shadows behind the boulders that were flung about the barren, blasted heathland where clusters of gorse and nettle lay in wait to snare the unwary. The bells fell silent and for a while it seemed that we had set out too late to catch the miscreants. The tinners said nothing, so for a while the only sounds were our boots on the rocky ground, the wash of the distant sea and a lonely owl that hooted from time to time. Cows stood still as statues on the cliff tops a good way off, as if they were on the very edge of the world.

We passed a ghostly circle of standing stones poking out of the earth at odd angles. A strange whining music filled the air.

"Listen!" I whispered.

"What?" said Gideon.

"Can you not hear? The maidens of the stones are singing."

"What you hear is the wind blowing around the stones."

"But there is little wind tonight."

"The sound is in your imagination, Sister Blight. These stones are the forgotten relics of an ancient civilisation, put here to placate the false Gods of a pagan faith, now all but forgotten." He stopped walking. "Perhaps we should turn back. I fear we set out too late to catch whoever it was that was ringing the bells." But at that moment the bells sounded again, as wild and unruly as before.

My stomach churned as we headed towards the squat shape of the church up ahead.

We reached the wall of the churchyard. Over the crumbling wall marooned grave stones poked out of the earth, not unlike the stone maidens on the open headland. A broad tree with darkness deep within it trailed its branches and the sight of it made me shiver. The bell ringing was ear-splitting and more crazed than ever.

"We go this far and no further, parson," said the man who was the spokesman for the two tinners. "If you do come upon a night wanderer, I suppose you has the power to exorcise him and send him fast to hell?"

"This nonsense about night wanderers is only an old smugglers' tale," said Gideon.

"Aye, but one of the miners saw a woman here not more than a month ago," said the tinner. "It was the dead of night she appeared, of a sudden, on the field path, dressed in black and all muffled up about the face. If I were you, I'd take a stout stick with me before going in there. They say the old parson of this church carried a horse whip with him when he laid the ghost of Wild Harris."

"Well, I intend to enter the church unarmed, gentlemen. I only ask that you wait here for me, so you can bear witness to the true explanation for the bell ringing."

Just then, the bells stopped their crazed clanging. We all looked at each other. Gideon climbed over the wall and made for the porch. Trembling, I followed him. The church door was open. Inside it was pitch dark. I wished Gideon had thought to bring a lantern with him.

"Who's there?" he called. His voice echoed from wall to wall and sounded afraid of itself. He moved into the deep darkness of the church, and I stayed close behind him, our footsteps loud on the stone flags. Some faint light showed under a big hole in the roof and lit the edge of an old pew.

Dwarfish arches showed pale on one side of the nave, but under the tower it was darker than ever. "I am not alone," Gideon called. Spirits echoed him all around us with their hollow, shivering voices, each repeating the words of the one before him. "I have men outside in support. Why not be sensible and show yourselves?"

A sudden loud snorting noise made me jump out of my skin. It sounded like a great beast blowing air from its nostrils. Then was a clomping on the stone floor, like hooves. A pair of moonlit eyes appeared in the darkness underneath the bell tower — eyes too far apart to be human. I thought I saw a pair of horns. It was the Old One, and those were his cloven hooves we'd heard. Beelzebub, himself, had lured us here. But the next moment there was a deep bellow that was answered by the baying of other creatures. Clattering hooves sounded on the stone flags, and one by one a herd of cows, white patches on their flanks, filed towards us. Gideon pulled me out of their path just in time, and I watched them butt one another through the door and out into the night. It wasn't the devil we'd found, but a few hungry cows that had come into the abandoned church and begun chewing on the straw bell ends. I was alone in the dark with Gideon, and for one brief moment at least, his arms were around me.

CHAPTER
FOURTEEN

On midsummer's eve, I mixed some hempseed with baccie and had a good smoke in Mamm's bedroom, sitting in my favourite straight-backed chair. When the right mood came over me, I crept out into the courtyard with a handful of the hempseed in my apron pocket. I walked about on the wooden doors of the fish cellar until my feet found the best spot for conjuring. It crossed my mind that Gideon would disapprove of what I was about, but hadn't the Good Lord made the medicines in the hedgerow, and given them their special powers? It was a cloudy night and the narrow alley out to the lane was pitch black. By rights, I needed to be a maiden for the charm to work, but I hoped the secret might be unlocked anyhow. I closed my eyes and chanted the spell three times, throwing hempseed around me.

> "Hempseed I sow thee, Hempseed grow thee,
> And he who my true love will be,
> Come after me and show thee."

It grew cold as deepest winter and my feet left the ground so that I stood on vacant air. Borne aloft by the spirits, I moved through a field covered in foggy dew until I hovered under a yew tree. The boughs sang with the voices of hundreds of birds. Slowly, a man loomed out of the mist with a scythe in his hand. He set about swinging the scythe under the shade of the tree, his back to me so I couldn't see his face. I began to shake along with the branches of the tree. I knew that if the charm was to work, then the wraith of my future husband would appear before me when I opened my eyes. It grew dark and all at once the birds became silent. Footsteps sounded close by, echoing against stone. Was my husband about to show himself?

He spoke. "Who's there at this late hour?"

I knew that voice. I opened my eyes and saw the fellow step out of the alley. My heart sank for it was only Nathaniel Nancarrow. He had seen me too, so it was too late to run into the cottage.

"What brings you here, Nathaniel?" I asked.

Perhaps I'd spoken more coldly than I meant to, for he stopped just outside the alley and came no closer. "I was coming up the lane and heard a voice. I wondered if something was amiss, it being so late."

"Nothing is amiss."

"Are you sure all is well with you? You don't seem yourself."

"I am well. You need not trouble yourself further."

"Well then, I'll bid you good night."

This appearance of Nathaniel, of all people, seemed to prove Gideon right. My charms were a worthless folly. I went back into the house, almost knocking over Tegen, who'd been hiding behind the door.

"Are you spying on me, Teg?"

220

"I heard voices and wondered who it was out there."

"I went out to take the air."

"I heard you talking to someone."

"Nobody of any note."

"Oh, Mary, how can you say that, when I know very well it was Nathaniel."

I sat at the table, tired and dismayed. Mamm snoozed in her chair. "So you were eavesdropping on me. If you want to know, I was chanting that old rhyme to find out who was to be my husband. When I opened my eyes, who should I see before me but Nathaniel."

"Then you are to marry Nathaniel!" she cried, her hand to her mouth.

"Marry Nathaniel? I could no more marry him than I could fly over the rooftops on a yard broom."

"And why not? He is a . . . I mean to say Nathaniel is a great friend to we Blights."

"You're cross with me, ain't you, Teg?"

"I'm going up to bed."

"I've still got some hemp, if you want to try your luck," I called after her.

When she'd gone, I tarried awhile, slumped at the table. I was just rousing myself to follow Tegen up the stairs when I heard Mamm's faint voice.

"You shouldn't tease her so, she's a good girl, is Teggie."

I got up to my feet with a sigh. "I didn't mean to wake you, Mamm. Go off back to sleep."

"Don't be running off now. Stay and talk awhile. We never jaw these days. Now, why don't you tell me who it was you tried to conjure with the hemp out there?"

"Never mind about that," I said.

"Going out in the courtyard at night throwing hemp about to conjure up a man's spirit — all you're doing is spreading seed for the birds to eat. It won't do no good, you know? No more than the Widow Chegwidden's herbs will cure me of the chronic."

"Don't say such things, Mamm! You'll get better, I know it."

"It was that minister you was hoping to see out there, and don't pretend otherwise."

I sat back down at the table with a sigh.

"You were ever a wilful girl," said Mamm. "The times I had to scold you when you was a little one, always in scrapes and getting folk's backs up. What a merry dance you led me, with no father about the house to show master. Fine and proud I was of you, just the same."

"Tell me about Dad," I said, meaning to head her off from talking about Gideon. "Tell me the stories you told us when we were small, how handsome he was, how brave, the way he was drowned trying to save the men in his crew."

Now she was all of a-tremble, straightening out her apron over her knees, and making a little pucker out of the cloth to wring it in her fingers.

"I tried to rear you decent and rear you ignorant, so if you learnt any wicked ways it weren't from me," she said, fretting. "I built your Dad up in your mind too much, maybe, when you was a scamp. I wanted you to hold your head up when you thought of him and try to be good and worthy." She gave me a furtive look.

"Maybe I put too many fanciful notions into your head."

"Aye, but he did die a hero. It's true, ain't it?"

"Oh, God help me! What have I done?"

"What are you saying of, Mamm? Tell me the truth!"

She moaned and writhed in her armchair. "He died at sea, that much is true. It was hard on me, I was carrying Teggie at the time, and it was a rare enough thing to get an honest day's toil out of him for he only ever worked when the fit took him. We was always scat, and I had to scrimp to get by. And where was he when my poor baby boys died? Up in the kiddlywink, drinking and gambling with his mates, that's where."

"So those yarns Loveday Skewes used to spread about Dad were true? He was no more than an idle gadabout."

"He wasn't a bad man, my pet, just a dreamer. It was his nature. He never liked to be tied down." I turned away from her in vexation, but she spoke on. "I see him in you at times. Look at me, Mary!"

Slowly, I turned round. She was pink in the face, her breath coming thick and fitful, her hand clutching at her throat. Quickly, I fetched a pot of the Widow Chegwidden's herbs from the stove, crouched by her and blew on the brew to cool it. I put it to her mouth, but she turned away.

"I hoped I'd live long enough to marry the pair of you off, at least. This foolishness that's come over you of late, Mary, it has to stop!" she wheezed.

"Be quiet Mamm, I beg of you," I said.

"Take a care for yourself. They be talking about you. The Widow told me this afternoon. I can barely breathe for fear of it?"

"What did the widow say? Tell me, Mamm!"

"Someone out there has a secret — one of the bettermost, she reckons. Some dark thing you was seen to do. Tell me you've nothing on your conscience, Mary!"

"It's muck and lies. I've done no more than what half the village does. You know where the tea and sugar comes from, don't you, Mamm, but you drink it all the same."

"Tegen says if you was to step down as teacher, you'd be off the hook."

I shook my head. "Tegen would say that. I ain't backing down."

"Just like your father. Listen to me, my girl. You must learn the sense of things, wise or foolish, according as they may happen — and not as you wish them to be."

On Sunday, I went to teach the class. As Aunt Madgie opened the door to let me in, I looked for a sign in her face that she might be about to spread a dark lie about me. But her cold and stony gaze gave nothing away. When I tried to move past her she put her crook in my path.

"You have stopped using the catechisms I gave you. Explain yourself," she said.

"I didn't like to use them. They are meant for children below seven years, but some of the doctrines might give the little ones nightmares."

224

"The doctrines are intended to scare them, so they will learn clean, frugal habits and proper restraint. How else will the children learn the virtues of duty, hard work and foresight, and know to shun the evils of luxury?"

"What does it gain a little child to be told that Hell is a dark and bottomless pit, full of fire and brimstone? Do we want to them to wet their beds at night?"

"You are too soft. It is little wonder one of the boys goaded you last week."

"Surely, larkish youngsters have always liked to goad their elders and betters." I stepped over her crook and slipped past her down the dark hallway.

"I will bring this matter to the attention of the Society, mark my words."

"As you please."

I squeezed past her and went into the kitchen where the class was always held. The children stood about in groups. The boys smirked at the sight of me and were in no hurry to take their places at the forms. The girls sat down quicker, giving one another sly little looks. Not one of them would look me in the eye as they sat down, a row of sour little pouts. They seemed changed since last we'd met. Even Sarah Pengilly, who I had made monitor and had thought my friend, looked down at the table rather than meet my gaze. Fewer of the children of the bettermost had come along, and the numbers were lower than before.

"Let us begin the Testament class," I said. "We will see what the Scriptures have to say about children who show no respect for their elders. Martin, you will read first." This was met with sneers and snorts from the bigger boys. Martin was a poor boy from Uplong Row, and one of the worst readers.

"Silence!" I snapped. "Turn to page three, all of you."

Martin bent over the table, his face close to the paper. As his eyes passed along the line of words he made low noises that had little to do with the marks on the page before him. The other boys shook with stifled laughter. After a short while Martin turned to me with a pleading look.

"Him don't know his halfabet, missus," said Kit Trefusis, smirking.

"Tell us, what do 'A' stand for, Martin?" said Peggy Combelleck. She sat across the table from Martin. She sounded kindly, but I didn't trust her.

" 'A' do stand for 'happy', don't it, Martin?" said Kit, and burst out laughing, which started the other boys off as well.

Martin looked from face to face, his bottom lip wobbling.

"Right to the top of the class, boy," said Kit, in a proper snot's voice with his nose in the air as though he were the teacher.

I wasn't going to stand for this. "Kit, go and wait outside the room until I'm good and ready to deal with you," I said. He took his time getting to his feet and dawdled out, slamming the door behind him.

"Eliza, you are to read next," I said. My voice was high and shaky. "And if anyone cheeks me again today

226

they can expect the stick on both hands. Have you all got that?"

Without Kit as ringleader, they were quieter, but my nerves were in shreds by the end of the class. When I'd sent them out I called Kit back into the room. He stared at the floor, sneering.

"You see this stick," I said, picking the nasty thing up from where Aunt Madgie had left it. "Look at me when I'm speaking to you, boy." He took no notice. "Very well. This is your last chance. If you're a bad boy again next week, I will beat you with this stick, and smartly too." He mumbled some words. "What did you say?"

"I said I ain't scared of the stick. I've had it at home plenty of times."

When he'd gone, it was a long time until I could breathe easily again. Wearily, I began clearing up the Testament books and stacking them on top of the cupboard. After a while, I heard Gideon talking with Aunt Madgie out in the hall. Hearing his voice out there, I had a fervent urge to get a sign from him, some proof he would protect me from those who blackened my name and spread dark rumours about me.

"I am sure the children are making adequate progress," he said to Aunt Madgie.

"Too soon to say," Aunt Madgie answered. "Your Miss Blight has yet to prove she can rule over the children in the way she ought. Lighting fires and other mollycoddling ways won't make them better soldiers of Christ."

"We should give her some leeway, Mrs Maddern. Perhaps by doing things in her own way, she will in time inspire devotion in the children."

"Devotion?" she said. "Well, you'd know more about that than me." I heard her crook tapping on the floor as she went into the back of the house. I tidied my hair as best I could, and straightened out my skirts under my hands. Luckily, I wore a plain black dress of the sort Gideon favoured. His footsteps echoed out in the hall as he came nearer, so I stepped into a shaft of soft sunlight that slanted down from the high window. Gideon stepped onto the creaking floorboards of the kitchen, and I could barely breathe, knowing he was there. I didn't look up until I'd gathered the books and put them in a pile. When I did, I found Gideon frozen to a spot over by the door, in a kind of rapt daze. He held some tattered old books in his hands.

"I have brought some copies of *The Child's Companion* and *Youth's Instructor*, both rather well-thumbed," he said. "And this too, an old geography. The covers are gone, I'm afraid, but I don't think the lie of the land has altered too much since it was published. I thought they might prove useful."

He came over and handed me the books. I opened them, glancing at a page or two before putting them in my basket. Gideon drew a breath as if about to say something, but instead he clapped his hands and rubbed his palms together. "Well, well, well," he said. "I've been meaning to speak to you — about the school funding and a few other matters. Suffice it to say, we have just enough subscriptions to continue for the weeks ahead. And we'll have another collection at the Lovefeast."

He went on for some time about all the things that needed doing for the Lovefeast, but I took none of it in. When he was done with his little talk, we left the house together and walked in silence to the end of Back Street and onto the little stone bridge. We stopped there for a bit, side by side, looking over the wall at the narrow river gushing down to the sea beneath us. I put my basket down.

"You are a little paler than when last I saw you," he said.

"It would suit me better if the class were held elsewhere," I said. "Where Aunt Madgie can't snoop on me."

"I can't help but agree. I see the strain she is putting you under. It's not too much for you, I hope?"

"I'll put up with it. And some of the children are doing well, I think."

"I am sure of it."

As he said nothing more, I picked up my basket and took a step across the bridge, letting him know I was on my way.

"Well now, before we part, I have just recollected another matter I wanted to mention," he said. His voice shook, which wasn't like him. "I've been thinking about that friend of yours, Johnenry Roscorla. After our encounter at the alehouse, I wanted to reassure myself about certain misgivings I had. You and he were close once."

"Once, but not anymore." I looked away from him, down the lane on the other side of the bridge.

"I only raise this, because I wouldn't like to think this rift between you and that young man was in any way related to your work in the Society," he said. "I feel it is my duty to say that, if you still have feelings for him, then your work in the Sunday school should not be a hindrance."

So, all along this was what Gideon had wanted to say, that I should go and wed Johnenry. I was mad enough to chuck the basket of books over the bridge and into the river.

"I don't love Johnenry, and I'm not quitting as school mistress," I said.

"Love isn't constant over time. Please consider what you have lost. I would be greatly at fault if I had raised expectations in some way, had perhaps made you feel you were above your neighbours."

"Well, I'm truly sorry to disappoint you, but Johnenry is walking out with Loveday Skewes now," I said. "And what about your own affairs? Is Mrs Stone over her illness? Is she back at home? And who was the woman from St Buryan who came to your house while you were abroad?"

He took a step back, as if I'd struck him. "I've done what little I can for Anne Treveil, I assure you," he said. "And I'm afraid there was another woman before her, both of them in the days before I was married. I did these women a great wrong that I can never undo. I would give them more, but Ellie counts every penny. She complains that we cannot hope to raise a child on what I earn as a minister. There, you have it. It's better that you labour under no illusions about me."

He turned from me and for a while stared down at the water churning underneath us.

"I only wish what is best for you, Sister Blight," he said.

"It's no business of yours whom I wed," I said.

Before he could say more, I dashed over the bridge and turned up Downlong Row. He soon caught up with me and we stood face to face. Before he spoke, he glanced up and down the lane to make sure we weren't spied upon.

"I'm concerned that we may have had a less than perfect understanding in the past, and perhaps I've been at fault," he said. "I confess that I've had a nagging doubt about my advocacy of you as school mistress, but I have tried to examine my conscience."

"I'm pleased to hear it. Now, if you please, my basket's heavy and I want to get home." I began rushing up the hill again.

"Whatever I have done, it was done in your best interest," he said, coming alongside me.

"Leave me alone! I'm weary of all your endless twaddle."

"Please, speak softly. Think how it will appear if we're seen quarrelling. I can't part from you until this is resolved."

I stopped, reached down the front of my dress and, after a moment's fumbling, found the scroll of paper that I kept on a string next to my heart. I pulled the string over my head and held Mr Wesley's hymn before his face. "Why did you give me this?" I asked.

"Surely, you have not misread my intentions?"

I tore the page up and threw the scraps at him. "I think it best if we never set eyes on each other hereafter," I said. "Some madness has come over me these last months, but I've come to my senses at last."

"Give me a moment to explain. Please, Sister Blight . . . *Mary*. On reflection, it is possible, I suppose, that in asking you to reconcile yourself to that young man, I was trying to remove a doubt from my own mind. Perhaps I wanted to be sure that all I've done with regard to you has been undertaken with pure and proper motives."

"If you have no feelings for me, why won't you just let me go?"

"I can't speak of this here in the lane. We could be overheard."

"Then go!" I shouted.

He flinched, then leant over me to whisper in my ear. "As you give me no other option, I will attempt to explain my position. It is possible that a man might, in all sincerity, mistake religious fervour for . . ."

"Louder, I can't hear you aright!"

He shut his eyes and took a deep breath. "It is possible that a man might mistake religious fervour for strong affection of a quite different order, and that my thoughts in relation to yourself may have been acted upon by . . ." He looked over his shoulder to make sure nobody was listening. ". . . Acted upon by a kind of unconscious propensity. As you insist on pressing me, I will admit to certain feelings for you."

"For God's sake, say what you mean in plain words, Minister."

232

He looked sorely vexed. "What I meant was that, yes, I do feel drawn towards you. But you must understand that everything has changed now that this, let's say attachment, is apparent to us both. We cannot under any circumstances be seen alone together at a future time. It would be unforgiveable to put at risk the work that's been done to establish a chapel in this cove. I am sure we are as one on this matter. A few months ago the old sickness threatened to overwhelm me, the despondency, the lethargy of spirit. I can't risk backsliding."

"You can't bear to think ill of yourself, can you?" I said.

"How can I forgive the unforgivable? Only Almighty God has that privilege, when Judgement Day comes. But if I'm to continue to do His work, I must have assurance."

"Perhaps if we were to lay out all the thoughts and deeds of any man from end to end, he would seem a hundred men," I said.

"Then how are we to sort the wheat from the chaff?"

"And what of me? What will I do? I have enemies in this village, and all the more so now that I'm school mistress."

"If you are ever in dire need, you may send notice to me. I'll do whatever is in my power to assist. I give you my word. That much I owe you."

He bowed, and went slowly back down the lane, his head hanging. But after only a few paces he stopped, and strode briskly back to where I stood.

"From this point on, we must take every precaution. I think it would be best if you absented yourself from the Lovefeast. In fact, I would ask that from now on you attend only those prayer meetings that are led by Mr Hawkey. Will you promise me that?"

"I will promise you nothing. What promise did you give those poor women you wronged?"

With that, I dashed back to the cottage. I charged upstairs and threw myself upon the bed. I was still lying there when it grew dark. A queer mix of feelings raged inside me. What was I to make of Gideon Stone? Wheat and chaff seemed all mixed up him. On the one hand, he was a soaring spirit who risked life and limb to save the souls of his fellow men. But in the shadows of his past lurked another man, a frail sinner, lost in drink and unable to master his base urges. He was either saint or sinner with naught in between. Couldn't he content himself with trying to be a good man, as best he could, without wanting to be an angel on high? A man like dear honest Nathaniel Nancarrow, who Tegen loved with all her heart.

Yet, I had nobody else I could depend upon, if my neighbours ever took against me. As the hours passed, I came to see that what troubled me most lay deeper in the darkness of my own heart, and I trembled to bring it to light. When first I knew Gideon, I'd thought him a man set firmly on a straight course, who wouldn't easily unbend from his duty. But I'd come to see he was a man like any other, with the same weaknesses and needs, and the secret to luring him off course might be found in his frailty, and not his strength.

CHAPTER
FIFTEEN

It was the afternoon of the day of the Lovefeast. I was bent over the table, up to my elbows in flour, taking out my grievances on the dough by kneading it with a murderous passion. Tegen was at her loom and Mamm snoozed in her chair.

Tegen left her needle fixed between the warp strings for another day. "Well, I'm beat," she said, slumping in her chair. "We're doing more work than we ever belonged to do these days."

"Aye, and good work is kept from us. It's because of me being made Sunday school mistress. We've rarely had to go shrimping other years, and when did we ever resort to filling a cart with sand to sell to the miners so they can sprinkle it on their floors?"

"I've even tried cutting griglans on the heath and making brooms with them, but nobody would buy them from me," said Tegen, yawning and giving her arms a stretch. "I wish you'd sing like you used to on baking days. It used to cheer me."

"I daren't sing with all my enemies waiting to catch me out in some sin."

"I do hear things, tittle-tattle. You should talk to Tobias Hawkey. He'll speak out against any mischief.

He'll be parson once the chapel's built and the minister's gone back to Newlyn, and he's well thought of hereabouts."

"I don't care for the man's home-spun sermons," I said, pushing my rolling pin over the dough.

"Well, I do," she said. "It was when 'Bias began leading the prayer meetings that I saw the light."

Realising what she meant, I let go of the rolling pin. "You're not telling me that you're under conviction, Teg?"

"I can't deny it. But I don't want it shouted from the rooftops. Is it too much to believe a day will come when hard work and sober living get their just deserts, as 'Bias says they should? I believe there'll be a reckoning at the Last Judgement. I'd like to see those cormorants who blacken your name standing before the Throne of Mercy when their time comes. God forgive me, I know that don't show Christian mercy."

We were quiet a moment. Buttery light streamed in from the open top half of the front door, flour dust swirling in it. Outside, swallows were swooping down under the eaves to feed their chicks, and the air was alive with their screeching cries.

"Suppose you offered to share the burden of the teaching with Loveday?" said Tegen.

"Share the teaching with her? I'd die first," I said, slapping a fresh ball of dough onto the table.

"Grace and the bettermost think Loveday should be teacher, by rights."

"Loveday's got Johnenry back, ain't that enough for her?"

236

"Oh Mary, at least stay away from the Lovefeast tonight, I pray you."

"I won't be told where I can go and where I can't. I've done no wrong. I've barely set eyes on the minister for weeks now. I am the school mistress. It's my place to be there."

"Look at you. Thin as a rush light. I swear there's no more fearful sight than a woman over-gone on a man."

"What makes you say such a thing?" I cried.

"I'm your sister. You can't hide things from me."

She looked me in the eye for a moment, and I realised she knew me better than I'd thought.

"Well, you needn't go worrying yourself," I said, going back to my baking. "The minister ain't after me. Last time we met he tried to pawn me off on Johnenry."

She shook her head. "Poor Johnenry," she said.

Hell or high water wouldn't have kept me away from the Lovefeast. Tegen and I got there late. As we came through the door, I saw Gideon up in his pulpit. He looked up, saw us there, and took a deep breath.

"Welcome, sisters," he said. "Your friends and neighbours will make room for you on the benches. We are listening to a short reading from Matthew." He found his place and began to read.

All the women were huddled together on one side, while across the aisle the men had plenty of room on their benches. Tegen tried to sit with the row of poorer women underneath the hissing and smoking tapers, the grease running down the walls behind them, but I pulled her away. We squeezed ourselves onto one of the women's benches. When we were settled, I glanced about me. The barn had never been so packed. There were new faces, people without clothes decent enough to go to the usual weekday prayer meetings. I was taken aback to find Nathaniel Nancarrow on the men's benches, and nudged Tegen to let her know. She turned pink from her neck to the tips of her ears. A double-handled mug filled with black tea was passed along the bench to me, and then a plate of bread and saffron buns. But I had no stomach for either food or drink.

It was then I saw the old woman in a mob cap and black dress who was sitting on the front bench. It was the first time that Aunt Madgie had shown her face at one of Gideon's meetings. She turned her head and her withering glance sent a shiver through me as I looked away. Her daughter Grace Skewes was alongside her. On the end of the row was Grace's daughter, Loveday, wearing a dress with wide shoulders and leg-of-lamb sleeves. She was simpering at Johnenry, who sat opposite her on the men's bench.

Gideon had stopped reading. I looked up to find him gazing out at the hearers. He read the next lines more slowly, looking up often, so we'd take note of the words.

"*A good man out of the good treasure of the heart bringeth forth good things: and an evil man out of the evil treasure bringeth forth evil things.*

"*But I say unto you, That every idle word that men shall speak, they shall give account thereof in the day of judgement.*"

I fell to wondering what the lines meant. Soon after, the reading came to an end, and he spoke to us in his own words.

"I see new faces here this evening. You are all greatly welcome. We have bread, tea, heavy cake, enough for all. Consider for a moment what has brought us together at this Lovefeast — especially in the light the gospel text from Matthew. What, indeed, do we mean by 'Lovefeast'? It is an occasion to come together with our neighbours in a spirit of harmony and trust, to celebrate the bonds of friendship and love between us. Let us put aside petty rivalries and forget past grudges in a spirit of open trust." Some turned and smiled at their neighbours, while others stared into their laps. "In recent weeks it has come to my attention that I, myself, have not altogether escaped suspicion, and have even been the object of censure." Murmurings spread along the benches at this. "I assure you all that my motives and conduct since I first arrived in this cove have at all times been honest and true. I am no saint. I have acknowledged at previous meetings that I have trespassed in the past, and we must ever be on our guard against temptation. In the same wise, I urge you to forgive your neighbour's transgressions. Remember the words of John: *He that is without sin among you, let him first cast a stone at her.*" At that, Loveday turned her head and looked straight at me, but I held her gaze.

"I bid you to forswear idle tattle and to look to your own sins before casting stones at others," said Gideon. "Very soon all our hard work to build a chapel in this

239

cove will come to fruition, and I will be gone from your midst. You will be in good hands with Mr Hawkey. Now, who among you would like to speak of their spiritual experience this week?"

Right away, I stood up and made my way to the aisle. I walked towards the communion rail, head held high, even though my legs trembled under me. For all I shook, I meant to put a stop to the whispering I knew was going on behind my back, and was hell-bent on taking this chance while they were all together under one roof. A hush fell over all as I halted at the rail, before turning to face the hearers.

"Is it right that a woman should stand at the communion rail to testify?" shouted old Thomas.

"It is only a wooden rail," said Gideon. "Sister Blight is welcome to stand and testify wherever she so wishes — and so may any other woman or man present."

"Dear friends," I said. "It is wonderful to stand here and feel God's divine love in this room."

"Praise the Lord!" shouted a coarse woman at the back.

"Old enemies are now become friends," I said. "Who would have thought it could be so, a few months back? I used to scoff when people said 'One and All!' But now I'm beginning to believe it, sisters and brothers."

"God grant it," shouted old Thomas.

"Hosanna in the highest!" called another man.

"But there's still strife between us women, isn't there? Work is kept from me, and from my sister. Black lies have been spread around this village."

A rumble was heard down on the front bench where the bettermost sat. "What are you saying of, Sister Blight?" cried Grace Skewes. "Who are you pointing the finger at?"

"Sister Blight," said Gideon. "May I ask you to restrict your testimony to a declaration of what God has done for your soul since last we met — and to refrain from accusations about your neighbours."

"I have been blessed these last few weeks, teaching the Scriptures to children, the little ones of some of you here," I said, without turning to look up at Gideon. "The children were willing to learn at first, but it seems as though a few of them have been given the wink to play up."

"Shame! Let Mary be teacher, if she so wishes," cried a woman. It was Martha Tregaskis, flushed with liquor, her nose red and swollen.

"I ask if there will ever come a time when we can love our neighbour as we love ourselves," I said. "As King Jesus told us to, instead of scheming to keep each other down?"

Grace Skewes stood up, and called to Gideon. "Are we to listen to a sermon from a woman?"

"I am only a woman and know it's not proper for me to take a gospel text," I said.

Gideon broke in on me. "Sister Blight, I think you have had your say," he said.

Grace Skewes sat down again and she and her neighbours put their heads together, mumbling. The rougher sort of women in the back rows were growing fractious.

"Come now, brothers and sisters, we are in accord, at least in all essentials," said Gideon. "So let's remind ourselves why we are here. If there are misunderstandings, then let us speak honestly. It will do no good if we shrink from one another or allow resentments to fester and grow into hatred. Thank you, Sister Blight, for raising these matters. Now, who else would like to exhort?"

I stepped away from the rail and walked briskly down the centre aisle. It was so quiet I could hear the rustle of my skirts and the beat of my heart. When I got to the bench where I'd been sitting, the women there would not look at me or make way to let me in, so I went on until I reached the back of the barn. I was riled and wanted to spite them all, so I strode towards the nearest empty bench on the men's side and sat down. Someone at the front gasped, and snide whispers spread around the benches. I looked straight ahead of me, pretending not to care.

Hearing a great sigh, I turned to see women fussing over one of their neighbours on the crowded benches opposite. "It's Aunty Merryn. She have fainted!" someone cried.

"It's no surprise, the way we're all packed in like pilchards, scarce able to breathe," another woman said.

"Such foolishness!" said young Cissie Olds, as she stood up and pushed her way along her bench to the aisle. She came across and sat next to me. The Widow Chegwidden and another woman followed her.

"Yes, come along, there is space for all," cried Gideon. "We don't want women swooning because of

242

quaint notions of propriety. Move across to the men's benches, if you will!"

"Have you lost your senses, parson?" cried old Thomas.

"I know of no commandment that says men and women shall not share a bench," said Gideon. "Didn't the Almighty place men and women in the Garden to work in harmonious partnership? Remember what the Apostle Paul said: *there is neither male nor female, but all are one in Christ Jesus.*"

Hearing this, Nancy Spargo moved across, with a couple of her friends in tow, although they looked less than sure about it. They sat on the bench in front of us. Before long, perhaps ten women had crossed the divide, while the men watched, aghast. I found myself sitting alongside four or five women, and with each new arrival I was forced to slide a little further along the bench.

Across the aisle, Tegen rose to her feet and stood there, as if stranded, in the middle of her row. Head down, she squeezed past the line of women and reached the end of the bench, whereupon she tried to step into the aisle, but fell headlong onto the ground. I was sure the woman at the end of the row had stuck out her foot to trip Tegen. One or two neighbours moved to help her, Tobias among them, but Nathaniel got there first. He helped Tegen to her feet, looking into her eyes with a tenderness I hadn't seen in him before. She dusted herself off, straightened her bonnet and pushed her hair from her face. I was on my feet and would have gone to her side, but she called to me, "Stay where you are, Mary!"

Nathaniel glared at the culprit, who sat at the end of the bench with her arms folded, her face turned away. "I am all right, Nat," said Tegen, softly. "Go and sit down now." Then, instead of taking her seat, she looked all around at the faces surrounding her. "I have something to say," she said. "I wasn't minded to testify tonight, for I was too afraid, or perhaps too proud. But now I might as well tell my news. Brothers and sisters, I have come under conviction these last few weeks."

"Thank the Lord!" shouted one of the men. Others answered with "Amens" and the like.

"I have kept it to myself until I was sure, but a great hope has filled my heart," she said, her voice stronger with every word. "For the first time in my life I've understood that God sees worth in all his children, however humble. And having that faith has made it easier to bear the hardship that Mary and me have known of late. There. That is all." She went and took her place at the end of the same bench where I sat.

"Thank you, Sister Blight," said Gideon. "I am greatly heartened to hear your testimony. It seems a good moment for me to come down from this pulpit and let Tobias lead our meeting. Tobias, come forward now and take your place!" Gideon stepped down from the pulpit, as Tobias took his place before the communion rail. Tobias would never go up to the pulpit, because he wanted to show he was one and the same as the rest of us. But my sights were on Gideon. Usually, he would sit in the front row of the men's benches when Tobias led the meeting, but that night he walked down the far side of barn on the women's side. When he came to my bench, he turned and came to sit down right beside me. This got them whispering down on the front benches where the bettermost sat. Millie Hicks rose to her feet. She was the staunchest ally of Grace Skewes and Aunt Madgie, and one of the biggest donors to the new chapel. I thought she meant to walk out of the barn in disgust, but instead she made the long walk down the aisle and sat down on the bench right behind me. I turned and looked at her and got a nod and a prim smile from her as she settled her sewing basket in her lap. All around me were smiling faces.

The good will was quickly cut short by three loud whacks, Aunt Madgie banging her crook against a wooden bench at the front. The old woman moved into the aisle, but would not stand at the rail where I'd stood. She looked out at the hearers, but where was her usual cold stare? She looked wounded, like an injured old crow. "If someone could give me a little water," she said. Grace Skewes ran forward and put a cup in her shaking hand.

"I am truly sorry that I was not in attendance at the meetings before now, friends," she said. "But I am an old woman and have been unwell of late. And I must confess I have been troubled by all I've seen and heard this night. I had never thought to hear so much dissent in a parish where we women have always held by one another." She took a sip of water and stooped to put the cup on the floor.

Alongside me, Gideon rose to his feet. All turned to look at him, and my face burned. He took a handkerchief from a pocket and mopped his brow. "We greatly appreciate your attendance here and you are welcome at all of our meetings, Sister Maddern," he said. "I think you have misunderstood the enthusiasm of your neighbours. None of us wants to sow seeds of discord. This is a Lovefeast, and you are bidden to celebrate God's divine love with all of us present. We have tea and bread."

"One moment, sir, if it pleases you," said the old woman quietly. "Others were permitted to testify so I only ask if I may say a few words. You will forgive me if my voice is less strident than some." There was a burst of clapping from the bettermost at the front, and shouts urging her on from others around the room.

Gideon sat down again, sighing and folding his arms.

"As I said before, we women have always been bound up in one another hereabouts," said Aunt Madgie. "Some of you young ones may not yet know that in this village we prevail against hardship because each knows his own place. Together we are as strong as the granite cliffs that shelter us. But if unity breaks down, then all will perish." She spoke with her true voice now, hard as gravel. "So, you want a revival in this village, do you, neighbours? Well, this is a nice kind of revival, I must say. I see one young fellow here tonight who has come for no other purpose than to moon at a maiden he's taken a fancy to." People followed her gaze to where Davey Keigwin sat. His young friends grinned at him and he was abashed.

246

"This has always been a village of God-fearing parents and dutiful and obedient children," she said. "Rectors have come and gone, and we have had to abide drunken priests betimes, just so we could take the Sacrament on Holy Days. But we are a proud people hereabouts, and will not bend before an ecclesiastical overlord unless he first wins our trust. We will hold with a good minister." She smiled at Tobias, who stood over at the communion rail. "And for my part, I enjoy nothing better than a good invigorating fire and brimstone sermon. I must confess, though, that I am not so taken with Lovefeasts or other new uplong notions. Nor do I like the sight of a woman parading about like a saint in light. *Pride goes before destruction, a haughty spirit before a fall*. Proverbs 6.18."

Gideon tried to rise to his feet but something held him back. I felt pulled along with him as he moved, and thought I must be sitting on his coat-tails. "Sister Maddern, let God be the judge of all of us," he called from his seat. "If you are finished your exhortation, perhaps now would be a good opportunity for us all to pray together."

"I have one last thing to say," said the old woman. All waited, silent and rapt. "Those who hanker after what does not belong to them are breaking the bond that has held this village together all these years. Uppish women are an abomination here. Lustful pride will be punished.

"An unmarried woman is a danger," she cried, all but shouting now. Tobias stepped in front of her and held up his hands, but her voice rang out clearly.

"Without little ones, women are worse than monsters. I have no need for Lovefeasts, nor tea, nor buns. It is not this life we should look to, but the next. Christ suffering on the cross is my constant inspiration."

Some of the women among the bettermost called out: "Blessed be His name!" and "Praise the Lord!" Others left their seats and stepped into the aisle. The women alongside me were angry.

"She've said enough!" said Cissie Olds.

"Somebody stop her mouth!" shouted Martha Tregaskis.

"Get down on your knees in submission before the throne of King Jesus," hollered Aunt Madgie, looking up into the rafters as if the roof might open and molten rocks hail down upon our heads. Gideon sat fixed in his seat, as if the old devil had turned him to stone. "Beg the Redeemer's forgiveness and bend to His will," she cried. "I will fight to the last breath to stop this village going to the devil. We will weed out wrongdoers and shine Our Saviour's holy light on their secret vices, their wanton ways and depravity."

She was drowned out by fractious voices. Half the congregation had spilt into the aisle. Some gathered around the old woman and cheered, while others quarrelled and jostled one another. Tobias went among the hearers, pulling apart those about to come to blows.

Gideon began to rise from his seat, and as he did so I found myself dragged up alongside him by some magical force. I fell forward and almost brought Gideon with me, but he took hold of me to keep me on my feet. All eyes were on us, as we held onto each other.

"Please, let us have order!" he shouted. I tried to break free of him, but could not. We seemed joined together. "Are we to have a ruction where there should be peace and loving kindness?" he shouted. Everyone gathered in the aisle and stared at Gideon and me. I tried to peer over my shoulder and find out what was amiss, and as I did so, Gideon jerked even closer to me.

"They be stitched together, see," shouted a young boy. He had squeezed through the throng to get a better view. Gideon took off his coat and then everybody saw what had happened. Someone had taken up a needle and thread and sewn a piece of cloth to my dress and stitched the other end to Gideon's coat. The Lovefeast was in uproar, with my enemies howling with laughter. Millie Hicks, who had sat behind us with her sewing in her lap, was nowhere to be seen.

III

HARVEST TIDE

CHAPTER
SIXTEEN

One morning, a week after the disastrous happenings at the Lovefeast, Tegen came rushing into the cottage. "What a to-do there is down in the harbour," she said. "There are notices up all over the quay. A hundred guineas reward, would you believe, for information on that devil they call the Porthmorvoren Cannibal."

"A hundred guineas?" I cried. "Can that be right?"

"A tidy sum, but it's right, for sure. I saw it with my own eyes," said Tegen. "I've always said there'd be a price to pay for wrecking. Take a look at this." She put the *Sherborne Mercury* on the table. "See here," she said, her finger on a column on the open page. The words swam before my eyes. "They've raised a campaign to match the fifty guineas the duke put up, and now respectable people from all over Penwith have put their hands in their pockets."

"Pity the snots didn't raise a few guineas for poor people hereabouts," said Mamm. I went over to plump her cushions, in part because I didn't want Tegen to see my face, for she'd surely have seen the panic in it.

"This Lord S— has lost three other ships this year alone, and two of them in Cornwall," said Tegen. She sat at the table, leaning over the newspaper. "It says so here. Every one of them plundered by wreckers." She shook her head, then began reading out the names of the ships. "The five-hundred-ton brig, *The Caroline of Brunswick*. *The Neptune*, an eight-hundred-ton cutter. *The Lady Lucy*. No wonder they mean to make an example of that cannibal! There's a rumour doing the rounds that someone in the cove saw what happened."

"But nobody in living memory has ever snitched on a neighbour," said Mamm. "Of course, nobody's put up a hundred guineas before now."

"With money like that, you could live like a queen, far away where nobody in the village would ever find you," said Tegen, a dreamy look in her eyes.

I went to the door, wrapping my shawl round my shoulders.

"Off to see for yourself?" Tegen called, as I shut the door behind me.

At the bottom of Downlong Row, I stopped to read one of the notices pinned to a post. It was the very same as the one I'd seen in Penzance that day with Mrs Stone, only the reward had been doubled.

"The constable was here at daybreak, putting them all up," said a voice right behind me. I turned to find Martha Tregaskis standing there. Her nose had a bend in it, having not set straight after the blow she got from Pentecost in the kiddlywink. "Gave me a fright, it did," she said. "You too, I seem. You look as if you've seen a ghost, Mary."

"I'm under the weather, that's all."

"Ain't been so much jawing about anything round here since your minister washed ashore," she said.

254

"He's not my minister."

"No of course he ain't, my lamb, but you know what I mean." She moved closer, frowning. Although it was early, I smelt liquor on her breath. "To think whoever did it is living in one of these cottages! The cannibal, I mean."

I nodded. I was frantic to get away from her, but afraid of looking guilty.

"The dead lady's husband is a fine lord and they reckon he'll stop at naught to find the wretch," said Martha. "If you think about it, a gentleman like that ain't going to let some country woman get away scot free."

"Woman? What makes you say a woman did it?" I said.

"Well, only . . ." She put a shaking hand to her face. "Only because that's what folk be saying."

"Who's saying?" I needed to know if Aunt Madgie was behind this.

"Well, I had it from Dolly Stoddern, if I remember right. Anyway, whether it be woman or man, I wouldn't want to be in their shoes."

"I'd better be off," I said.

"If I hear any news, I'll be sure to let you know," Martha called after me.

I muffled my face with my shawl and walked to the quay, briskly so nobody would bother me. Though I kept my head down, out of the corner of my eye I saw that every barn in the harbour had a reward notice pinned to it. I told myself that nothing had really changed, the story had been all over the coast for weeks. Yet it seemed to me that every neighbour I passed gave me a wary look. Dolly Stoddern had told Martha the cannibal was a woman, and Dolly was close to Grace Skewes, Aunt Madgie's own daughter. And Betsy, Dolly's daughter, was the best mate of Loveday Skewes. If Aunt Madgie was to falsely accuse me to anyone, it would be to one of them.

All that day I couldn't sit still in the cottage, but kept going out to walk up and down the lanes. In the afternoon a squall sent a batch of the handbills whirling around the village. They got caught up in bean plants and in roof thatch, wrapped themselves around hogsheads in the harbour and the masts of boats, stuck to the cobbles of the quay and got covered in muddy footprints. Some just blew round and round in little eddies in the lanes. That night, as I lay awake in bed, I had a mad notion of rushing out and picking up as many of them as I could and putting them out of sight.

The following morning, I took the stone idol out of the drawer where she'd been hidden since Gideon's arrival in the cove. The idol was wrathful after being left in the dark so long. When I tried to summon answers to my problems, she was silent. I began to think she really was a cold and senseless rock, as Tegen had always said. But perhaps I was not making myself plain. There were things I could not speak of in the cottage, perhaps dared not even think. I put the idol in my basket and set out for Tombstone Point.

In the orchard above the village the boughs creaked under the weight of ripe apples and I stumbled over windfalls, brown and riddled with wormholes. The lark trilled on high, but it was a forlorn and empty sound she made now that her young had left the nest. A great brown spider crouched in a trembling web, the pattern on his back richer than any embroidery. I passed through the narrow lane of grimy cottages where the miners lived and reached the headland. All around me vast black clouds were hurled across the heavens by the gusts, and down below the grey and heartless ocean stretched clear to the Americas.

I reached Tombstone Point, and sat myself down upon cold granite covered in lichen and moss and crow droppings. Off across the headland, trees huddled in a dip, keeping an eye on me. The high branches floated silently in the wind as if underwater, beckoning me to another world than this. Down below, the sea called me into its depths.

I asked the idol what I should do to bring my troubles to an end. She frowned. "Tell me!" I pleaded. "I suppose you judge me because you think I meant to steal a married man from his wife?"

The idol's face clouded. I got to my feet and shook her in my hands. She grew heavier, so that my arms ached. "You think me weak and selfish," I said, stepping closer to the cliff edge. I thought of Lady Rosemount in the novel I'd found under Ellie Stone's bed. She too had stood upon on a precipice, ready to throw off all restraint. Did the idol want me to leap off the cliff? She glowered at me, reading my thoughts. A heat came off her and her face glowed red as the sunlight that was just then streaming through the clouds. All the while a screaming sound rang out of her, maddening to the senses. She began to shake with such a passion I could barely keep a grip on her. Her powers pulled me closer to the cliff edge. I looked at the sheer drop, my mind as wild as the violent waves that raged and broke against the rocks below. Another step and all my fears would come to an end — but so would all my hopes.

The world became a chamber of echoes, gulls screeching as they bore themselves on the gusts, the wind soughing in the bent and stunted trees that clung to the stony earth, rocks singing their ancient song. Fine hairs grew out of every part of me, too fine to be seen by human eyes. They probed like snail horns into the unknown, quivering with every new sound or movement. I lost all form as if I was made of water and held apiece only by my will.

It grew dark, even though it was not yet midday. I gasped for air, opening my watery mouth and letting out a mournful sea lament, swathed in thick white swirling mist that poured from inside me and covered the ground so I couldn't see where the cliff top ended. The ground beneath me began to pitch and roll. When I saw the water raging far below I closed my eyes. And I threw the idol over the cliff.

A week later, Tegen and I were working on the squire's farms. There was no let up, as the longer it took to bring the harvest home the more likelihood of bad weather spoiling the crop. For long hours we followed a staggered row of men who hacked at the brown barleycorn with their scythes, the backs of their necks black with the sun under their billycock hats. Whenever they reached the end of the field, they walked back and started again at the other side, and on and on it went. The giant Pentecost set a killing pace for the rest of the men, and ribbed them mercilessly if they couldn't keep up. There must have been four score women behind them, some who would never see fifty again and others as young as six. We toiled and moiled, bent double and scorched by the sun. Tegen and I had no breath spare for talking. We needed all our strength to scoop the corn into sheaves and twist the straw binders round them. The barley was tough and spiky and left scratches all over our arms. As the day wore on, our tempers got more and more frayed.

It came time to touch pipe and a group of us women flopped down in the shade of an old elm. Tegen and I sat in a slump a little apart from the others, and took our crust and slice of meat from the squire's man. There was water and a pot of beer for each of us. I watched Tegen bite on the dry crust and pull a chunk of it away in her mouth. I looked at her in her coarse shirt and filthy apron. Her sunbonnet was low over her eyes, her face blotched and her sunburnt throat and chest a livid red above a thin line of snow-white flesh that showed below her shirt. It was because of me that she had taken on this work. Only the lowest people worked the harvest, slaving from dawn to dusk for a few shillings when the crops were finally gathered in, and the right to collect faggot wood on the five-mile walk home.

I moved closer to Tegen so we could speak without being overheard. There were damp patches under her armpits, and she smelt of sweat. It was a minute or two before I had the heart to speak.

"You'd never turn against me, would you, Teg?"

She frowned at me. "What makes you ask that?"

"Something's hanging over me. I'm ashamed to speak of it."

"Well, there'll be way round it," she said, "as long as it's not to do with those reward notices." She looked at me a moment, swatting a dozy bluebottle away from her bread. Then her eyes opened wide. "Oh lor!" she cried. "You never . . ."

"I only took her boots," I whispered. "I didn't do the rest, I swear. But Aunt Madgie saw me by the woman's body and I'm sore afraid she'll accuse me of it."

Tegen stared at me, frowning.

"You believe me, don't you, Teg? You know I'm not the cannibal?"

She nodded her head, wearily. "I just thought of all those dire things Aunt Madgie said at the Lovefeast. The woman's mazed. She might say you did it, and snitch on you."

"I can't sleep nights for fear of it."

"Then you know what you've got to do. Let Loveday become school mistress. And keep away from that minister. I've never trusted him. There's a darkness about the man I can't fathom."

"It's not the minister's doing. Anyhow, you're bound to say that, Teg. Always worrying what the neighbours will think."

"All a woman has in this world is her good name. Save yourself, while you still can. Listen to what 'Bias says. Hard work, decency and self-reliance will reap their own reward."

"It's always 'Bias this and 'Bias that with you these days."

"My faith is what gives me strength. If I were you, I'd pray to God that nothing bad comes of this."

"Suppose Aunt Madgie snitches on me anyhow, even if I stand down as teacher? I've got to get out of this village, whatever it takes."

"But think of it, a woman like you, without a penny to her name. What would become of you?"

I pulled a tuft of grass out of the earth. Tegen looked at me and seemed to read my mind. She shrank away from me.

"Oh, Mary!" she whispered. "You're as mazed as that old woman. Even now, you're dreaming about that minister. I beg you to wake up and come to your senses. Find a man in the village and forget this madness."

"You mean a man like Nathaniel Nancarrow?"

She gave me a fierce look.

"Don't worry, Teg. I saw you two at the Lovefeast, and how he looked at you. You must tell him what's in your heart. You belong to each other. Anyway, you're welcome to Nathaniel."

"What say you? He's not good enough for you but I'm welcome to him, is that so? Why, only a great, puffed-up foreigner with high and mighty ways is good enough for Mary Blight, I suppose. You'd better come to your senses before it's too late."

I looked down at my raw, cracked hands, the filth under my nails, the ugly freckles on my arms.

"I'll pray for you," said Tegen.

"Save your breath. I don't want the same things you do. We're different as different."

"Go your own way then, and end your days in gaol or the poorhouse. Or worse." She shifted away and supped her beer with her back turned to me. I looked away across the empty field in a fair hump.

"It's fine for you," I said. "You never hoped for much out of this life, but I do. I'm not throwing myself away on a fool from the village." Something sharp struck me on the back of the head, and Tegen's crust of bread landed on the grass beside me.

"How would you know what I want?" she said. "You don't know me, you don't see what I'm like."

I turned to look at her. I'd never known her so vexed. "What are you saying of? 'Course I know you. Don't be upsetting yourself. This rotten work has us both in a temper, that's all."

"I'm sick of you, and the troubles you bring," she said, getting to her feet. Some of the women looked up at her, but for once she took no notice. "You're on your own from now on," she said, wiping her hands on her apron. "I've got my loom and a bit put by from all the cloth I've sold. You can look after yourself, and good riddance to you." And with that, she hoisted up her skirts and made off across the field.

That night I was awakened from troubling dreams by a soft voice. "Is that you, my lamb?" It was pitch dark and I had no inkling where I was at first. It came back to me. I was in the chair downstairs, alongside Mamm. Dying embers shifted and dropped softly in the hearth. The kitchen came to life in the pink glow, the table and dresser, the settle. Dr Vyvyan had been to call on his rounds earlier in the week. He'd said Mamm had rheumatic fever and wasn't long for this world. Her last hours were being measured out in long, even breaths. I reached for her hand and felt her blood pulse slowly under her skin. It was hard to believe her blood would ever stop moving through her veins. I didn't know how long I'd been asleep, or how late the hour. It was my turn to wait upon Mamm, and Tegen was snoozing upstairs. Not in the bed we usually shared, but in Mamm and Dad's old room. It was the first time we'd ever slept apart. We hadn't spoken a word to each other since the row in the barley field.

"Mary?" A rattling death rasp. "Is that you, my lamb?"

"I'm here, Mamm." I whispered. Dim and pink, she faded before my eyes, a spirit sinking into the other world. "My three sweet boys, all lost, one after the other," she said. I put my ear close to her face and felt her breath cool on my cheek. "No more'n babes, they was. Do you hear they calling me?" She took one more deep breath like a long, shuddering snore, and then she was suddenly quiet, as if surprised at herself. The room turned strangely cold. I sat there in the gathering daylight, and heard the deepest silence I had ever known.

CHAPTER
SEVENTEEN

I was on the top floor of the derelict old salt house in the harbour, mending a net. Slow and irksome work, but what choice had I? At least keeping my hands busy took my mind off the empty feeling I'd had in the fortnight since Mamm had passed away. It didn't help that I'd fallen out with Tegen and we hardly spoke, not even as Mamm was laid in the earth. I wanted nothing more than to take my sister in my arms, but when I saw the sour pout on her face I couldn't bring myself to.

Outside in the lane, I heard women's voices. Realising it was Grace Skewes gossiping with Millie Hicks, I let the needle fall and felt about for the wretched thing down where the mesh was spread on the floor, listening to the voices below in the lane.

"A fine day for doing your laundry," said Grace. "Surprised you wasn't blown away up there, in this wind. There be a storm coming, I seem."

"I believe so. That's why I went and got the job out of the way. I has a terror of the house being struck by lightning at night and people finding me with dirty pillowslips on my bed. I want all to be decent even if my end do come upon me sudden."

Grace laughed. "You is a fine example to us all, Millie."

They were quiet a moment.

"Well, the very sight of a neighbour who might have a bit of news to share is most cheering," said Millie. "It ain't that I be eager for a slander. It do give me qualms to hear measly tales about my neighbours. Only there be some matters that people has a right to know of."

"I will hold my tongue and let others keep theirs," said Grace.

"The same goes for me."

I knew they were set on blackening me, so I left the net hanging on a hook and crept over to the window. So eager was I to get a peek at them, I almost put my foot through a hole in the floorboards. The window pane had been blown out long since so I could see them down there clear as day, standing just a few yards away. I leant over as much as I dared, but tried to keep out of sight. It was then I saw Grace's daughter Loveday was with them. Millie's baskets of laundry were set down beside her on the cobbles. What fine linen she had!

"Well, at least Johnenry has seen the light where that one's concerned, and not before time," said Grace, smiling at Loveday.

"And has you set a day for the nuptials yet, my girl?" said Millie.

Loveday nodded and simpered, while Grace spoke on her behalf. "First Sunday after Martinmas. And we hope you'll be in the pew alongside us on the day."

So Loveday had wormed her way back into Johnenry's heart! I was almost tempted to win him back just to spite her.

"Well, that one have lost Johnenry, for sure, but she's still got her hooks in the minister, playing the modest maiden," said Millie.

"For my part, I were never taken with the minister," said Grace. "I only offered him hospitality out of respect for his calling, and gave money for the chapel in hopes it might improve the conduct of the baser sort in this village."

"The same with me," said Millie, her long, pointed nose in the air as if some smell offended her. Seemingly, they'd forgotten how they'd been all over Gideon like a plague of lice when first he came.

"Have you heard anything about the two of them?" asked Grace.

"Nobody I know of have seen them together. This morning I was in Downlong Row, minding my own business as usual, and who should I bump into but Dolly Stoddern. She's neighbours with the woman. She said she was pruning her beans last night and happened to go up her Jack's ladder and peek into you-know-who's courtyard."

"Yes, and then?" urged Grace.

"She saw naught awry," said Millie.

"Perhaps the minister saw through her charms in the end," said Grace. "He's barely set foot in the cove this last month and when he's here he spends all his time working on the new chapel. The building's all but finished. Perhaps there's nothing in the tale."

"Maybe, and I would never spoil a neighbour's good name for a pastime," said Millie. "But a lone maiden is always a danger, I seem."

"Quite so. It would be better for all if she found herself a man of her own, instead of stealing other women's," said Loveday.

"She'd rather lead the fools on," said Millie. "And if you ask my opinion, none would have her anyhow, not if it really came to it. She's never been ready with soft answers and men don't take to a scold." She lowered her voice. "Some say she do have the look of a sea pellar about her."

"Or a merrymaid. Webbed feet, I shouldn't wonder," said Loveday, giggling.

"Well, I am not one to judge, but if any wrong have been done in this village, then the truth has a way of coming to light," said Grace.

"Providence will always punish false pride," said Millie.

My blood turned to cabbage water listening to them. A few yards away, Aunty Merrryn's old devil of a cat was crouching on a harbour post, watching a little wagtail pecking around on the slipway. The cat kept so still you'd think he was made of the same granite as the post he sat upon. What I heard next, gave me a fright.

"Now, all we need is for that minister to come to his senses and make Loveday Sunday school teacher," said Millie.

"As soon as the chapel's built and the minister gone, people in this village will make her stand down," Grace said. "There be ways of bringing people down a peg or two hereabouts, if needs be. And if that ain't enough, we know there is someone highly placed in this village who has a secret, and she's biding her time until she has cause to let the secret out."

The three sneaks nodded at each other, sharing knowing looks. Just then, the cat leapt off the post and pounced on the bird. A little wing flapped in his jaw.

Something made Loveday turn her head up towards the window where I was watching, and just in time, I ducked out of sight and took a step back. The next I knew, my foot had stepped into thin air and I was tumbling backwards, reaching for the window frame to no avail. I landed on my back with a loud thud and a creaking of floorboards. My skirts cushioned the blow, but I jarred my tailbone. I sat up, pulled my leg out of the hole and got to my feet. By the time I reached the window again, the women had fled.

I went back to my stool. My backside throbbed where I'd landed on it, and my head reeled as I fretted over all I'd heard. Aunt Madgie was looking to spread lies about what she'd seen on the beach that morning. I wondered how much part those reward bills had played in all this. Aunt Madgie wasn't long for this world, but Grace Skewes and Loveday would be keen to get their hands on all that lucre. Aunt Madgie had already made the threat all those months ago when they summoned me to her house in Back Street. And after her vile words at the Lovefeast, she seemed capable of anything. It was as if she truly believed she'd seen me take the earrings. Perhaps, she'd grown feeble minded and her memory was failing her. Or maybe in her hatred for me, she'd come to believe me guilty, and remembered what happened that morning not as it truly was, but as she wished it to be.

I stewed over my plight all that day. It came to me that the only way to save myself was to go to Aunt Madgie and tell her I'd stand down as Sunday school mistress. After all, she and her cronies had already poisoned the minds of the children against me. But if I took that step I'd be cutting my only tie with Gideon, and any dim hopes I had of a better life. Fear won out over desire in the end, and I resolved to go to Back Street and tell the old woman that I was quitting as teacher. Loveday was welcome to it.

The next day I left the cottage with leaden heart and limbs, and turned onto Downlong Row on my way to Back Street and Aunt Madgie's house. I was lost to all around me as if smothered by a dense and numbing fog, so at first I didn't see the short, stout fellow climbing the hill towards me with a waddling gait. The stranger was red in the face from the climb, with white whiskers. I was about to walk right past when he raised his hat.

"Good day to you, Miss Blight," he said, huffing and puffing. I remembered that queer foreign accent and gruff voice. It was Mr Dabb, the Justice, who I'd last seen at a dinner in that fine house in Newlyn. "I didn't give you a start, I hope?" He peered at me from under his bushy eyebrows.

"No, it's only that I hadn't thought to see you hereabouts."

"Well, I must go wherever duty calls me."

"Your business is with the mines, I suppose?" I said.

"Not on this occasion. I've come in my capacity as Magistrate."

"Nobody is in trouble, I hope,"

"Well, we shall have to wait and see about that. My visit relates to our old friend, the Porthmorvoren Cannibal. You'll have seen the notices I had pinned up."

I nodded.

"You've heard nothing, Miss Blight? No rumours?"

My throat was so dry it hurt to swallow, and my heart was beating fit to bust. "I'm afraid I've heard nothing," I managed to say. "I wish you luck with it. By the way, how is Mrs Stone? Have you seen her of late?"

"I have indeed, only this week. We're fast friends now. Wonderful woman, Mrs Stone. She's taking a great interest in this enquiry, you know? Now, would you be so kind as to tell me which of these lanes is Back Street? I think I might have missed my turn."

"You're going to Back Street?"

"I'm visiting Mrs Maddern. You'll know her, no doubt."

So he'd come to see Aunt Madgie! I put a hand out to support myself on a neighbour's wall.

"Are you unwell, Miss Blight?" He looked at me closely. "You look quite drawn. You're taking care of yourself?"

"I lost my Mamm lately, and haven't been myself."

"I'm very sorry to hear that. Please accept my condolences. Well, as we're heading in the same direction, why don't we walk together?"

When we'd walked a little way down the lane, I plucked up courage and asked, "You'll be talking to Aunt Madgie about the cannibal, I suppose?"

He leant towards me and lowered his voice. "Let's just say, something has come to light that may be of significance. Mrs Maddern may be able to shed some light on it, I'm reliably informed."

"Well, here we are," I said. "That house along there with the posts outside is the one you want."

"Do take care of yourself, Miss Blight," he said, shaking my hand.

I waited on the quay for a little while, before rushing home. Once I was safely inside, I stood with my back against the door for a long moment, trying to catch my breath. After I'd calmed down, I dropped into a chair at the table, turning out of habit to look at Mamm in her old armchair, but the chair, with its frayed arms and crumpled cushion, lay empty. I burst into tears at the sight. I longed to tell my troubles to Tegen, but she was at Nathaniel's, helping his Tamsin look after the little ones while he was out fishing, not that she'd had much time for me since the row we'd had during the harvest.

The slow hours passed, and my thoughts could find no place to rest. As the day wore on, I fancied that voices were plotting against me out there. Who was this person, I wondered, this Mary Blight that they spied upon and slandered? I felt a prisoner in my own home, fearful of the groans and clicks inside and rustling without. Darkness fell, so I lit a taper and put it on the table. It hissed and the smoke made my eyes itch, eyes already sore from weeping.

I must have dropped off, for I was roused by three soft thumps on the front door. I leapt to my feet, thinking it must be Gideon. I drew my shawl about me and ran to the door. Outside there was a smell of alcohol and sweat and a dark-haired man staggered out of the night.

Johnenry! It was only Johnenry.

"Quick, get in here before you're seen," I said. "What are you thinking of, coming here like this? Are you sure you nobody saw you?"

"I saw a light in the cottage. I go his way every night so nobody will think it strange to see me pass by. I'm due on the night core in an hour. I'll be late and my pay will be docked, but damn them to hell." He stood there, not knowing where to put himself. He coughed — a dry, hacking, rattling noise.

"You'd better have a good reason for calling on me at this hour. What if Loveday finds out you've been here?"

"She's got no claim on me."

"Oh wisht! What are you saying of?"

He sat down across the table from me. In the queasy light, he looked sickly and drawn. He coughed again.

"It's the mine that gave you that cough, isn't it?" I said.

"I started working shifts in the bal to save up for the wedding with Loveday. But there ain't going be no wedding."

I thought of Loveday getting her wedding linen together for after the nuptials and then getting this news. "Why are you doing this? What madness has come over you?" I said.

"I hear you and the minister have fallen out." He smiled, a grisly sight. "He ain't been seen near you for weeks."

I was trembling now, fearing what he'd say next. "What are you doing here, Johnenry?"

"It's not too late for us, Mary."

"Shush! You've been drinking."

"I'll treat you as you deserve to be treated."

"No more foolishness," I said. "Things are bad enough for me already, without this. You must go."

"We can get away from here. They'll give us a cottage near the mine. We can start a new life."

Wasn't this what I wanted, to flee the village and all my troubles? I thought of summer days long ago when Johnenry and I lay on the rocks at Tombstone Point, dreaming about what would become of us.

"I'll never let you down. I'm not like your parson," he said.

"I'm not running away with you," I said. "I'm fond of you, as a sister is of a brother, but I don't love you, Johnenry. I am sorry to say it, truly I am. Now you must go. Go to Loveday. Get down on your knees and beg her to take you back."

"I've loved you since I was in my thirteenth, Mary. I'll never love another."

"That's enough." I stood up and went to the door. "I'm going out to see if the way is clear. Follow me into the alley in a moment, and I'll signal when it's safe for you to go."

He stood up. "Mary, I . . ."

"Quiet now!"

How loud my footsteps sounded in the dark, clacking on the timbers over the fish cellar. I went to the end of the narrow alley and looked up and down the lane. It was clear, so I waved for Johnenry to follow me. He squeezed past, taking me in his arms. I felt the stubble on his chin as his mouth tried to find mine, but I struggled free of him. "Never!"

I pushed him out of the alley and into the lane, and ran back inside.

Sometime later there was another rap on the door. I gave no answer but there was another knock, so I opened the door a crack and found Johnenry out there.

"You're not coming in," I said. "Get on your way." I slammed the door and bolted it.

It was quiet for a while, then a kind of howling began, like an animal caught in a trap. Johnenry was still out there in the courtyard and calling my name over and over. When I could bear it no longer, I opened the door and threw a pail of water over him.

"Be gone with you! I never want to see you again."

The next morning I was awoken by a loud banging on the front door. Still half asleep, I crept downstairs and opened it, half thinking I'd find Johnenry standing there, but the courtyard was empty. I went down the alley, and looked up and down the lane, but no one was to be seen. It was only when I went back that I found a reward notice had been pinned to the door. I tore it off and crumpled it in my fist.

I got dressed, trying to think of how to free myself from the trap I'd fallen into, and I remembered what Gideon had said. If the worst came to the worst, I could call on him. But how was I to reach him? And did he still feel the same way? He'd barely set foot in the cove these past weeks.

At that moment, I heard voices out in the courtyard. It was Tegen and Tobias Hawkey, the preacher. I ran to the dresser, taking up a pen and ink and sat down at the table to scribble a note on an old envelope. Having no time to seal it, I folded it and put it in my apron pocket.

Sir,
You will quickly guess who writes this note. You once told me I could turn to you if I were ever in the direst need. That moment has come. I beg you to meet with me on Friday next at that place we once went to at night to rid this village of a foolish superstition. Go before sunrise so that you will not be spied upon or followed.

I would not ask this of you, were I not in the gravest peril. While it will be some risk to you, I will avail to shield you from any dishonour. In hopes that you will heed this plea,

Your servant,
X

As I finished, Tegen plodded wearily into the kitchen. I rushed out and through the courtyard. Tobias was walking briskly down the lane. I called after him and he turned about, retraced his steps and followed me into the courtyard.

"I have remembered your mother in my prayers, Mary."

"Thank you, that's kind. You won't mind me asking a favour of you?"

"Not at all."

"When are you next going to Newlyn?"

"On the morrow. I have a meeting with Mr Stone."

"That is lucky, for I have a note for the minister." I took the note out of my pocket and handed it to him. "Will you give this to him, as soon as ever you may?"

"It's to do with the Sunday school, I suppose."

"Of course. I think the minister would prefer that you didn't peruse it. There are some confidential matters to do with the funding."

"You may depend upon it." He looked at me and frowned. "You're wasting away, Mary. Your Mamm's passing has taken its toll on you, I fear. I wonder now, how are you getting on in your soul?"

"Let's talk of this another time, 'Bias. I've work to do."

He took a step closer to me. "You have a true friend in me, Mary. If there's aught that's troubling you, don't suffer in silence."

"You've heard some nonsense about me, perhaps."

"I've no time for loose talk. I only ask that you don't cut yourself off from human fellowship."

"If you wish to help me, give this note to the minister."

He put the note in his jacket pocket. "I should warn you that Mr Stone hasn't been himself of late."

"Has he been taken ill?"

276

He thought for a moment. "We must pray for him."

"He is sick then?"

"I'd rather not speak of the man's affairs."

"And what of Mrs Stone?"

"She is returned to Newlyn."

I might have swooned had not Tobias caught me by the arm. "If you have something on your conscience, Mary, it's best that you to share it," he said.

"Give the note to the minister, 'Bias. That's all I ask."

CHAPTER
EIGHTEEN

Friday came. I waited in the old church a long time in darkness thick as tar, my back against a pillar, afraid to move because of the thumps and creaks and scratching all around me. The old ruin was no more than a great, cold tomb, full of the bones of the dead. In daylight's first glimmers, the pews took ghostly form, and a pale shape with outstretched wings dropped out of the black depths of the tower and floated over my head through the nave. At first I thought it an angel fallen from Heaven to scare me away, but it let out a shivering hoot before it turned about and flew back into the tower. It was only an owl, home from its night haunts. Outside on the moor, the world slowly filled with sound, of birdsong, the lowing of cows and the bleating of sheep. And yet there was no sign of Gideon. I had almost given up hope when at last the church door wrenched open and footsteps sounded on the flags. The steps came to a halt a few feet away. I could make out a tall figure in the near darkness.

"Make yourself known to me if you are here. Speak," he said.

"Over here," I whispered.

He walked over and stood before me, broad and solid.

"I hope you've good reason for summoning me here. I hadn't intended to come to Porthmorvoren again until the chapel build was complete. And that was to be my last visit."

"I have no one else to turn to. I fear Aunt Madgie may accuse me of a dreadful crime any day now."

"I doubt it. You country people are notorious for being thick as thieves."

"You saw how she railed against me at the Lovefeast. And the other day I saw the Justice go to her house."

"What possible crime have you committed that the better part of your neighbours aren't equally guilty of?"

"I didn't do it. It's all muck and stink. But Johnenry came to the cottage the other night and asked me to wed him, and when I refused, he woke the whole village with his bawling. He's left Loveday for me, and that's another nail in my coffin."

He put a hand to his forehead. "And these trifles are what possessed you to drag me all the way from Newlyn?"

"No, there's worse, far worse. I think Aunt Madgie might have told the Justice I'm the cannibal," I cried. "That's why I called for you. I can hardly breathe for fear of it. She saw me by the body that morning and with blood on my lips. I own to that. It was because . . . I am too ashamed to admit it."

"But you did not commit that dreadful act?"

"How can you even think it? I took her boots, that's all. I hit myself in the mouth with one of them and that's where the blood came from. I know that's wicked enough in its own right, but I swear to God I'll never do such a thing again. That day when Pentecost gave you a hiding, and you told me how you came under conviction, I believed that I could raise myself up from what I'd been. I swore from that day I would never go wrecking again. You told me the Maker's saving grace was for all sinners, so long as they believed."

"I'm hard pressed to know just what it is you do believe, Mary Blight."

"My neighbours will take against me, and after you're gone and there'll be nobody to defend me."

"My deputy Tobias will exert his influence to prevent the villagers admonishing you too severely."

"You would not stand there so unfeeling if you knew all the strife that has befallen me. Even my own sister has turned against me. My dear Mamm is dead, and lies out there in that cold soil."

"I will pray for her soul. However, circumstances constrain me from doing more on your behalf. I've had good cause to avoid you in recent weeks, as you are aware. After the unfortunate antics at the Lovefeast, I thought it was all the more important we were not seen again in each other's company. I couldn't allow anything or anyone to put at risk the establishment of a proper place of worship in this cove."

"I'll flee this village then. I'm not safe here," I cried.

"Do not upset yourself any further. Here, please." He held out a white pocket handkerchief. "If you insist on fleeing the village, I can offer you a little money. I can also furnish you with a written reference that might help you secure work elsewhere. Then again, it might not, given my own current circumstances. However, I must counsel you against this course."

"But if that old woman tells the Justice I'm the cannibal?"

"It's your word against hers. She hasn't a shred of evidence. Without a doubt, it will be hard on you, but in time the differences between you and your neighbours will heal. We must all surrender to God's will, and think of the life to come."

"So this is why you're here. To give a sermon and throw me a few coins?"

"I came here because I gave you my word."

"But you had to creep here before dusk, and run the risk of being seen. Didn't you come because you wanted to see me again?"

"On the contrary. I came here to put an end to this once and for all. My wife has come home."

"You don't love her," I said.

"Our conversation is at an end." He turned and walked towards the door.

"Run away, then," I called. "I see you now for what you are — a weak and cowardly man."

His stopped, then slowly turned and took a few paces towards me. "Very well. As you are intent on provoking me, perhaps you should know something of my present circumstances." He reached inside his jacket and pulled out a folded piece of paper. "Here. Read this."

I sat on the end of a bench, opened the paper and found it was a letter.

To: Mr Gideon Stone
IN UTMOST CONFIDENCE

October 3rd 18—

SIR, — As superintendent of the Penwith circuit, it is my duty to inform you that two complaints of a grave nature concerning your conduct have been submitted to the circuit office. Should the claims be proven true, they would amount to a serious breach of the discipline of the Conference. The claimants are two women, below named:

Mrs Louisa Trevellick of St Just, aged twenty-seven;
Miss Anne Treveil of St Buryan, aged twenty-four.

I do herby summon you to a meeting at the super-intendent's office in Penzance at 11 a.m. on 21st October with a panel of three lay and three ordained members of the Society, whereat you will have the opportunity to respond to the statements of the two claimants. I advise you to prepare your own state-ment in advance of the meeting. A fair copy of the claims made against you is appended to this mis-sive.

The panel will consider whether the matter can be reconciled to the satisfaction of all parties. Should we fail to achieve reconciliation, however, I will be obliged to refer the matter to a disciplinary hearing of the Methodist Conference.

I advise you that forthwith you are suspended from your ministerial duties until further notice.

Due to the serious nature of these complaints, I must advise you that, should the charges be established, the committee is required to take steps up to and including an order that you cease to be in full connexion, i.e. you will be dismissed as a minister.

I am, sir, your most obedient servant,
Mr J— W—
Superintendent,
Penwith Methodist Circuit, Cornwall

After that, I could think of nothing to say. He broke a long silence with a cough. "So now you understand," he said. "This is the consequence of my surrender to base appetites. We must subdue such desires. We're not like the animals. God has endowed us with moral faculties."

A shaft of light lit his face and I saw how careworn and lined he was, with deep shadows under his eyes.

"But that same God who made the animals also made you," I said. "Can we always be so sure what God wants of us? It seems to me that we can no more deny our Nature than the birds or beasts of the field."

He laughed, a dry and bitter sound. "I hadn't thought to hear such sophistry from a plain, uneducated woman. Remember we're in God's house. Take care not to blaspheme."

I got up from the bench, and took a step towards him. "We both need to escape our troubles. Millie Hicks stitched us together that time, and shamed us, but weren't we fastened to each other all along? You chose me because it was meant."

"I chose you as Sunday school teacher, not as . . . Or at least I gave myself to understand . . . That is to say . . ." He threw his head back and groaned. "What a fool I've been all these months. I made myself believe the Holy Spirit was working within me and construed strong emotion as proof of faith. But it was something else." His fists were clenched.

"So, you are like other men," I said. "Is that so bad? I wonder if anyone in this world is just what they seem. Everything is show in these times. Even your wife has her secrets."

He turned and glared at me. "I warn you not to insult my wife."

"The face she shows the world is not the one I saw."

He stepped towards me, bracing himself as if he might strike me. Before he could, I ran to him and hugged him, my head on his breast. He turned his face away and raised his hands aloft.

"Every step I take, a snare is waiting for me," he said.

"It doesn't matter to me what you've done." His heart pounded under my cheek. "God made you the man you are."

"No more," he said, trying to push me away. But I squeezed him in my arms until something inside him seemed to give.

"Sister Blight, end this madness now, please, before . . ."

He seized my wrists, freed himself and staggered backwards, but I took his hands and put them around

284

my waist. In a moment, we were kissing. He threw his coat down on the cold stone slabs under the tower at the back of the church and we lay down beside each other. His hands roved wherever they pleased, handling me as if I was I was a priceless china-clay doll that might easily shatter. He raised my skirts and gazed at my limbs with the wonder Adam must have shown for Eve when first he beheld her in the Garden. How hot and heavy he was when he lay on top of me. He slid into me without let or hindrance, and I threw my head back, falling upwards into darkness too deep to fathom.

CHAPTER
NINETEEN

Afterwards, we stood together in the church.

"Will you abandon me now?" I asked. My throat was dry and my voice no more than a croak.

"No, not after this," he said, patting the dust from his coat. "We are meant to be together for good or ill. It is no use denying it."

"But what of your wife?"

"I will do whatever is required." He was still and silent a moment. "You and I will need to move somewhere we're not known, and I fear I'll have to resign myself to a less exalted calling. We must act quickly, given your situation."

"And you're sure you'll do this for me?"

He nodded. "We will endure whatever hardship awaits us together. Be here in this church, ready and prepared, on the Sabbath by the stroke of one of the church in Paul. That gives me time to put matters in order as best I can in Newlyn."

"So soon!" I had to steady myself against a pillar.

"Above all," he said, "do nothing to arouse suspicion. Be patient. Let us pray God will in time forgive us this great wrong if we lead sober and decent lives hereafter."

Before we parted, he pressed me hard to him as if to embolden our resolve for what lay ahead. I left the church first, leaving him to follow a little later so we were not seen together. I went down the headland in steady drizzle, but nothing that day could have dampened my mood. The wide earth seemed new and strange. In this blissful daze I at last reached the top of Downlong Row. Fish bones and egg shells flowed down the gulley, and it was hard not to slip on the greasy cobbles.

As I got near our cottage, three figures loomed out of the misty rain, standing in a line and blocking my path. Two of them were boys from the Sunday school — Thomas Penpol and the troublemaker Kit Trefusis. The other was a bigger lad, Kit's older brother Matthey. Where the younger boys' faces were smooth and boyish, Matthey's had hardened into that of a young man, with a line of dark fluff over his top lip. As I got closer to them, I saw they had no intention of moving out of my way.

"What game is this, my lads? Come along now, and let me pass," I said.

Kit Trefusis was the first to speak. "We know where you've been. You were up in the church with the parson."

"Things have come to a pretty pass in this village when big brave lads like you think it right to accost a lone woman in the lane," I said. "I have been in the church on my own, sheltering until the rain stopped." I looked at each of them in turn. The younger boys wouldn't meet my gaze, but Matthey scowled at me.

"Let's go, leave her alone," said Thomas, trying to move away. He shivered, his hair flattened to his forehead by the rain.

"Stay where you are," said Matthey, in his grown man's broken voice. He folded his arms. Thomas stared down at his feet, scudding his shoe backwards and forwards.

"I'm surprised at you, Tom," I said. He avoided my eye, and glanced at the older boy for his cue.

"Tell the harlot what you saw," said Matthey.

"Don't you dare call me such names, Matthew Trefusis! You're going to regret this, I'll make sure of it. Step aside, and let me pass."

"Tom followed the parson up there and saw the two of you leave after," said Matthey, stepping towards me. "They was in there a long time, wasn't they, Tom?"

"That is enough," I said.

"Did you let the parson f— you, or just let him have a feel?" asked Matthey. "Admit it, and we might let you go."

"Get along now, Tom, and you too, Martin," I said. "You've been led into this and I know you're ashamed of yourselves. If you go now, we'll say no more about it."

Tom and Martin squirmed. The bigger boy leered at me, but I met his gaze. "This is the last time I'll tell you. Get out of my way, boy."

Kit sniggered at hearing his older brother cut down to size, and Matthey punched his arm, not playfully but brutally. The younger boy winced and his eyes filled with tears as he rubbed his arm. Matthey slowly stepped aside, leaving me just enough room to slip through, so I had to push past him. I walked briskly down the hill, losing my footing, which made Matthey laugh. I reached my own alley and rushed down it and across the courtyard.

Only force of will got me to busy myself about the house. My joyous mood had been well and truly spoilt, and in its stead was a sickly dread. Be patient, Gideon had said. But how could I be patient when I'd been spied in the church with him?

I packed my basket, choosing three dresses, some shifts and petticoats. I took the old stocking that I hid in the rafters with all my treasures inside it, the silver hair pin and some other jewellery I might be able to sell, and coins that would help fund our new life together. I wanted something to remind me of Mamm, so I took the sugar nips. She'd always had a terrible sweet tooth, and so had I. When I was done, I sat and waited, not knowing what to do with myself.

I wrote a note for Tegen and left it in Mamm's room for her to find after I'd gone.

My dearest Teggie,
When you find this I will be on my way to a new life far from here. No doubt you will hear the rights of it before long, but please don't judge me too harshly. When it is safe, I will send you the address in the hope that you will visit. It has been an agony to me, holding all my worries inside, and thinking of how I always used to share every secret with you.

I have had a heavy heart ever since our quarrel and I would give the world to be able to take back my words that day during the harvest. I said that you didn't want anything out of life which I know is not true. I haven't held you in the regard that you deserve and I am sorry for it. I've have been caught up in my own nonsense, and not seen that you have grown to be a fine woman with a woman's wants and hopes. You are not the shrinking child of old, hiding behind my skirts. I am so proud when I remember the way you stood up and testified before all at the prayer meeting. And I should never have mocked Nathaniel, who is a good man, brave and honest and true, which is a rare thing in this world. I see how he feels about you and pray you'll be together before long.

I want you to have my Bible as it is too heavy to carry across the moor. It breaks my heart to leave you behind, but I console myself with the hope that we will be together again before too long.

Your ever-loving sister,
Mary

Thinking about my sister made me weep and wet the page I was writing on, so I sprinkled some sand on the words to stop them fading away.

On Saturday, the day before I was to be reunited with Gideon, I was woken up by a hubbub down in the cove. I got down there to find a great scrum of women by the harbour wall. Then I saw that do-gooder Miss Vyvyan in their midst and, to my horror, Mrs Stone. They were raised as if on a stage. Mrs Stone looked haughty, but pale with shadows under her eyes. Alongside them were two other women I remembered from Miss Vyvyan's dinner party in Newlyn. Miss Vyvyan looked about her, rubbing her palms together with relish, as though she were heartened to find the village in such dire need of her help.

"A good morning to all of you ladies. If you'll allow me to introduce myself and my companions. My name is Miss Vyvyan and I have with me Miss Elliot, Mrs Cotterill and Mrs Stone." There were murmurs of surprise among some of the village women at the mention of Mrs Stone. As for Mrs Stone herself, she gazed grimly ahead of her, as Miss Vyvyan carried on with her talk. "We are representatives of the West Penwith Benevolent Society for the Relief of Indigence, and have been allocated to this district to report on cases of need. We have brought no funds with us today, I'm afraid." Some of the women grumbled to hear this. "However, we will be drawing up a list of the most needful among you, so that gifts of money, or clothing if more suitable, can be made at a later date." This got them all jawing, so she had to bide her time before going on. "We will first meet with the leaders of your local Methodist Band to discuss the fairest way to distribute the funds." There was more groaning about this, as it meant the bettermost would have the biggest say in who got any money. "Porthmorvoren, being somewhat remote, has been overlooked in previous tours and we hope to rectify this in the coming weeks. Now, my companion, Mrs Stone, would like to say a few words. Mrs Stone, if you will."

Mrs Stone cleared her throat and looked out over all our heads. "The village of Porthmorvoren is of special concern to me for reasons of which I'm sure you're all aware." This got the women murmuring again. "It cannot have escaped your attention that this village has become a by-word for moral turpitude, ever since the wreck of *The Constant Service* — and the depravity that tragic loss occasioned." There was a rumble as neighbour turned to neighbour, talking of the cannibal. "The entire region is appalled," said Mrs Stone. "Horrified by what took place. For too long you've been allowed to ... that is to say, you've been neglected. Our founder, Mr Wesley, inveighed against wrecking and smuggling, so you must understand it is our moral duty to subdue and govern those among you who even now yield to this heinous crime."

"We has natural rights to the goods," shouted Nancy Spargo. "Not that I would ever stoop so low ..."

"You have no such rights," said Mrs Stone. "But this is not to the point. What I mean to say is ... In the past we have been used to give doles to the poor, regardless of their moral character. However, I am of the opinion that relief should be preceded by an enquiry into the habits and conduct of the party concerned. Charity works best when it's deserved. Otherwise, what will our donors think?"

The village women began squabbling about who amongst them was most deserving of alms.

292

"It is my belief," said Mrs Stone, "that the sure way to instil clean, frugal habits in people like yourselves, as well as a love for country and inclination to industry, is through religious education." She took out a pocket handkerchief and wiped her brow. "And I should like you to know that I have particular concerns about the Sunday school in this village."

Some of my neighbours turned their heads to gawp at me.

"Those who are without blame will be helped," said Mrs Stone. "But felons will be punished. A great lord has put up an award. You will have seen the handbills."

She was drowned out by the voices of the women. Meanwhile, someone was pushing through the crowd to get out, and in a moment Martha Tregaskis stepped free of the main body of women, looking very pale in the face. She staggered a little way off, then bent forward and retched onto the stones of the quay, leaving a steaming puddle of puke that reeked of bile and spirituous liquor.

While all eyes were on Martha, I slipped away and rushed home. Once in the kitchen, I paced about, my thoughts racing. There was a knock on the door, which made me jump. I was surprised to find Miss Vyvyan standing on the threshold, alone. She came in, beaming at me like we were old friends.

"Mary, I am so pleased to see you again." She looked round the cottage and found it so distressful she clasped me to her breast. She took a step back, still holding me by the wrists, and frowned as she looked into my face. "Oh, Mary, you are a bag of bones! And how you shake! We must do something to help you."

"Will I fit you a cup of tea?" I asked.

"I can spare a few minutes, so yes, how kind. Look at this place! You deserve so much more," she said. "I dreamt of you last night, by the way," she said, sitting at the table.

"You dreamt of me, ma'am?"

"Call me Rebecca, please! Yes, I lay in bed awake for a long while, thinking about my visit today, and I tried to imagine your living conditions. And I'm sorry to say they're entirely as mean as I'd envisaged."

"I do my best."

"Oh heavens, Mary, I'm not blaming you. Anyway, let me describe my dream to you. Did you ever dream of flying when you were a child?"

"You mean like a witch, ma'am?"

She smiled. "Yes, perhaps so. Well, it was like that in my dream. I soared into the air, higher and higher until I was up in the clouds. I could see that great stretch of water, the Atlantic Ocean, and how it connects the shores of Cornwall with the islands of the West Indies. I saw great ships laden with rich cargoes blown by the trade winds across the waters from one side to the other, and I witnessed the unforgivable wrongs done to thousands upon thousands of human beings, those poor souls, the Negroes, who have been transported in chains to those far away islands. And here on our own beaches I saw the petty crimes of the coastal people for what they are, an attempt by poverty-stricken wretches to taste a little of the luxuries taken for granted by their betters. I thought of you, and I realised that you are only a paler cousin of those poor souls treated with utmost brutality in the plantations. You are links in a chain."

"I have no Negro cousins, ma'am."

"I'm sure not. I was speaking figuratively."

"I wouldn't want you to think I was a wrecker, either, ma'am." I put her tea down on the table.

"What a lovely teacup," she said, holding it before her with raised eye brows. She gave me a knowing smile. "I want to assist you, Mary. You'll let me, won't you?"

I nodded.

"I'd better go — they'll be looking for me." She got up, hugged me again, and off she went. She hadn't even touched her tea.

After that I spent the morning and well into the afternoon waiting and fretting in the cottage. It seemed an age. Mid-afternoon, there was a knock on the door and this time I found Mrs Stone standing there. When I'd got over the fright, I let her into the kitchen, where she stood in silence, looking about her in disgust, and giving off a fearful chill. Without a word, she took a crumpled note out of her pocket and gave it to me.

"This was left under a stone outside my house in Newlyn, where anyone might have found it," she said. "Read it."

FROM ONE WHO WISHES YOU WELL.
I AM TRULY SORRY TO BARE BAD
TIDINGS BUT YOU HAVE THE

RITE TO BE INFORMED THAT BEFORE A RELIBEL WITNESS Y^R HUSBEND HAVE BROKE THE 7TH COMANDMENT WITH A SERTAIN MARY BLITE OF PORTHMORVOREN.

"What do you have to say for yourself?" she said.

"It's lies. I have neighbours who want to see me ruined."

"Do you think I'd make an accusation like this without first establishing the truth? My husband has already confessed to it."

"Please, ma'am . . ."

"Be quiet! While I've been doing the rounds here today, I've been enquiring about your character. Mrs Maddern, a decent, respectable woman, was most anxious to enlighten me about your misdeeds."

"Aunt Madgie hates me and so do her family."

"Mrs Maddern witnessed you commit an infamous crime."

"She did not!" I felt light-headed and had to sit down. "I'm not on trial here," I said.

"Not yet. But Mrs Maddern has agreed to come forward to the Justice."

"She wouldn't do that. She knows I didn't do it. And besides, nobody snitches in this cove. Aunt Madgie, least of all."

"This time her conscience must have got the better of her."

At that moment Miss Vyvyan returned.

296

"Rebecca, it's come to my attention that this woman is a moral degenerate," said Mrs Stone.

"You astonish me, Ellie."

"I have strong grounds for what I say. A neighbour of Miss Blight, a woman of a good family, witnessed her molesting the dead body of Lady S— on the morning the poor woman washed ashore in this cove. Mrs Maddern will testify that Miss Blight had blood around her mouth, so it is self-evident that she is responsible for the heinous crime that has scandalised the region."

"It's not as it seems, Miss Vyvyan," I said.

"With great reluctance, Mrs Maddern has breached an age-old custom among the country people in these parts of never informing on a neighbour," said Mrs Stone. "She has written a letter to the Magistrate, which I have in my pocket. I will personally deliver it to Mr Dabb tomorrow, after attending chapel."

"I didn't take the earrings. It's Aunt Madgie's word against mine. She's no proof," I said.

"Oh, I have proof enough, Miss Blight," said Mrs Stone. "I have long suspected you. You forget the time I caught you in my bedroom, trying to steal my linen. And I know you stripped the woman of her boots, for I have them in my possession still."

"I took the boots, but I didn't take the earrings."

"Do you believe a jury would countenance the idea that a woman capable of pulling the boots from a dead woman's feet would have scruples about stealing the greater prize — a pair of gold earrings? Now you see, Rebecca, this is the person you elected to take under your wing. Mary Blight is the Porthmorvoren Cannibal."

"Taking a pair of boots is hardly a felony," said Miss Vyvyan. "And her efforts as Sunday school teacher show good intentions, which must surely mitigate?"

"Well, we shall find out soon enough whether others are as tender-hearted as you," said Mrs Stone.

"Go ahead, Ellie," said Miss Vyvyan. "I'll catch up with you at the quay. I'd like to speak to Miss Blight."

When she had gone, Miss Vyvyan sat down at the table with me. "This is an unfortunate business. I'll do whatever is in my power to help you," she said. "But I warn you it is little enough."

"What will become of me?"

"Your prospects are not advantageous. Lord S— is intent on making an example of somebody. There are ways of persuading juries and the Duke has the means to get his way. In the first instance you'll be sent to prison, awaiting trial."

"And if they find me guilty?"

"I'm afraid the penalty will likely be excessive. There has been months of prurient interest in the case and the region's reputation is tarnished. A judge is likely to make an example of you at the assizes. It's not fair, I know. Lord S— has amassed tremendous riches on the back of slave labour. For all his paintings and antiques, let alone the preposterous 'gothic ruin' he has erected in the grounds of his estate, the man is no more than a pirate. You must flee this village as soon as possible. Mary, is there somewhere you can go?"

"There is somebody who might help me."

"Then you must go to them as soon as ever you can." She gazed across the table, frowning. "Who knows what you might have accomplished in other circumstances."

CHAPTER
TWENTY

The Sabbath arrived. Would Gideon be true to his word? Before I found out, I had one last ordeal to endure — the Sunday school class.

Aunt Madgie opened the door of her house in Back Street with the same cold look as always, giving nothing away. Along the hall I could hear the children, their unruly voices muffled by the kitchen door. I waited for the old dame to call me to task for my failings as she usually did, but she stood aside to let me past without a word.

When I opened the kitchen door I was near deafened by the rowdy voices of the children, who stood in little groups around the room, pushing, shoving and teasing one another. With horror, I saw that Thomas Penpol and Kit Trefusis were there. They knew I'd been in the church with Gideon, and I was sure they must have passed it on to the other children.

"Quiet! I demand silence right this minute," I shouted. The children carried on, heedless, but I could tell they had heard me. "Shut your mouths this minute, every one of you!" I cried. "Do you hear me?" I took up the stick that lay upon the dresser. "If you do not do as you are told, every last one of you will get a stroke of

300

this on both hands." My voice was high and strained, and I knew I showed more fear than mastery. Aunt Madgie's vile catechisms were spread all over the table. I picked them up and handed a pile to the child at each end of the table to pass along to their classmates. All the while, I felt the old witch listening and ill-wishing me behind the door.

Once I'd taken my place in the chair at the head of the table, I set the stick down before me and began reading aloud from the catechism. The children listened in silence to the fate that awaited them in Hell. My nerves were as frayed. After about a quarter of an hour, I felt calm enough to look up at them.

"Please, Sister Blight," said Kit, putting his hand up.

"What is it, Kit?"

"I need a piss." Every boy and every girl broke into giggles, except poor Sarah Pengilly, the class monitor. I picked up Aunt Madgie's stick and slammed it down on the table so hard that the wood split. I put the bent stick down again, and looked from face to face, fighting back tears.

Kit smiled sneakily at his mates. "Sister Blight, what do harlot mean?" he said.

Sarah gasped, and looked up at me. The others looked at each other, but weren't bold enough to glance my way.

"What do it mean, Sister Blight? Do it say in here?" said Tom Penpol. He waved his catechism and looked to the others for backing. They were in uproar by now, Kit and the other boys patting Tom on the back to spur him on. "Kit's big brother says you should know," Tom said, sniggering.

I got to my feet and took up the broken cane, twisting the end until it snapped off, and throwing the shorter piece onto the table. Tapping the stick on my palm, I glared at Tom Penpol.

"I won't have you speak to me this way," I said. "Come over here." Tom climbed over the laps of the others, making a meal of it, and came to stand before me with an impish smile on his face to show he wasn't afraid. But he had turned fearfully pale.

"Hold out your hand," I commanded. Tom wiped the spit off his chin with the back of his hand. He wasn't laughing now.

"The stick be broke, Sister Blight," he said, with a sniffle.

"You dursn't hit him with that custiss, Sister, he will get splinters," said Peggy Combelleck.

"Keep your hand steady, boy," I said, raising the stick.

He put his hand out with the fingers curled a little, and he flinched as I raised the stick higher still. Closing my eyes, I brought the stick down — more smartly than I meant to. I must have missed his palm and hit him across his little fingers, because I heard the wood strike bone. He whimpered and his hand shot into his armpit. He screwed his face up tight, and a tear rolled down his cheek.

"I'm going to fetch my Mamm," he bleated, breaking into a sob. "She will bring her rolling pin and give you what for." He slipped past me and ran to the door, opened it and dashed down the hallway. Out in the hall, the front door creaked on its hinges and slammed shut. The other boys were already climbing out from the form and running after him. The girls hesitated, then followed the boys out. Only my little friend Sarah Pengilly was left, trembling in her seat.

I went into the hall and right away heard the old woman's crook striking the floor as she loomed out of the shadows of her house. She blinked as she entered the hall. The children had left the front door open and let in a shaft of dusty light. I was in a hot temper and the sight of her only kindled it the more.

"Are you content?" I said. "I have tried your way and this is my reward for it. A mutiny."

"You were never equal to the position," she said. She spoke calmly, with only the slightest hint of a taunt in her voice.

I took a step closer to her. "You have brought me to this. You have connived to bring me down."

"You have brought this on yourself, my lady. It is not my doing."

"You think you can stand in judgement over me," I said.

"The Almighty will judge you, not me."

"He will judge you too."

"I have no fear of the Redeemer's judgement."

"If you are as pious as you pretend, then why do you never round on your neighbours when they breach the Sabbath?" I cried. "How is it that you sanction wrecking and smuggling? Your notions of right and wrong are a pretty puzzle, I seem."

"The people's livelihood comes before all else," she said, holding my gaze steadily.

"The Almighty will see into your heart on Judgement Day, and call you to account for the lies you've told."

Her eyelids drooped and she began to recite some scripture under her breath. "*Yea, all will know thy base cravings, thou agent of perdition. The Lord will punish the haughtiness of the daughters of Zion who walk and mince as they go, with stretched-forth necks and wanton eyes. Isaiah 3:16.*" She quaked, like one possessed by demons. "*He will uncover thy secret parts, and instead of beauty there will be branding.*" Only the whites of her eyes showed under her eyelids, as if she looked backwards into the darkness of her own soul.

"Listen to yourself. You are mazed with bitterness and envy," I said. "An ill-wishing, cold-hearted witch. A false old relic whose time is nearly past."

Her eyelids began to quiver, then she struck me hard across the face. I tasted blood, and my fingertips dripped red when I took them from my mouth. Before I could stop myself, I'd slapped the old devil back with all my might. Her crook clattered to the floor as she staggered backwards, cracking her head against the wall. For a moment she didn't move, her head on one side, her gaze downwards. When she spoke it was in a thin rasp.

"I saw you on the beach that day. I know you did it." She tried to lift her chin to look me in the eye, but couldn't. "You want me dead to stop me standing before the Magistrate."

304

"I did no more than steal a pair of boots," I whispered, putting my mouth close to her ear.

"You bit that lady's earlobes off to get your grubby hands on her jewels." She slid further down the wall as she spoke. "To inform against such as you would be . . ." Her eyes closed as she slid onto the floor. There was a smear of red down the wall behind her.

I put my fingers to her neck and felt for her pulse among the folds of wrinkled skin. Her lifeblood throbbed slowly, the merest twitch under my thumb. What would befall me when she came round? The old woman was weak, and it would have been easy enough to put my hand over her mouth and snuff the life out of her once and for all. It was no more than she deserved, but I could never have brought myself to do it.

I looked up and down the hallway, and saw little Sarah Pengilly standing alone by the kitchen door, watching me and fumbling with her apron.

"Don't fret, now, Sarah. Aunt Madgie has taken a fall. Will you fetch the Widow Chegwidden to look at her? And let her kin know she's had an accident and hurt herself."

The girl nodded her head quickly, and moved down the hallway, pressing herself against the wall to keep clear of me as she passed.

A moment later I heard one of the boys shout out in the lane, "It's the gallows for 'ee now, harlot!" Then his feet pattered into the distance.

I wasted no time in running home, picking up my basket, and rushing up the hill to the headland. Huge black clouds churned and raced across a vast sky. When I saw the church ahead of me I felt a tremor of unease, but I pushed on and stepped into the dark building. I put my basket down, and sat in a pew, shivering in the draught. I looked over my shoulder at where the bell ropes hung under the tower, half expecting to see Gideon standing there. The church had seemed enchanted on that other morning, but now it was dark, drab and dirty. I thought of the hour I'd spent with Gideon lying under the tower and a faintness came over me.

It was a good while before I heard the distant sound of the bell in Paul tolling the hour. It set my heart thumping. He would come now, surely he would. I waited a while longer, then, impatient and uneasy, walked out of the church. Heavy rain had begun to fall. I went through the porch into the graveyard, my feet sinking into the soggy turf, and peered beyond the dripping trees. There was nobody to be seen. I could hear a distant rumble of thunder, a storm rolling in off the Atlantic.

I went back inside and waited, shivering in a creaky, worm-eaten pew, water dripping over the stone flags from the hem of my skirt. Doubts bred in my mind like rats in a cellar. As the long minutes passed, and lengthened to hours, my mood shifted from frantic hope to despair and at last to a kind of daze. The light was fading and the church falling under deeper shadow. It would be dark within the hour. The roar of the tempest grew louder as each moment passed, and now and then a flash of lightning lit up the church. He was not coming.

I pushed hard on the church door to get it open, and the gale slammed it shut behind me once I'd left. Up on the tower the leering granite crone squatted and held her gaping *kons* open with her hands, a torrent of rainwater gushing out her and falling onto the stone cross that lay beneath. The cross had toppled and now lay flat on the earth, broken in two. A high wind was at my back, whipping in off the sea and blowing me this way and that. Gulls were sent shooting pell-mell over the cliff tops. Before long, I was wet through with freezing rain. Below me, the grey sea raged, and tall waves rolled in from afar. A gust knocked me onto all fours, and when I got up, I found I could lean back against the gale with all my weight and the wind stood me upright. In that instant, there was an almighty thunder clap overhead. The earth shook under my feet. An eerie glow lit the sky as it was rent by flashes of jagged white lightning, and the air smelt scorched. I ran wildly down the steep bluff until I reached the street of blackened miners' cottages, which at least buffered the wind. At last, I turned onto Downlong Row and ran into the cottage.

I dragged myself up the stairs, my wet clothes weighing me down. I took them off and dried myself as best I could. I caught sight of myself in my frayed white shift in the rusty oval looking glass in Mamm's old room. It was like seeing a ghost. A shirt hung out of a drawer, so I seized it and threw it over the mirror. Then I went back downstairs, tossed my wet clothes in the laundry tub, mopped the floor, and sat at the table. I was all alone. Tegen was looking after Nathaniel's children while he sailed to Marazion to visit his sister, who was poorly.

As the stillness and quiet of the cottage settled about me, I saw everything as it really was, naught but lies and falsehood. What a fool I'd been! Gideon Stone wasn't the man I'd dreamt he was, but an adulterer, a canting, cowardly liar, a drunkard, a stone picked up at the tide's edge that sparkled when wet, but when dry showed itself to be as drab as any other pebble on the beach. I went into a blind rage, beating the wall with my fists till I could bear it no more, throwing the metal pail across the kitchen. Still my anger hadn't abated, so I took fistfuls of my hair in my hands and tried to tear it out by the roots.

Weary and beside myself, I dropped onto a chair at the table, and let the angry tears flow. I thought my grief would never end, but after a hundred shuddering sobs I became quiet. I laid my head down on my arms and fell into a heavy sleep. When I awoke, it was night.

CHAPTER
TWENTY-ONE

I sat in the kitchen in the dim amber glow of a rush light. The storm had moved off over the moor and a hush had fallen over the village. Every rustle in the thatch, every buffet of the window unnerved me. I heard a cough outside and near jumped out of my skin, but I told myself it was just a neighbour passing by in the lane. A moment later there was a snigger, so I went and stood with my ear to the door. After a while there was a knock, then two more loud raps on the door, and next a horn blasted so loud that it could only have come from one of the seiner's speaking trumpets that the fishermen used out on the water. It must have sounded right outside the door. A fearful rantan of drumming and shouting began. Peeking out of the window, I saw my neighbours out there shouting and jeering, beating kettles, pans and tea trays, while others blew whistles and horns. They sounded like a hunting party of lunatics. It was a long while before the din came to an end.

In the quiet that followed, I heard a woman ask, "Who is it this time?"

"That ginger hussy," said another. "A bad turn out she is, needs taking in hand."

"She stole Loveday Skewes' man when they was all but at the altar," called another voice. "And she turned the minister's head too, afore that."

"I know the wench. A cheat and a scold, and proud as Satan. Give a woman like that her head, and soon she'll have the whole village by the heels."

"She tried to murder Aunt Madgie, I knows that for a fact."

"And they say she be the cannibal?"

"Aye, and the rest of we has been tarred with the same brush. We've never had so many Preventive Men crawling over the village as in these last months. I hope she hangs for it."

There was another bang on the door, and a call for me to show myself. I had no choice but to face them, so I opened the door and stood on the threshold. The little courtyard was packed to the gunwales with sneering neighbours, and as soon as I showed myself they began jeering and cursing. Betsy Stoddern was to the fore, but there was no sign of her mate Loveday Skewes, even though she'd surely put them all up to it.

"That's enough now!" I cried when there was a lull in the shouting. "You should be ashamed of yourselves, tormenting a lone woman."

"How do we know you be alone?" said Betsy. "For all we know, you might have one of your fancy men inside."

That got them shouting again, so I had to wait before I could speak. "You've had your sport," I said. "Most of you hardly know me. What right have you to judge? Go home now, all of you."

"Don't be uppity with us, madam!" said Betsy.

"How many men you got in there?" shouted some idle fellow, to screams of laughter.

With horror. I saw that huge lummox Pentecost barging his way through the throng towards me, towering over the others. As he got closer I saw his tiny eyes, his bent nose with its patchwork of breaks and his pocked slab of a chin.

"Don't you dare lay a finger on her!" shouted a woman at the back of the courtyard. I knew that voice — it was Cissie Olds. So at least I had one friend. But Pentecost had already got behind me and thrown his huge arms round me, pinning my arms to my sides. He lifted me as if I weighed no more than a cloth doll. As my feet left the ground, I back-kicked him with all my might but to no avail. He carried me towards the alley that led onto Downlong Row, the crowd parting to let him pass. I couldn't bear the filthy looks they gave me. We reached the alley and the big fellow could hardly fit inside, having to stoop to get me through. I heard a donkey braying at the other end, and I knew then what was in store for me. There was to be a Riding, and I was the one to be shamed.

Pentecost carried me out of the dark tunnel into the torchlit lane. I was too frantic to take it all in, faces all around me looming out of the dark, piercing shouts and laughter. He hoisted me above the heads of the rabble and threw me onto the hard floor of a donkey cart. It stank of hay and rotten apples. Cissie Olds got a knee onto the cart and tried to climb in after me. "Let her go, you devils!" she shouted, as she was pulled off and dragged away. The cart jolted on its way and lurched from side to side as the jittery donkey pulled me slowly down the steep hill. I huddled in a corner, holding my knees to my chest, trying to hide my face, while my neighbours pelted me with potato peels and rotten eggs. Young lads leapt up to spit at me, and women, flushed with drink, threw back their heads and roared with laughter.

My rush of panic slowed to a deep dread, as I picked out the faces of neighbours, young and old, filing behind the cart, some carrying horn lanterns aloft, putting the thatch at risk. The mood was like Christmas Tide or when the fair comes to Penzance. Children had been taken from their beds to see the show. Billows of bitter smoke blew into my face, half blinding me and making my eyes stream.

When we reached the quay I heard raised voices, men reciting lines in the way of actors in a Mummers' Play. I couldn't catch their words but there were bursts of laughter from those who'd gathered to hear them. Three large effigies were mounted twenty feet in the air on high poles, down at the western end of the harbour. The crowd was more scattered down there, and as the tide was out some had climbed down onto the sand to dance around a great bonfire that blazed there. The cart was led to the front where space had been cleared for it under the effigies. I was jerked and bumped about as the nervous donkey started at every sudden loud bang.

Closer up, I saw who the tall effigies stood for. One wore a dress with straw stuffed up the sleeves and poking out of the cuffs. She had long orange locks

312

made of yarn that hung almost to her feet. The others were men, and Gideon was so like the real man that nobody could fail to know whom it signified. The last was surely meant to be Johnenry, as he had a miner's stoop on his head. The men who held the poles and spoke for the effigies wore masks with horns and big gaping mouths, horrible in the murky light as they leered out of the shifting smoke. The one who held up the effigy that was meant to be me, jiggled her about and spoke in a high-pitched, snot-nosed voice.

"Oh, come closer to me, minister, so I can feel the Holy Fire!" he said.

The one who spoke for Gideon, shouted back in a deep and fruity voice, "This will be a Lovefeast you won't forget, I promise you, Sister." Then Gideon began chasing "Mary" up and down the quay, while she squealed or beckoned him with a sultry moan. The drunken crowd laughed their heads off, among them the ruffians who spent their time loafing in the kiddlywink, and the miners from Uplong and their wives, and some of the children I used to teach the gospels to. High up on its pole, my effigy leapt to escape the hand of Gideon groping for her rump, and every time he managed to touch her there was a trumpet blast.

Nancy Spargo stepped into the place cleared for the players, her plump arms swinging at her sides. She berated the crowd. "What are you devils doing by the woman?" she bawled.

"What's the matter with you, missus, get away with you," a ruffian shouted at her.

"Look at the poor soul!" said Nancy, pointing at me. "You may depend she got trouble enough to bear already. 'Tisn't for we to punish her." The mob jeered, but Nancy took no heed, tramping over to me to help me off the cart. When my feet touched the ground, my legs trembled so much I could hardly stand, but Nancy held me in her arms.

Just then I heard Tegen's voice. "This isn't justice," she was yelling. "You should know better. Where is your Christian mercy?"

"Hark at her, little Tegen Blight," someone shouted, and the rest jeered or bellowed with laughter.

Hearing my sister's voice, I searched her out among the people surrounding the Mummers and soon saw her weaving her way through the crowd towards me. When she reached me I fell into her arms. All was forgiven between us without a word needed. We held each other close for a long moment but — too soon — Betsty Stoddern pulled us apart.

"You two can pet each other later. We ain't finished here yet."

"You have no right to treat my sister this way, as God's in Heaven," said Tegen, standing between me and Betsy.

"This be how we do things hereabouts, and always has done," said Betsy. "It's meant. She'll get a little fright and mend her ways. Now, you run off home, Tegen, if you ain't got the stomach for it."

"You're not getting away with this, Betsy, you big ape!" cried another voice. It was Cissie Olds. She had several other women alongside her.

"It's all out of envy of Mary," said Cissie to Betsy. "Where is that Loveday? Come on, step out here, Loveday Skewes, and stand up for yourself this once."

I realised the Mummers had put a stop to their play, and all eyes were on us. There was a flurry of jostling as the mob turned to one another to ask about Loveday's whereabouts. In a moment, someone flushed her out from where she'd been lurking at the back of the crowd. Cissie and another woman ran over and bundled Loveday to the front. She sidled up to Betsy, with her nose in the air, making sure not to look me in the eye.

"So this is your idea of One and All, is it, Loveday?" said Tegen.

"What is you saying of?" said Loveday. "None of this is my doing,"

"And where is that mother of yours?" asked Cissie. "And Millie Hicks, and all the other schemers behind this Riding?"

Loveday bit her lip, all of a tremble like the little coward she was.

Betsy took her part, squaring up to Cissie. "Mrs Skewes and Mrs Hicks be at home like the God-fearing, upright people they is," she said.

Nancy Spargo came over to Betsy, rolling her shoulders like a wrestler loosening up for a bout. When Betsy turned to face her, Nancy pulled up her sleeves and looked up into her eyes. "You leave Mary alone now, Betsy. If you want to pick a fight, I'm your woman," she said, poking her own chest with her thumb. "I be pig ugly already so a smack in the mouth means naught to me." Some of the men shouted at the women, hoping to see them slug it out in public. I looked around for Loveday, but she'd taken her chance to slip away while the crowd's eyes were turned from her.

At that moment, a fellow in a long coat stepped out of the crowd towards us. There was a huge cheer at the sight. It was Ethan Carbis and he wore a mop on his head that was meant to be a judge's wig. He stopped a few feet in front of me and the rabble gathered behind him. Carbis opened a roll of paper he had in his hand. He began to read in the voice of a landed gent, while the crowd howled with laughter.

"*My Lord Mayor, Ladies and Gentlemen, and poor honest country people,*

"*I hereby charge Mary Blight of this parish with the following offences:*

"*Stealing another woman's betrothed out of envy . . .*"

The crowd bayed to show their reproof.

"*Teasing young Pasco Hurrel until he threw himself off Tombstone Point . . .*"

"Shame on her!" someone shouted.

"*Having improper relations with the minister, Gideon Stone . . .*"

They hissed and hooted, and with each new charge the catcalls got louder.

"*Committing sacrilege in God's holy church . . .*

"*Striking a devout and respectable old lady of this parish, Marget Maddern, with intent to cause injury;*

"*Chewing off a woman's ears to steal her earrings, and thereby bringing a plague of Preventive Men to this cove and disrupting the trade of respectable people.*"

When he'd finished, he waited for the riotous shouting to end before looking down at me and saying, "Have you anything to say in your defence, Miss Blight?"

"Aye, I have something to say. The most of it is lies, and the rest is no worse than others here have done."

Betsy shouted me down. "If you showed any shame and admitted you'd done wrong we'd go easier on you," she said. "You has brought all this on yourself. Why can't you ever lean to the common way?"

"Let me hear an 'Aye' from all those who say she is guilty," called Carbis, looking round at the crowd behind him. There was a great blood-thirsty roar of "Ayes". "And a 'No' from those who say she is innocent." Some answered on my behalf, but they were few.

"Guilty as charged then! I sentence you to be taken from this place . . ."

Carbis was cut short by the sound of loud drumming at the eastern end of the quay. The mob fell silent at the sight of a lone, tall, dark figure standing there in the flickering light of the bonfire flames, smoke trailing past him. He looked more like a spirit than a flesh and blood man. In one hand he held a big frying pan and in the other a stout wooden club. He began to walk slowly through billows of smoke towards the crowd, his stride slow and stiff. As he drew closer, I saw that it was

317

Gideon Stone. His face was unshaven, his coat caked with mud.

But before he could reach the rabble, that great oaf Pentecost stepped out from the midst of them and lumbered towards him, his great arms swinging at his sides. Gideon drew to a stop and waited. Of a sudden, the mob began whistling and hooting. They had seen Martha Tregaskis stagger into the open and go rushing towards her husband, holding her skirts up so as not to trip over them. Pentecost turned and scowled at Martha, the little black holes of his eyes peering out from under his brow. She drew up to him and seized his arm in both hands.

"I won't have this!" she yelled, trying to pull him away, like a woman possessed. "I can't bear no more of this wickedness. I can't!"

"Will you never learn your place?" said Pentecost. "Take your hands off me and get out of my sight."

"I won't go. You'll have to kill me first!" she cried. But Pentecost only sneered, and took her by the scruff of the neck. He lifted her as if she were a cloth doll, and flung her to the ground, where she landed with a dull thud and lay there groaning.

Next, Pentecost stepped towards Gideon until the two men stood face to face, a yard apart. "So you want another wrestling lesson, do you, parson?" he said.

But as the words left the brute's lips, Gideon swung the frying pan he held in his hand and fetched a bone-crunching wallop to the side of Pentecost's head. For a long moment, Pentecost stood his ground, and I feared it was the end for Gideon. But then the giant's head began to roll on his shoulders, his legs went from under him and he fell heavily. There were gasps all around at the sight of the big man lying there, out cold.

Gideon threw down the pan and it clattered on the stone. He walked over to Carbis and stood before him, glaring.

"That's enough playing the fool for one night, fellow," he said. Carbis cowered and stood aside, taking the mop off his head. "I see my work in this cove is not yet done," Gideon said to the rabble, his voice hoarse. "I demand in God's name that you put a stop to this outrage immediately. Did we not build a chapel to God up on that hill yonder? And yet I return here to find you reduced to a condition of pagan savagery, a baying mob meting out a punishment to a defenceless woman."

"He's come for his strumpet," shouted a man in the crowd.

"He've had a bellyful. See how he sways from side to side," said a woman at the front of the crowd, mimicking Gideon by swaying herself.

"Repent and atone for your sins before it is too late!" he bellowed, his voice echoing all over the harbour. "You who have sinned know who you are." He looked around at them, his face gleaming with sweat, the veins standing out on his neck. Few would meet his gaze.

"Listen hard to what I am about to say — you will learn no more important lesson than this," he cried. "Do not believe that when it is all too late, when your life is passed and you are no longer able to come and kneel in the house of God, do not think that at that moment when you stand before the Almighty, and are found wanting, and your bodies are fit only as food for worms, and your souls are damned to burn in torment in Hell's fires, forever without end, do not think, I warn you, as you cry pitifully, imploring the Lord to permit you to repent and mend the errors of your ways, do not dare to suppose that God our Saviour will hearken to you and admit your soul among the ranks of the saved. Do not think it. For it will be too late."

People fell to their knees and bowed their heads in prayer. Others shuffled away, muttering darkly to one another.

"When you have breathed your last, and you stand before God, and know you have squandered every minute and every hour when you might have mended your ways, when you beg forgiveness of the Redeemer, do not think that by kneeling at that late hour as some of you do now, in abject terror, asking the Almighty to pardon your sins, that you will be forgiven. You will not. You will be past forgiveness. Your own tormented cries and those of your neighbours will ring forever in your ears as the molten rocks fall around you through all eternity and the fiends of Hell torment you. Your cries will go unheard by God, and even the blessed in Heaven who mourn your fate will not be able to help you, for you will be damned for all eternity, you who would not be saved."

A scuffle broke out, neighbour turning on neighbour, and wives tried to move their husbands out of harm's way. I took my chance and slipped away along the quay. Gideon followed me.

320

"Mary, I must speak with you."

I turned on him. He took a step backwards when he saw the look on my face.

"Such a ranting spirit you have!" I said. "I hope you go to hell with the rest of them. How can you stand there, shameless, when you left me waiting in the church all those hours?"

"I am here now."

"What use are you at this late hour?"

I turned up Downlong Row, blind to where I was going. Down in the harbour, the mob had all but forgotten me as they set about each other.

"You have good cause to be angry, but I beg you to hear me out," said Gideon, following close behind. "I must warn you that my wife has been to see the Magistrate. The Customs Officer will be here at dawn. You must prepare yourself."

"I know it. If you'd come when you were supposed to, I'd have got on a coach at Bodmin hours ago."

"It was no easy matter to walk out on my wife. I came as soon as I could, walking across that moor in the dark at great peril to myself."

"Aye, but only after a spell in the alehouse. You can go back to Newlyn, for all I care. I want no more sermons out of you. I've had my fill of perfect love in the next life and sober self-reliance. To think you have the gall to turn up here, half drunk!"

"I'll do my utmost to help you. I will stand by you in these times of trial. Mary, I beg you to put your trust in Divine Providence."

"To hell with Providence! You weren't on that cart being spat on."

We reached the door of Gideon's chapel. The building seemed no more than a humble barn set apart from the villagers' homes. Gideon felt in his pocket and took out the keys. He went inside and I followed him. I could smell the liquor on him, mingling with the scent of sawdust and freshly sawn timber. In the moonlight, I saw two rows of backless benches facing the pulpit, which was almost lost in shadow.

"I have waited all these months to enter this place," he said, walking down the aisle. "I had hoped for more, a manifestation of the Holy Fire, a consuming flame within. Not this emptiness."

We passed the front pews with their high backs, and I was filled with fury as I thought of the Skewes and Hicks families and those of their ilk sitting there out of the draught. Gideon knelt at the Communion rail, clutching his hands before him.

"We must endeavour to believe without signs or miracles," he said. "Perhaps the Redeemer wants me to see that this is no more than a building meant for worship, and nothing on this earth is permanent."

"Such a picture of piety you make, kneeling there with your hands in prayer," I said. "If I were you, I'd pray forgiveness for what you've done to me, and to those other women. Or will that count for nothing on Judgement Day?"

"Think of what I have lost — my calling, all my work over ten long years come to naught. This chapel . . . Do you know what that means to a man like me? I must do

what is right in God's eyes . . . The balance of my mind
. . . I came here this night to do my duty by you. I will
stay with you until the constable arrives so you won't
have to endure the wait alone. And I'll do all in my
power thereafter to save you."

"Do your duty by me? Save me? Have you forgotten
it was I who saved you? I wish I'd left you to drown.
The truth is, Gideon Stone, you're either drunk on
holiness or drunk on liquor. You put yourself above me,
always the master, too puffed up with male pride to
think ill of yourself. You will save me, you say, but it
isn't you who will do hard labour, or feel the noose
about your neck. And to think I once thought you
halfway to being an angel!" My anger gave way at last
to tears. "I thought you knew me, for myself, as no man
had done before," I sobbed. "In your arms that day I
felt blessed, and I'm not ashamed of it. I thought that
God must have dearly loved his children to have given
them that secret gift."

He stood up and faced me. I saw he was moved by
my words. He opened his mouth to speak, but the
chapel door swung open and someone stepped into
the church.

"They are here!" I cried. "They've come for me."

"Mary, is that you?" said the newcomer.

It was a voice I knew well. "Nathaniel!" I shouted. I
ran to him and threw my arms around him.

"I've just now sailed from Marazion," he said. "I saw
the flames from across the bay and feared the village
was burning down. What in God's name has occurred
this night?"

"The King's Men are coming at day break, Nat," I said, wiping away my tears on my apron. "They mean to put me in gaol. Aunt Madgie told them I'm the cannibal. She said she'd seen me do it."

"You're no cannibal, Mary," said Nathaniel. "I've known you long enough to be sure of that."

"What am I to do?"

"Is there somewhere you can go?"

"I have an aunt in Looe."

"Then we need to stir ourselves. We'll take my boat."

As he spoke, I saw Gideon leave the chapel.

After fetching my basket, and bidding a tearful farewell to Tegen, I rushed down the lane, frantic to flee the cove before the Preventive Men could catch me. But soon I heard footsteps behind me, and quickened my pace. My pursuer called my name, a woman's voice. When I turned, I was shocked to find Martha Tregaskis limping behind me, clutching her side and wincing. She stank of liquor. I let her come alongside me.

"Forgive me, Mary," she said.

"This isn't the time, Martha. I've got troubles enough without taking on yours."

"I can't bear it on my conscience no longer," she whined.

I pushed on, leaving her behind, but after I'd taken a few more steps, her meaning struck home and brought me up short.

"It was you that morning. You did it!" I said. "You're the cannibal."

She snivelled, and stared at the ground. The side of her face was swollen from where she'd landed after Pentecost had thrown her to the ground earlier. "My hands were cold," she whimpered. "I could barely move my fingers. And after all, the lady had passed away. What use were those jewels to her?"

"Do you have them still?" I snapped, thinking there might yet be a reprieve for me.

"Sold! And the money long gone. Pentecost stints on the housekeeping and I've eight mouths to feed. If there's no food on the table I get a beating." She lifted trembling fingers to her eye, which was no more than a slit in the bulging flesh of her eyelid.

"How could you stand by tonight and say nothing?" I said. "Shame on you! When the Preventive Man gets here you must tell him it was you that did it. They'll show more mercy, I seem, with you a married woman and a mother."

She backed away, looking about her as if afeard the constable might show up right then. "But who's to take care of my children?" she whimpered.

I took hold of her and shook her hard. "You must do what's right, do you hear?"

"No! I can't. Pentecost swears he'll break every bone in my body if I breathe a word of it — and bury me on the moor." She broke free of me and went hobbling back up the lane, rubbing her sore hip.

"Wait!" I called, chasing after her and gripping her fiercely by the arm. "Did anyone see you that morning? Tell the truth now."

"Not a soul."

"You're sure of it?"

She nodded, and with that my last hope sunk, for none would believe my word against hers, not when Aunt Madgie had come forward as a witness against me. "God damn you, Martha Tregaskis!" I cried.

Precious minutes had been lost. I reached the quay and rushed down the steps onto the beach where the dying embers of the bonfire glowed through fine spray. There was light enough to show Gideon Stone standing by a mooring post, the very same he'd leant on when we'd first talked all those months ago. Flakes of ash fell like snow all around him. The feeling of that time came back to me with great force, and rage mingled with longing in my heart.

"This is the last I'll see of you," he said.

"You have the whole world to save. I wish you luck with it."

"My only wish is to save your soul for all eternity."

"I can't wait that long. I'm not giving up all for Perfect Love in the hereafter. I'm a feeling woman and I want love in this life, perfect or otherwise. And if not love, then at least life."

"I wish you knew how hard this is for me."

"When you sober up, you'll see it all in a new light."

"I'm sober now, believe me, and miserable as any man that ever lived."

From out in the darkness, Nathaniel called, "We must make haste, Mary."

As I walked towards the water's edge, Gideon called out to me once more. "I will find you. I'll come to Looe."

I turned to face him, one last time. "No, Gideon. When the moment is passed, you'll think better of it. I shan't wait for you another time, only for you not to show."

"I'd get on that boat with you if I could, Mary. God knows I would! But my every limb shakes with terror at the prospect of being in a boat again."

Without looking back, I waded out towards Nathaniel. He leant over the gunwales and lifted me into the boat. I'd never put to sea before, and was perhaps the first woman from the village ever to do so. The sea wasn't firm and steady underfoot like the land, but shifting and slippery. I sat on the bench to the fore, and heard Nathaniel in the stern grappling with the oars, before turning the boat about with short strokes.

There was a loud sploshing out in the water. A figure was wading towards us. Nathaniel stepped forward, his bulk dark against the night sky. He had an oar in his hands, ready to bring it down on the head of a Preventive Man, if need be. The wading man reached the boat and gripped the sides, hauling himself up until his head and shoulders leant into the boat. Then he swung his legs over the side and landed with a great thud on his back, setting the boat swaying wildly from side to side.

It was Gideon. He crawled on hands and knees in the bottom of the boat and raised himself with a great to-do onto the bench alongside me.

"Shall I throw the fool overboard?" shouted Nathaniel.

"Not just yet, Nat!" I cried. I turned to Gideon. "What do you think you're about?" I said. "Get out of this boat, now."

"You heard her. Jump out, preacher," shouted Nathaniel. "We've no time to waste."

"I'm coming with you, Mary," said Gideon.

"Are you mazed?" I said.

"I shall hold fast to you, even if it kills me," he stammered. He was shaking so hard the bench wobbled beneath us.

"He'll get us all killed!" shouted Nathaniel. "Listen to him, the fellow's scared out of his wits. I hadn't reckoned on a chicken-hearted land lubber aboard." But despite what he said, I heard the scrape of the oars in the rowlocks and the splash of the paddles and I knew he was rowing us out of the harbour. Queer thumps sounded under the hull and I could only wonder what lurked in those unseen depths. "The sand bar be off to the west, so it's only they rocks yonder we need worry about," Nathaniel shouted.

"God help us!" groaned Gideon.

Soon after, the wind began buffeting my ears and cold spray stung my face. We had cleared the harbour. The boat pitched and rolled harder than before, creaking and straining as if it might split in two at any moment. My stomach lurched at every rise and fall of the swell.

Nathaniel moved over to the boat's mast. "We're gathering steerageway, I durst break out the sail," he said.

By the time he'd gone back to the tiller, the sea was slapping against the sides of the boat as it heeled to the wind. Then I thought I heard gunshot, and for a fleeting moment feared the King's men were on our tail, but it was only the canvas flapping and cracking in the wind. Gideon and I were thrown from side to side and my knuckles ached from clutching the bench beneath me. Every time the boat leant over, the pair of us slid together, and gallons more freezing water slopped inside. Gideon's head was bowed, and under the roar of the wind I heard him pray for deliverance.

Perhaps Nathaniel heard his prayers, for he called out, "We'll have rounded the Lizard before it gets light. I know these waters better than any Preventive Man."

Soon we got onto a more even keel, and I was able to collect my thoughts. I remembered the day I first saw Gideon lashed to a barrel in the harbour, and I saw what it must have cost him to get on board a boat again. And now he'd set himself on a course with no way back.

I put my mouth to his ear. "It looks like we shall have to do for each other after all," I said. I put my hand on his, and felt how firmly he was gripping the bench.

Not daring to move his hands, Gideon leant towards me and perhaps meant to kiss me, but at that very moment the boat pitched and threw us apart.

"How confoundedly strange that it should turn out this way," he said.

"Perhaps it was meant," I said. "God works in a mysterious way."

We sat on our bench to the fore of the boat as the ropes strained and the sail swelled, pulling us towards the new day on choppy waters. To the east a thin grey line showed on the horizon, the coming dawn. From where I sat with my back to the future, I could see the village where I'd spent my whole life. It was a dimly lit island afloat in the night, while the rest of the world was no more than a dream.

Acknowledgements

Thanks to the writers and tutors at New Writing South, in particular Susannah Waters for her help with an early draft, to my agent David Headley, and to everyone at HarperCollins HQ, in particular Kate Mills for safely steering *Wrecker* out of the harbour and into open water.

Other titles published by Ulverscroft:

HOMECOMINGS

Marcia Willett

At the end of the row of fishermen's cottages by the harbour's edge stands an old granite house. First it belonged to Ned's parents; then Ned dropped anchor here after a life at sea and called it home. His nephew Hugo moved in too, swapping London for the small Cornish fishing village where he'd spent so many happy holidays — and now other friends and relations are being drawn to the house. Among them is Dossie, lonely after her parents died and her son remarried. And cousin Jamie, coming home after more than a year, since his career as an RAF pilot was abruptly cut short. Both have to adjust to a new way of life. As newcomers arrive and old friends reunite, secrets are uncovered, relationships are forged and tested, and romance is kindled . . .

THE POSTCARD

Fern Britton

Life in the Cornish village of Pendruggan isn't always picture perfect. Penny Leighton has never told anyone why she's estranged from her mother and sister. For years she's kept her family secrets locked away in her heart, but they've been quietly eating away at her. When an unwelcome visitor blows in, Penny is brought face to face with the past. And a postcard, tucked away in a long-hidden case, holds the truth that could change everything . . . Young Ella has come back to the place where she spent a happy childhood with her grand-mother. Taken under Penny's broken wing for the summer, the safe haven of Pendruggan feels like the place for a fresh start. Soon, however, Ella starts to wonder if perhaps her real legacy doesn't lie in the past at all . . .